TRUE SUCCESSOR

True Successor

A Novel of the New Roman Empire

Joseph H. Levie

iUniverse LLC
Bloomington

TRUE SUCCESSOR
A NOVEL OF THE NEW ROMAN EMPIRE

This is a work of fiction. All of the characters, names, incidents, organizations, and dialogue in this novel are either the products of the author's imagination or are used fictitiously.

iUniverse books may be ordered through booksellers or by contacting:

iUniverse LLC
1663 Liberty Drive
Bloomington, IN 47403
www.iuniverse.com
1-800-Authors (1-800-288-4677)

ISBN: 978-1-4759-7069-2 (sc)
ISBN: 978-1-4759-7068-5 (hc)
ISBN: 978-1-4759-7067-8 (ebk)

Library of Congress Control Number: 2013900459

Printed in the United States of America

iUniverse rev. date: 9/11/2013

FOR HALLIE, MATTHEW AND JESSICA

CAST OF CHARACTERS

IN SAPODA
Mikail de Ruyer, a young Roman political officer
Karita, the manager of The Blond Horseman, a tavern
George Hoffman, secter chief of the Political Department
The *Headman* of Sapoda
A *Blacksmith*
Feydor, the Blacksmith's assistant
Jelem, a Mongol Sergeant

EN ROUTE TO AND AT ST. GEORGE'S CASTLE
Gaspar Nodiameau, a retired soldier
Colonel Christopher D'Hagen, Vice Commander of Imponza Castle
Aetius daCosta, Proconsul of the East, nicknamed "the Paladin"
Hugh Pannonius, the Proconsul's senior aide
General "Dan" Lauzac, a cavalry general
Andrew Kloffheim, Deputy Chief Political Officer
Sergeant Major Sodermann, an old fashioned soldier
Colonel Raul Valla, an old friend of Hugh Pannonius
Willem, a bodyguard

IN AND AROUND THE CITY OF AACHEN
Charles Martel IV, Emperor of New Rome. His friends and family call him "Martin".
Genvira Honora, Empress of New Rome. Everyone calls her "Jenny".

Dorcas daCosta, lady in waiting to the Empress. The Paladin's daughter
David daCosta. The Paladin's son
The Old Emperor, Emperor Scipio Augustus deceased, the previous
    emperor
The Old Empress, deceased, the previous Empress
Prince Frederick, the Emperor's first cousin
Prince Clovis, Frederick's father, deceased
Agatha, Frederick's wife
Conrad, Frederick's son
Louis Duval, chief political aide to the Emperor
Albrecht Desle, the senior aide to the Emperor
Giuseppe Sforza, the Imperial Chancellor.
Valerian den Olivese, the Magister Militium
Alejandro de Ausundas, the Mayor of the Palace
Thomas Marsalia, the Chief of the Political Department
General Biakarione, the Emperor's chief military aide
Simonides Klephas, the Byzantine ambassador
Augustus Walsenburg, a friend of Prince Frederick
*Augustus Wittelsbach, Francisco de Medici, Louis de Bourbon, Mariano
    Viscoti, Otto Hapsburg,* leaders of the Grandee party
Giovanni Mazzeo, Roman Senior Ambassador
Isaac de Bergeros, another Senior Ambassador
Andivius Hedulio, First Speaker of the Witanagemot
Victor Bibenda, a tax examiner
Hildegard, an assistant
Erich Himmelfarb, a bureaucrat
Emmerich Bader, a go-between

IN ROSTOCK
Phillip Ganz, a valet
Evander ("Ev") Leyden, a *spy*
Arturo Fidelibus, Count of Mecklenberg province

THE PARIDES COMPANY
Stephen Hoffman, managing partner of the firm
Demitrius Hoffman, resident partner, Aachen
William Hoffman, resident partner, Rostock

Julian Parides, resident partner, Vienna
Marinus Liebkind, chief clerk, Aachen,
Hector Phillipadros, chief clerk, Vienna
Leonidas Angelos, clerk, Vienna

MONGOLS
Subatai, a senior military officer
Kaidu, politician and general
Osorian, a general
Ochir, a very important Mongol
Bekter, a diplomat

A WORD WITH
THE READER

True Successor is a novel of alternate history. Many people have wondered what would have happened if the Roman Empire had not collapsed. Here I posit that in the Fifteenth and Sixteenth centuries, a series of able Emperors of the Holy Roman Empire succeeded in transforming it into a new Western Roman Empire, ostensibly by returning to its roots in Charlemagne's empire. In this world, Emperor Frederick II, who ruled Germany, Italy, Sicily and Burgundy, did not die in 1250, nor was he defeated by Pope Innocent IV at the battle of Parma. Rather, he won his battle and lived on for twenty years. Thereafter, the Empire acquired the rest of France in stages, mostly by marriage, Spain and Tunisia by conquest from the Muslims, and Poland and Hungary by expansion to the East.

In the Fifteenth and Sixteenth centuries a series of strong Emperors ending in Karl VII and, after his death, his wife, Clara, rebuilt the ramshackle Empire into the "New Roman Empire" in a process they called the "Refoundation". There were disturbances, but the Thirty Years War never happened. Although many of the religious and civil tensions that led to that catastrophe existed, the Emperors avoided the final catastrophe. Some of those tensions have not entirely gone away. The panRoman policies mentioned in this book are the Emperors' programs to curb the former upper nobility's remaining preferential and semi-feudal local rights.

The currency of The New Roman Empire is the denarius. In 1812 the denarius was worth about two 1812 dollars. The five denarius coin was "the good one," and the ten denarius coin "the big one."

PROLOGUE

January 19ᵗʰ 1783
Aachen

THE SNOW BEGAN JUST before dawn. By mid-morning, all Aachen and the enormous Imperial palace at its heart were in the grip of the year's worst blizzard. The heavy snowfall left the palace white and silent. By half-past two its rooms and corridors were quiet and empty.

Prince Clovis, whose brother was the present Emperor, Scipio Augustus, was alone, awaiting his final visitor in his cold, high-ceilinged office, a large and luxurious marble room with silver furnishings, hung with tapestries depicting the triumphs of Julius Caesar. Though there were fireplaces at both ends of the room, Clovis stood at the window, which he had left slightly open. He liked the cold because he thought it sharpened his mind. Clovis made a fine figure: a tall, middle-aged man in an ermine-lined jacket, burly, and glowing with health. He had used the blizzard as an excuse to send his staff home, leaving no one else in this room or its antechamber. He wanted no witnesses to what was to come. A few minutes before, an unfamiliar servant had entered the room, quickly made a fire in the second fireplace, and departed as silently as he had come, leaving Clovis alone at his window to watch the snow bury the garden and turn its trees into lace.

A year ago his brother had the Emperor passed him over for the title of Crown Prince in favor of his own son, the twenty-six year

Charles Martel, whom the family called Martin. Clovis took Martin's promotion as a personal insult. Although direct succession was usually the rule, in theory the ablest of the four thousand descendants of Charlemagne could receive the appointment. Clovis was fifty-three and in the full strength of his maturity. A soldier in his youth, he had served the Empire in its long wars with the Mongols and helped to establish a neutral zone between the Empires. Later he had been ambassador to the Danes, governed Cuba, the Empire's outpost in the New World, and acted as his brother's Proconsul in Tunisia before returning to Aachen.

Disaster had followed within a year of Martin's appointment; Scipio Augustus had a stroke. Since then he had been unconscious, and he would soon die. As Crown Prince, young Martin had automatically become Regent. As such he would succeed to the throne. Clovis meant to make sure the young thief would never be Emperor. *Too bad,* thought Clovis. *The boy's likeable enough, but the Empire needs a man. Martin can't deal with the Mongols, the Caliphate and the Byzantines on the Empire's borders. The generals might be able to manage the fighting, but who will manage them? At home things would be even worse. The great aristocrats—the Grandees—will roll over both the boy and Karl VII's panRoman policies like a carriage over a flat stone.*

Clovis had quietly approached the senior members of the government. Those discreet men were careful never to say so directly but they let him understand that if Martin disappeared they would not contest his succession. Only one obstacle was left, the Chancellor, second only to the Regent, to whom the armed guards protecting the palace reported. That morning Clovis had received an unsigned note in the Chancellor's unmistakable spiky handwriting. And though he had thrown the paper in the fireplace, he remembered its words perfectly: *"An unexpected opportunity has arisen. I will be in your office at five o'clock. Wait for me."* Clovis was relishing his anticipation. The boy would be dead tonight, and Clovis would be Emperor tomorrow.

The Emperor of New Rome repeats his coronation oath in his own words and swears to it. When he finishes, the crown of Charlemagne is placed on his head Clovis smiled as he imagined himself being proclaimed Emperor:

"He shall be known as Clovis, the fourth of that name, Emperor of New Rome and the Western Roman Empire, happy, glorious, triumphant and pious, doer of justice, first magistrate, no despot but lover and protector of the Roman people and their Empire, defender of the true faith and true successor to Charlemagne."

He smiled, savoring the vision and the words *True Successor to Charlemagne,* but the smile disappeared when the door opened suddenly, and the room filled with armed men who closed the door behind them. Clovis recognized Martin, Aetius, Martin's illegitimate half-brother, and three of the young men in their circle: Giuseppe Sforza, Major Valerian den Olivese, and Alejandro de Ausundas, along with half a dozen junior army officers.

"What's this, Martin?" Clovis demanded in an angry voice. His nephew faced him to say, "Uncle, it's over. The Chancellor provided me with the note to send you. He's not coming and never was. My own grooms, Otto and Fabian, have confessed they were to stage an accident and make it appear that my horse threw me and left me dead. The two guardsmen who were to do the actual killing and your man Rossini are dead too. I killed them myself."

"That's a lie."

"I have their confessions."

Clovis stood mute and ashen-faced.

The Crown Prince went on, "I loved you more than I loved my own father. You knew it. You always told me you loved me."

"What matters is what is best for the Empire," the older man said in a flat voice." I would have spared your life."

"No one who has confessed has said so, and you would have needed to display my body. If you want a public trial you can have it. I will see that you are convicted. That will destroy your wife and ruin your children's lives. Frederick and Cornelia will live out their lives as the impoverished and despised children of a traitor." He paused before continuing "But, if you take poison here and now, we will announce your death as a heart attack. I will not blacken your memory. I will treat Aunt Vera and your children as family. Little Frederick will have a prince's upbringing and career and when the time comes, I will find Cornelia a good husband."

Clovis stared at the mosaic Imperial seal inset in the marble floor at his feet for a long minute as if to say farewell. Then he asked, "Is there no other way?"

"None."

Clovis stood for a minute before finally nodding. "Give me a few minutes to pray." As he sat down at his desk, he turned to Aetius to spit out venomously, "I suppose, dear nephew, you have the poison in your pocket. The bastard doing his legitimate brother's dirty work."

"Indeed," Aetius replied. He turned to the Crown Prince, "Martin, you must not be here for the rest of this. Have the soldiers escort you back. We four will stay."

The Crown Prince nodded and left.

A short time later Clovis said "Amen" loudly and, still seated, opened his mouth. Sforza and de Olivise seized his head and pulled his jaws open. Aetius took the vial out of his pocket and poured its contents into Clovis's mouth. Then Sforza and de Olivise forced Clovis' jaws together and held them in place. For a minute, it seemed as if Clovis had changed his mind as he struggling with them in a grotesque wrestling match. Then all four men together forced Clovis onto the floor, the chair crashing down with him and held him there even after he started to writhe in convulsions. His breathing first turned deep and rapid, then stopped. In a few minutes, all movement had ceased. Aetius took out a small pocket mirror and held it up to Clovis' mouth and nose. After a minute, he nodded and said to Sforza, "I've made the arrangements to have the body found. You know what to do. The Imperial Physician is expecting you, Giovanni."

The assassins left, closing the door quietly behind them. On the floor Clovis' twisted mouth still seemed to be in pain. His open gray eyes glared angrily at the ceiling in silent accusation. Soon, he would be found and those eyes would be closed. It had all been arranged.

Book One

Mikail

April 1812

CHAPTER I

Mikail

THE YOUNG POLITICAL OFFICER had a girl in the village. He had met Karita a year ago when he had visited Sapoda to talk to the headman about smuggling. Close to the main road running through the neutral zone between the Roman and Mongol empires and only ten miles from the Mongol border, the village of Sapoda was a natural way-station for smugglers. Mikail had been spending most of his time on smuggling cases for no better reason than that his chief thought them important. No one else did; the Zone had always been a haven for smugglers.

The Sapoda headman was also the local man of substance. He owned the mill, some other property, and The Blonde Horseman, the only tavern in the village. His daughter Karita, a very young widow, was not on good terms with her stepmother so she managed the tavern and lived there on the second floor. When the headman housed him at the Horseman, Mikail had noticed the petite blonde waiting on him when her clever hands made a show out of deboning his fish. He spent the evening flirting with her. For her part, Karita seemed to like what she saw. Mikail de Ruyter was six feet tall with dark brown hair, blue eyes, and a trim little mustache anchoring his sunburned face. He had given his dinner order in Ukrainian, the language of the western provinces of the Mongol Empire. She came over to his table, bringing a bottle of wine and then surprised him, first by sitting down and then by unexpectedly speaking Latin. "The Inn's very best," she said with a friendly smile, uncorking the bottle. Surprised and delighted, he showed it by smiling and thanking her for the wine in the courtliest

3

Latin he could command, adding, "I could listen to you all night. I had almost forgotten how lovely my own language sounds until I heard you speaking it. How did a girl like you get here?"

"I was born here," she said. "My parents moved to Imponza when I was a baby. When I was seven, my mother died, and we moved back. Father remarried, but my stepmother and I do not like each other. We all agreed I would be happier with my uncle and aunt in Imponza, on the other side of the river. I went to school there in the Empire and came back here to get married. My husband died within a year, and I've been running the tavern ever since."

"My sympathy on your husband's death," Mikail said.

"It was an arranged marriage. Daddy thought he was doing the right thing, but it was a terrible mistake." She paused and studied his uniform, "What brings you here, red jacket?"

Mikail laughed, "Your father and my uniform. I'm here to talk about the smuggling problem with the headman of Sapoda while I drink his sour Dragonhead leaf tea, because I hope to be a diplomat some day. The smuggling is upsetting my chief, and I can't see why. If you live here, you have to know that everybody in the Zone is involved. Yet, your father insists with a straight face, there is no smuggling here."

Karita made her face look angelic. "Smuggling? Here? How could that ever happen?"

"Besides making my day a lot brighter, whatever are *you* doing in Sapoda?"

"I really don't know," she sighed, "although making your day brighter sounds like a good idea."

The bottle of wine had launched his best evening in a very long time. She so obviously enjoyed stretching her spirit's limits and showing how pleased she was with their encounter, that he found himself talking to her seriously. There were plenty of blonde beauties in the Zone villages, but no lively, articulate girls. He told her how lonely and bored he was, how his chief's patronizing ways irritated him, and how uncomfortable he was about his prospects for advancement. Officers of the Political Department were supposed to collect information and increase Roman influence if they wished for promotion to the elite Diplomatic Service. He had liked George Hoffman, his sector officer, but George had unkindly returned the favor by dead-ending Mikail at a desk, fussing over trivia. That was no way to build a record for transfer to the Diplomatic Service.

As Mikail opened up to her, Karita responded. She felt that she had been nowhere and done nothing since her schooling had ended. Her brief, arranged marriage with a rich old man from the next village had ended after a year when his horse had fallen on him. Karita did not miss her husband, but she was lonely. She hadn't grown up in Sapoda and didn't have a single friend there. The men were clods, and the Blonde Horseman bored her. Her stepmother was a figure out of a nasty fairy tale. She yearned for a better life in a bigger world.

He commiserated. She was too pretty and vivacious for a small town in the neutral zone between Rome and Mongolia. After three hours, Mikail felt happier than he had been for a long time and told her so before he finally dragged himself upstairs.

Not long after, there was a knock on his door, and in she slipped, pink and blushing, barefoot in a lacy white chemise. When morning came, Karita went downstairs to make a hot breakfast and brought it for them. Afterwards, they sat on the bed, arms around one another, and talked for hours. Mikail marveled; this girl was a laughing brook in a stony desert.

As he left, she stood on tiptoe to tell him with her parting kiss, "Thank God you came, I was going to run away next week. I had already started to pack."

That had been exactly a year ago. Since then, he had seen her as often as he could get to Sapoda.

He had written Karita to say he would stop by on Thursday and stay over before going on to his monthly meeting with his sector officer, but here he was on Tuesday, two days early to surprise her with a one-year anniversary present, a turquoise necklace that echoed the color of her eyes. Mikail wasn't at all sure what her father knew (and if he did, whether he wanted others to know) about his daughter's lover. So rather than wearing his uniform, he was dressed in a peddler's hooded coat that cast his sharp features into shadow, a costume he often had occasion to wear. Not everyone in the Zone wanted to be seen talking with the Emperor's political officers.

Mikail put the necklace into his pack, tied up his horse in the woods a mile from the tavern, and sauntered down the road, enjoying the hundred shades of green in the first blush of the Moldavian Spring. He began to think about putting the necklace around her smooth lovely neck that night. He would wait until she was naked to have the pleasure of seeing it hanging between her generous breasts. The thought of bedding her caused him to whistle in anticipation. Certainly, she was the best thing that had ever happened to him, and he kept thinking ahead to the night's pleasures, but—a dash of cold water—it had to come to an end. The Political Service might ignore an officer's affair with a Zonian—its junior officers were young, unmarried men with healthy appetites and that was how the Service liked them—but Karita was an extreme conflict of interest made lovely flesh.

Nor would his family be of any help. His father was long dead, and Lucas, his ambitious older brother, was head of the family. Lucas loved Mikail, mentored him, had gotten him this job, and still was his most important supporter, but he insisted so often and so vehemently that he was not a stuffed shirt that he ended up proving the contrary. Worse, Lucas and his wife, especially his wife, would consider Karita an embarrassment to Lucas's own career. As the head of a Roman family, Lucas had a legal right to prevent an unsuitable marriage. Still, Mikail felt that he and Karita could go on for the present with clear consciences. Karita had no one else, at least that he knew of. He wouldn't stand in her way if something better came along, would he? He had told her so, and they were both of age, weren't they? As if to prove he was right, the sun came out from behind the small cloud that had hidden it.

He emerged from his daydream smiling and looked around. A few hundred yards before the tavern a tannery and smithy huddled near the stone bridge over a small, fast flowing stream two hundred yards down from a water-driven mill. Together they comprised Sapoda's tiny industrial district. The tannery's stench and the smithy's fire kept them away from Sapoda's reed-thatched wooden houses. Approaching the two establishments, still glowing with love, Mikail couldn't believe what he saw. Not fifty yards away, riding down from the village towards the smithy, were three uniformed Mongol cavalrymen and a string of horses trotting on a lead held by a middle-aged sergeant with a grizzled mustache. The two soldiers riding behind the sergeant looked very young, probably recruits. A Mongol cavalry detail was as out of place on this country road as a line of spangled circus elephants, yet there was nothing clandestine about these riders. They sat in their saddles as if they knew exactly where they were going and belonged there.

The three turned off the road towards the smithy. The instant he saw their backs, Mikail slipped into the woods and crouched between the broad trunk of an old oak and a boulder to observe them. The smith's helper came out of the shed, and the sergeant bawled at him, "Hey, Fydor, send out big-muscles-and-tiny-brain. I have paying work." The sergeant's Ukrainian had an accent, but was not bad. *He's been here before and done this*, Mikail thought. Sure enough, the blacksmith was already standing in the door, primed to return fire by loudly telling his helper, "Fydor, ask the horse's ass on that horse's ass what brings the great Khan's worst sorrow here to honor us."

One of the troopers started to snicker, but as the sergeant began to turn in the saddle, he quickly changed his expression.

The sergeant retained his dignity by pretending not to have heard the insult. "Horses need reshoe," he told the smith. "We pay same as last time. How long you take?"

"Easy enough," the smith answered. "You in a hurry?"

"Yes," the Mongol said, "We have job to do on somebody here Thursday. Then must rejoin our tuman fast as can ride. Big operation on the way, probably next week. Our big man wants us, buttons shiny, ready to go."

"Then take your men to the tavern for an hour," said the smith. "Have a drink, and when you come back, I can tell you how long I'll take. But do me a favor, Jelem. Don't force yourself on that pretty little blonde. The last time was ugly. She's has a hard enough life, and right now she's probably crying her eyes out in the kitchen because we both know who's going to get hurt by that little job that brings you to Sapoda."

Those soldiers are looking for me, Mikail thought. *Looking for me and no one else. Why else would Karita be crying? They knew when to expect me. I've been betrayed.* Crouched behind his rock he was very frightened. Political officers lived and worked in foreign territory without diplomatic immunity. Why had the Mongols singled him out? The Mongols had a reputation for cruelty and torture. The idea of falling into their hands was terrifying.

A sense of urgency that was close to panic overwhelmed him. *I can't stay here, I'll be killed. My duty is to warn the Emperor that an invasion is coming. The Mongols will be over the border, raping, pillaging, and burning our cities as they did in the past. I'm the only one who knows!*

He realized he had to get back to his horse, his maps and his weapon. The compass in his pack would enable him to go cross-country through the woods. *Move now! Move now!* He'd get rid of his uniform and clean out his saddlebags so he could pass a checkpoint. *But what about my silver card identifying me as a political officer? I'll have to find a way to hide it. I'd better be well away before tomorrow. They'll be sending out parties to watch the roads. Move! Don't wait! Move!*

He pushed down rising terror and took out the compass. Once the Mongols were out of sight and the smith and his helper had returned to their smithy, he ducked into the woods and started back, carefully watching where he stepped. He worked his way through the woods, keeping under cover and parallel to the road. *Move now! Move now. Now! Now!*

Twenty minutes later he found his horse and started to breathe normally. He poured the contents of his saddlebags out onto the ground and hastily sorted through them. His correspondence, a Latin-Ukrainian dictionary, a pocket copy of Virgil, Galilean binoculars, the manuals stamped with the Emperor's portrait or the Imperial Political Department seal and anything else that might shriek ROMAN! and made them into a small pile. He added his uniform to the heap and carried it into the woods where he scratched a shallow hole in the ground with his short sword and covered it with a flimsy layer of dirt, leaves and sticks held down by small rocks. They'd be found, but by then it shouldn't matter. He checked his weapons, a standard short sword that really was no more than a long dagger and a crossbow covered in a cloth sheath, along with two-dozen spare bolts. They would not attract attention; most travelers carried a weapon. The crossbow was only good for a single shot before reloading, but the bolt it fired could kill within two hundred feet.

Not much of a believer, Mikail said two Paternosters and tried to remember the right formula to commend his soul to God. He could not recollect the exact words and hoped God would accept the heartfelt intensity of his feelings. He started to put distance between himself and the village, carefully keeping to a moderate pace that would not attract attention and trying not to let the horse feel his anxiety. Not, he reflected, that there was much chance of his mare's pace drawing unwanted attention. George did not believe in buying good horseflesh for his junior officers. He liked to say in a droll way that that fancy horseflesh gave a junior officer an improper perception of his importance. George's own mount, of course, was another story.

It was almost ten a.m. Concentrated thinking now would distract him as he traveled. He could consider his position when he stopped to water the horse or let it graze. Survival tactics had been part of his training in Trier and in the annual refresher course. His instructors had preached over and over against the dangers of inattention. By half—past one, after the few people he passed had barely looked at him, he began to feel better. Finally, he spotted a small stream next to a grassy clearing and turned the mare's head towards it. His teachers had insisted that once you were out of immediate danger, you should do exercises to calm your mind and then take time to consider what to do next. While his horse grazed, Mikail settled down to think.

Although he had come down this very road just a few hours before, he could hear the instructor's voice saying, "Careful, careful, take nothing for granted," as he took out his map. It revealed that in a few miles the road would fork, with the right turning towards the official border between the zone and Roman territory, the Velina, a narrow river less than a hundred feet wide, thirty miles away. Once across it, there was another thirty-five miles to the Pruj, a much broader river. The space between the two rivers was Roman territory but empty countryside in which the only sign of Roman presence was a military road constructed long ago to move troops up to the border when necessary. The area was uninhabited, except for smugglers and a few fishermen. It would not be safe. Mongol patrols might already be roaming it.

To reach safety Mikail had two rivers and over seventy miles to cross. His three-year-old mount would be tired long before he was safe. He had a good head start but the Mongols had numbers, experience, and plenty of remounts. His horse could ford the Velina, and afterwards, the Roman highway offered easy traveling, but it would not be safe, especially where it ran through open countryside and swamp. He might risk the forested road by daylight, but once out in the open, he would be too visible. When he finally arrived at the Pruj he would need a way to cross the big river.

As he rode he kept alert. It would be wise to replenish his supply of food, if only to keep his mind unclouded by hunger. It was too early in the year for berries or fruit, and he didn't have time to grub for edible roots or ferns, but a peddler could bargain for a few loaves of bread without being conspicuous. The first town after the fork was Gadowa, but he would not pass through it because it was on the wrong side of the fork in the road. Gadowa held a fair every Friday. If a farmwife asked him, he would say he was going to the fair. But wouldn't a peddler with nothing to sell be suspicious? He would say that his partner was already in Gadowa with their trade goods, and he wanted something to eat in the saddle as he rushed to catch up with him. Before he reached the fork he stopped at a wooden farmhouse in front of a large grove of linden trees, which meant the farmer kept bees. Near the house he found himself enjoying the early spring flowers and colorful blossoms on the bushes while listening to a goldfinch sing before he remembered that men were hunting him.

The farmwife was working in her kitchen garden when he walked over and told her his story, which elicited no reaction. She sold him two loaves of bread, a few big pieces of cheese, and some boiled ham for a fair price. He had been right about the bees; he could hear them buzzing in the field. Mikail liked sweets. He asked the farmwife for a piece of honeycomb.

"Don't have any left," she said. "They've bought all our hay too and practically everything else we were willing to sell. We used to see wagons and equipment now and then, but for the last couple of weeks it's been like the Emperor's birthday parade."

Mikail took a chance and asked, "Who are they and what are they doing here?"

"I don't rightly know," she said, "but there are more of them almost every day. Whatever they are going to do, they are going to do it soon." She looked at him in a kindly way and added, "Don't ask me too many questions whoever you are. It isn't healthy for either of us."

Mikail thanked her and once out of her sight urged on his horse's pace. When he came to the fork he saw three horsemen waiting in the shade of a spruce tree by the road leading to the Velina. *Courage*, he told himself, *perhaps they aren't Mongols. Anyhow, it's time to find out whether I can pass a checkpoint. They can't be looking for me already.* As he came nearer he observed that the horsemen were indeed Mongols and seemed to be looking for someone, but their profiles showed they were watching for someone riding towards Sapoda. He slowed down to avoid suspicion and passed them without stopping.

He kept to the road until late afternoon when he had to decide about crossing the Velina. Mongols at the crossroads meant the ford would be watched. He could avoid it by swimming his horse over the steam a mile or two away, but a night crossing would entail wandering blindly through the woods. His mare might break a leg. Better to wait for morning and cross above the ford. He found a patch of shrubby, interwoven mug pines and thorny bushes that afforded a good view of the road behind which he could hide. He led the mare into the woods, took off its saddle, and tied it to a beech tree, keeping his crossbow and short sword with him, the spare bolts in his pocket. Still anxious, he walked back to the road for a second look to reassure himself he would not be visible. It was already dusk. Feeling hungry, he nibbled at a piece of one of his loaves and a bit of the ham; it tasted like a feast.

Now Mikail had the time to think things through. *It had to be the headman, Karita's father. Did he have a motive to betray me? Did he want to end her relationship with me? She never told me he had complained to her, and a Roman political officer would be a good catch for his girl. That would please him. How could her father know of my arrival if she didn't tell him? So could it have been Karita herself? No, she must have been indiscreet—the whole town seemed to know about us—but she wouldn't be a party to trapping me. Karita loves me, loves me more than I love her.* (There was a stab of guilt as he thought this.) *She has not been acting any more than I have; her passion is real. And she cried when she thought the Mongols were going to kill me. Nor is she the sort to tell people, let alone her own father, when she was going to have an assignation with a lover. Certainly if the village knew of our affair then her father must have known, but why must he be the one who told the Mongols?*

All right, then how did Karita herself know when I was coming? I told Tvar, George's messenger, to stop at the tavern on his way to deliver my weekly report to George. He was to give my letter to her when no one else was present. But I didn't tell anyone about Tuesday. That was to be a surprise. The Mongols thought I was coming on Thursday. Who knew about Thursday besides Karita? Tvar? Tvar is George's stooge but I don't think he can read. Anyhow, my love notes always are put into a second envelope, which is also sealed.

Who else could have known about Thursday? George? Certainly. I told him so myself. I put a note in with my weekly report telling him I'd arrive Friday afternoon in time for the meeting "because of a personal matter on Thursday night." I knew he wouldn't mind because the sector meeting was set for Friday night, and he would know where I was, which is what he always insists on, but he didn't know about Tuesday. That was my own last minute idea. George has known about Karita for months. I told him myself over drinks, several drinks, and now that I think of it, George paid for them, which isn't like him; he's miserly. He told me in his worldly manner that so far as the Service was concerned my love life was mine to do what I pleased, but that I must always avoid mixing my personal and professional lives. It has to be George, damn him! Pretending to be my friend and mentor, so kind, so helpful, and all the time betraying me. I used to like him, he knew it, and he'd have taken advantage of it to have me killed.

This just isn't possible, Mikail thought. *There must be another explanation.* But, once started, the thought was irresistible. It answered the obvious question: how could the Mongols have kept their presence in the Zone a secret from all the Emperor's political officers there? *Maybe they didn't have to try very hard; perhaps George isn't the only traitor in our little group. It's such an easy trick if George tells the Mongols the location of every political officer. Then the Mongols just keep away from us and make sure any Zonian knows what will happen to his family if he tells us. George knows just what the Mongols need, and what they need is exactly what is in my weekly report. He never gives extensions for the weekly report. It makes sense for the Mongols to arrest or kill all the sector's political officers just before they attack. Probably everyone else is dead or captured and that's why the Mongols are hunting me.*

What do I know about my supervisor? George never talks about himself or his personal feelings. He had a couple of years in Aachen and has important friends there. Since then he has been in the field for ten years, which is unusual. He's really good. He speaks all the languages, can talk easily to anyone, knows the regulations forward and backward, and has a great understanding of process. He always knows exactly what all of his people are doing. He couldn't have missed knowing his section was infiltrated.

Then, too, before he came to us he was supervising a dozen officers down South and due for a promotion to the Diplomatic Service or a good job back at Saint George's Castle working for the Paladin, until he fell afoul of that oddball, Hugh Pannonius. The rumor was that Pannonius wanted to discharge George for some violation of regulations, but the Paladin himself gave him a second chance. ["The Paladin" was the nickname of Aetius Da Costa, Proconsul of Dacia Commandery.] *A sector with only five or six officers was no promotion for so experienced an officer. It was a demotion, no matter what everyone said. General wisdom claims the Paladin prefers the indirect path. Maybe it was his suggestion to George that it was time to go. George's the only one of us who speaks Mongol. I twice asked to go to the language course at Saint George's, but he wouldn't let me put in my application.*

The sound of many horses coming closer interrupted Mikail's reveries, and with them came sudden, unwelcome light. Cavalry was coming down the road, led by riders bearing torches. Twenty troopers followed the torches *Must be an advance guard,* thought Mikail, and flattened himself against the ground behind his cover. A long column of horsemen riding two abreast followed the advance guard. The column moved on the trot but still took a long time to pass. Mikail estimated that there must have been at least five or six hundred horsemen, trailed by a wagon train. Once they were gone, Mikail started to rise to stretch his muscles until he realized that if there had been an advance guard, there might be a be rear guard too. He put his ear to the ground and heard approaching hooves. He hurried to hide as two rearguard contingents quickly passed. The entire formation had moved swiftly, a well-disciplined body of regular cavalry moving into position.

Too close to the road to rest safely, he found a place a few yards further back where he could hear any movement and see whoever passed. It was very late when he fell into an uneasy slumber. After an hour or so, he was roused by the sound of hooves—a single horseman in a hurry. One horseman should be no problem, but to Mikail's consternation the rider stopped, dismounted twenty feet away to tie his big stallion to a tree, and started into the woods, carrying his sword. From his place of concealment, Mikail could see him moving by the light of a partially obscured moon; the distinctive onion dome of his Mongol dress helmet—he seemed to be in dress uniform, which was peculiar—made him easy to follow. Mikail had taken his loaded crossbow with him and now unlocked it. The Mongol seemed to have heard the click because he froze for a minute, looking around. Mikail stood rooted. He stopped breathing, afraid the man could hear his beating heart. But the Mongol must have concluded that it was only a small animal scuttling on the forest floor and went a little further into the woods to squat to take care of nature's call. *He'll finish and go*, Mikail thought with relief. Then the stallion neighed and, to his horror, he heard his mare whinny in response. The Mongol jumped out of his squat, picked up his sword, and called out something in his harsh native tongue.

Mikail instantly realized he couldn't let the man leave; there'd be a search party on him within the hour if he did. He knew with absolute certainty that he either killed this man or died himself. But he had an advantage; he was between the Mongol and his charger.

Holding the crossbow behind him, Mikail stood up, making a loud scuffling noise. Alerted by the sound, the Mongol saw or sensed Mikail's presence and, holding his sword high, poised to strike, he charged toward him with a scream. There was moonlight enough behind him to make him a perfect target. Mikail couldn't miss. He pointed the crossbow at the attacker's heart and pulled the trigger. The bolt audibly smacked into his chest; a choking sound and the man fell backward onto the forest floor.

For a little while Mikail felt nothing. Then his sense of time returned, accompanied by the most intense feeling of urgency. He reloaded, and although the man was surely dead, shot him a second time. The victim was in full dress uniform with ornate epaulets, a red, heavy, silk-lined cloak, a damascened helmet, and a small enameled armor gorget covering his neck. Mikail realized he had just killed an important officer. His uniform probably meant that he had been rushing to make a grand entrance at the start of day when he took over his new command. Mikail would have to pull his body deeper into the woods for safety's sake, but right now he needed to dispose of the stallion quickly. If a passing rider saw an officer's mount tied up at the roadside with no rider nearby, he would investigate. Mikail walked back to the road, untied the stallion's reins, and led it well into the woods, where he shot it, with regret but no hesitation, squarely between its beautiful eyes.

As the horse crashed to the ground, he noticed it was carrying oversized canvas saddlebags. When opened, they contained maps, something that looked like a metal fan, a field telescope, a heavy, oddly shaped piece of metal with raised Mongolian script cast into it, and two packets of papers in oilskin wrapping with official seals. He took everything and, feeling like a grave robber, put his hand into the corpse's pocket for his identification papers. He found them. They were written in an elegant hand on embossed paper with a red seal affixed. After a moment's thought, he cut off an epaulet and added it to the saddlebags. Before he left, he looked into the face of the man he had killed to memorize it, then pulled the body further into the woods. There was no time to dig a grave for man or horse. Mikail hoped there were no wolves in these woods.

Killing the officer changed his plans. Now he could not pass the most cursory search or try to talk his way through a check post. Ignoring the risks of riding at night that had frightened him only an hour ago, he rode carefully for three or four miles, staying parallel with the river before giving his horse or himself a chance to rest. *I was happy and in love this morning*, he thought. *Now I'm a murderer and spy running for my life.*

CHAPTER II

Old Gaspar

MIKAIL WAS IN THE saddle at first light. Using his compass, he worked his way through the forest parallel to the Velina for several miles before turning towards the water. Once near the river, he followed its bank, looking for a place where the stream narrowed and trees on both sides blocked a scout's line of sight. It took him longer than he expected, but he finally found a fordable place where he swam the mare across the stream into what was technically Roman territory. Ten minutes later he stopped to rest his horse and breakfast on bread and cheese. His map showed the river Pruj more than thirty-five miles away, surrounded by a flat, swampy river plain. When he got there he would have to abandon the mare because the silhouette of a man on horseback would be visible for miles. The Pruj was too broad and swift to ford, he would also need to find a boat.

The map did show two ferries and a bridge over the Pruj, but they all were out of the question. One ferry was downstream at Ocania where the Roman road through the empty area ended at the Pruj. The Mongols would be sure to watch it. The other was upstream but too far away. Further down river to the south at Imponza was a fortified bridge protected by a strong, well-garrisoned Roman fort on the far side of the river. Imponza would be ideal, but its approaches would be too well watched.

The only safe crossing Mikail could imagine was on a smuggler's boat. All right, if he was going to need a smuggler's boat, why couldn't the smuggler smuggle *him*? For the past several months Mikail had done little but collect information about them and their trade. George had wanted to know who the smugglers were, where they lived, where they crossed the Pruj (a subject of obsessive interest) and a great deal more. Mikail had wasted months on the issue over his protests that these pointless investigations were keeping him away from fieldwork. Now it all seemed worthwhile, because he knew just whom to use: Gaspar Andiacus Nodiameau, whom everyone, including the man himself, called Old Gaspar. A former Roman soldier in the Imponza garrison, he had been cashiered without pension for drunkenness on duty, insubordination, and petty theft, and expelled from Imponza. In pursuit of his endless assignment Mikail had passed a memorable night drinking with Old Gaspar.

Mikail found the charge of drunkenness persuasive, but only if you judged drunkenness by the bulk amount of alcohol consumed because Gaspar never showed any effect from the hogsheads he swallowed. In his cups, Gaspar insisted he had been framed by his battalion Sergeant Major, who wanted his wife. The story could be true; the Sergeant Major was now openly living with the woman. The law did not allow divorce, but military custom was tolerant about arrangements. Gaspar had said he no longer wanted the woman back. What he wanted was his pension. If he could get his pension rights back, he would go home and turn honest. Mikail had promised Gaspar to see what he could do and suggested to George that he could eliminate a major smuggler by getting Old Gaspar his pension. It wouldn't even cost the Emperor a single good one, because the garrison's pension chest could just reverse the windfall it had taken by forfeiting Gaspar's twenty-five years of contributions. George had listened to Mikail's earnest presentation, laughed at his bureaucratic cleverness, commended his ingenuity, and promised to look into restoration of the pension, all of which Mikail had dutifully reported to Old Gaspar. In fact, George had done nothing at all. Soon thereafter, the smuggler project had been discontinued and Mikail reassigned to prepare the sector's annual budge. George had presented it as a promotion, but Mikail hadn't been fooled. *I got close to something important that is rotten in Imponza*, he thought, *If I get out of this alive, that Sergeant Major will bear investigation.*

So he'd go see Gaspar. The old rogue lived in a shack near the Pruj. Mikail knew where it was, though he'd never been inside. Gaspar did his drinking at the tavern. He drank with everyone, but didn't invite officialdom home.

He saw a large hill a mile away. From its top he could use the field telescope he had taken from the dead Mongol to search for their patrols to the north and to view his route south toward Gaspar's cabin. He rode to the far, southern side of the hill and tethered his horse at its foot. He started to climb, trying to keep under cover. Halfway to the summit he heard men talking loudly above him. They seemed to be discussing an interesting professional topic in a language consisting of explosive consonants. Mongols! They were walking down the hill on a path that would eventually bring them out on the north side. Mikail hid behind a tree. He saw several officers who carried slates and map cases. Telescope cases hung from their belts and one held an abacus. The latter stopped to use his abacus for a minute before returning to the conversation. A pair of enlisted men followed, carrying measuring tripods and rolled-up signal flags, *Surveyors and engineers then, not a search party*, Mikail thought. Shaken but relieved, he waited twenty minutes after they passed out of sight before climbing to the summit.

Nothing had prepared him for what the telescope showed when he swept it north. On both sides of the Roman road an army blanketed the land like grass over a thickly grown meadow. For the next fifteen minutes he used his telescope to traverse the panorama as he had been taught, first in small left-to-right slices and then by swinging the lens back and forth to pick up movement. When he put the telescope down, the immensity of what he had seen in the pleasant morning light made him dizzy. How miraculously lucky he had been! Had he crossed the Velina two or three miles earlier he would have run into the midst of this horde.

His first impression was of a land where great patches had been shaved off Earth's natural beard of vegetation. The great spaces so created were roiling with endless men, horses, and encampments. The camps were all built to the same pattern, a rectangular grid for the soldiers' tents and adjacent lines for their horses. All the roads were dense with traffic. Long caravans of construction materials were heading down the Roman road towards the Pruj. Mikail noted that one caravan consisted entirely of flat-bottom barges. There were even a few camels loaded with equipment. In many of the clearings there were stacks of supplies and fodder, and in others, large tents presumably serving as warehouses.

It was nearly eight o'clock. Kitchen fires still smoked but breakfast was over. Much of the army was still doing morning exercises: Long files of sweating soldiers in loincloths were running in place, playing leapfrog, or paired off and wrestling with each other. But the presence of horses was the most noticeable thing that struck him: being watered, being fed, being groomed, being exercised, waiting patiently in long lines in front of portable smithies, or galloping as their riders charged down a painted line shooting at targets shaped like a man on a horse. In the largest clearing cavalrymen riding small, lithe Mongol horses were being drilled in tactical maneuvers, going from line to column and back at full speed or scattering out of formation to avoid imaginary volleys before quickly reforming.

He looked for infantry but saw none. Except for a few artillerymen practicing loading their guns and the men still at their exercises, all the soldiers were cavalry. He carefully scanned the camps looking for heavy artillery or any siege train equipment. There was none. New formations were still riding down the Roman road, but this army was almost ready to move.

Suddenly Mikhail was reminded how sinister an omen those engineer officers had been. Several hundred arriving cavalrymen led by a rider in an orange cloak unexpectedly turned off the road. Followed by open carts in which Mikail could see tents, equipment, and building materials, they turned onto a narrow path toward a cleared space just below him at the foot of the north side of the hill. When he looked down he observed that space had been marked off with string, latrines had already been dug, and piles of hay were stacked at neat intervals. Mikail could even hear the distant sound of bugle calls. In fifteen minutes, the first soldiers would be close by, and soon someone would be climbing his hill.

Mikail finished scribbling his notes and completed the map he had been drawing, He could not resist, unwisely, standing for one minute more to enjoy the grand Breughel tableau below him. Then he tore himself away to run to the far side of the hill. Southward the countryside seemed empty. He scrambled down the hill, taking no notice when his jacket tore on a thorn bush, and, once mounted, galloped south to find Gaspar. If an observer on the hill noticed him, hopefully he would assume that a single rider moving away from the great army was a Mongol scout.

For the rest of the day and well into the following night, Mikail rode through dense woods. Now he had to find Old Gaspar. The way to his cabin ran through scruffy empty country that took the rest of the day and the entire following night. It was all slow going. Mongols scouts had passed through the empty countryside; he saw their hoof prints whenever he crossed a road or path. Always alert for the enemy, solitary in the dark night forest, Mikail's fear transmuted into loneliness. *If the Mongols find me and kill me, nobody will ever know and nobody ever will care. Not even Karita. She will think I abandoned her.* He kicked the mare's sides to make her move faster, but the tired beast barely responded. By sunrise he started to feel better. The light helped and he could see that he was approaching the last ridge before the forest gave way to the Pruj's swampy flood plain. It was time to abandon his horse. Mikail emptied his saddlebags into his pack and took his weapons. Saddle, tack and harness, all went into a pond. He gave the horse's rump a good hard slap and watched her run away.

Gaspar's cabin looked more like a large shed than a house. He had used his soldier's sense of terrain to site it on a dry hillock in the middle of a marsh. The elevation gave him a good view, and a nearby stream permitted him to move cargo through the swamp down to the river. Mikail approached carefully. A well-situated nest for a smuggler might also be a good place for a wide-awake Mongol officer to station a few men, but there were no tethered horses or other indications of enemy presence. He noticed a small rise at the water's edge and, fearful of what he might discover—he recollected the last time he took a distant view— he crawled to a position where his telescope could search the horizon. He saw engineers at work a few miles down river but nothing closer.

All roads seemed to end two miles down river at a large construction site. Opposite the site another similar construction faced it on the shore of a large island that divided the river. The two sites so mirrored one other that one expected to see a bridge across the water to connect them. Mikail was puzzled until he noticed an engineer riding a horse into the river toward the island. The horse seemed to be walking below the surface of the river. Of course! The bridge was *under* the surface of the river, suspended from or supported by piles driven into the river bottom. Mikail had heard of such things but had never seen an underwater bridge. He pointed the telescope at the surface of the river and found ripples that could be caused by underwater piles. Scanning the shore of the island, he saw nets and tarpaulins covering objects that must be boats. Mikail realized that he had finally found the real explanation for George Hoffman's obsession with smugglers; because they crossed the river, smugglers were likely to discover what the Mongols were doing. So they had to be watched and, if necessary, bribed or killed. Clever George had put him to work watching the smugglers on behalf of the Mongols!

He hurried towards Old Gaspar's cabin. No smoke rose from its chimney. Mikail knocked but at first no one answered. He knocked again and heard someone coming slowly.

A wiry, bandy-legged, small man with a sword in his hand opened the door, saw Mikail, and ordered, "Get inside. Fast!" Mikail saw pale bleached-out blue eyes, a pinched nose, and an almost-white moustache astride a skinny face under a disorganized mop of graying hair. His voice was high pitched, and his eyes blinked constantly. The picture created an entirely misleading semblance of old age. A second look showed a healthy, well conditioned man with muscular arms, a solid torso, and strong, outsized hands. Mikail had heard other smugglers swapping stories of Old Gaspar's endurance and cleverness.

In fact, Old Gaspar was hardly old, probably in his mid forties. "Old" was a nickname. In a flash of sympathetic insight the visitor realized that Gaspar's adoption of a third-person description of himself as "Old" was his private joke. Something had driven the man to join in the use of a mocking nickname. Or he might simply prefer to be underestimated. Either way, the misnomer had impaired neither his strength nor the cleverness evident in his suspicious pale blue eyes.

Mikail stepped inside the shed and, against all common sense, immediately felt safe. In no way did the cabin's neat, clean interior resemble its ramshackle outside. It was the home of a retired soldier standing ready for inspection. The wooden walls were whitewashed, the floor varnished and swept and the bed made with tight corners. Cupboards lined one wall while framed commendations hung on another next to brackets to hold the sword now in his hand. The furniture looked home-made by an experienced carpenter. There was a Franklin-style stove for warmth with a woodpile next to it. Surprisingly, a lithograph of the Emperor and Empress hung next to the mounting for the sword.

"Surprised, ain't you? Why should ye be? Visitors ain't likely to be friendly, so the outside don't attract them. Don't mean Old Gaspar likes mess," his host said. "I ain't surprised to see you. You got nowhere else to go. Stay inside. Soon as anyone sees you, you're a danger to me. That bastard George Hoffman has been here three times with a squad of soldiers alooking for you. He's put a price on your head. Nowadays he looks so slick and pleased with himself you could puke. What do you want from me?"

Feeling lightheaded, Mikail answered, "Breakfast to start. I'm looking for a smuggler to take me over the river. Can you tell me what's going on?"

"Sure," the older man replied as he hung up the sword. "Least ten thousand Mongols, maybe much more, are going to be over that river in a few days. Now tell me fast, why shouldn't I kick you out before friend George makes his fourth visit?"

"You do get down to business in a hurry," Mikail replied. "For one thing I'm carrying a weapon. That's always a good reason to talk. A better one is that nothing good is coming for you from the Mongols or George. Your smuggling days are over. Get me across the river and I'll pay and pay well. I tried to get your pension back, but your friend George killed the idea. You owe him nothing. You owe me the favor of a long conversation."

"Talk to you? Sure. Only not here," Gaspar said. "Can't afford to have you found here. I was going out to chop wood."

"I'll carry the ax."

"All right. I have a place we can talk in peace," Gaspar said. "There's food there Think I'll take a couple of tools."

He led Mikail into the swamp by a path that looked worse than it was to a pair of great oaks growing out of the side of a tussock with twisted, ancient roots half again thick as a man's waist. The gray trunks and roots had grown into each other so that together they looked like a large rock. Gaspar walked over to the side and slipped through an opening not apparent from the path. Mikail followed him into a dug-out space that resembled a root cellar. Gaspar found candles and lit them. "Used this place to store things," he said. "There's nothing much left. Dried fruit and hardtack is over there with kegs of water. We can talk now without worry."

Mikail took a piece of hardtack and some dried apples. He offered an apple to Gaspar, who took it. The two men sat companionably on an embankment and munched away. The sharing somehow reflected the start of a friendship.

Gaspar broke the silence. "Before we get down to business," he said, "what did you do to upset friend George? Anyone who can upset him that much has to be a friend of mine, but he hisses like the snake he is whenever says your name. I asked him what it was all about when him and his Mongol friends last paid me a visit. He wanted to make me think he was friendly, but all he would say was he had to threaten to kill a girl's family to keep her mouth shut. She wanted to tell you what was going on."

Mikail's heart jumped. He explained what had happened.

The older man grimaced, "You had better luck with your woman than I had with mine. Not that George was trying to beat you out. What George loves is money."

Feeling lighter, Mikail went back to business. "Gaspar, you're an old soldier. Do you know what's going on?"

"Course I do," Gaspar said. "All us smugglers talk to each other. Least we used to. Now it's mostly complaining how the Mongols ain't letting us do business. The Mongols are getting into position to invade. My guess is they cross the river in two weeks, maybe less. Going to come over down at the island where they have a funny bridge under the water and upriver at the ferry crossing where the army road ends. They took over the ferry, along with the local boats, including mine, damn them. My guess is ten, maybe fifteen thousand men, are on Roman soil now, with thousands more still in the Zone, all cavalry. Their security is mighty good, real professional. I can describe the engineering works pretty well, and I know enough to give a good description of the troops to any Roman staff officer. Would too, except the Mongols grabbed my boat, and nobody at Imponza is going to take my word for anything. So far I've 'scaped arrest 'cause I have Mongol friends who used to be my suppliers. But that's all over, and George seems to be someone important. Sooner or later he's going to arrest me. Or kill me. The man's turned rabid. What can you do for me?"

"They know me at Imponza," Mikail said. "Until six months ago I was in and out of there almost every month. I know D'Hagen, the Vice-Commander pretty well, because he used to be in charge of support for political officers. I have the political officer's silver card that requires the military to support me. How can we get over?"

"Couple of miles from here there's a village of fishermen. The Mongols didn't want them to disappear from the river. Too suspicious. Boats still go out every day with Mongol crews but one of 'em kept a rowboat. It's tied up on a creek near his house. I thought 'bout that boat the minute I saw your face. Before then I was leaning to riding the storm out underground here. The fisherman keeps his oars locked up in his house, but I'm a pretty fair carpenter. I can make oars. You willing to risk your neck? If they catch us in the river trying to cross, they'll kill us."

"Oh, I'm willing," Mikail said, "My family are Lowlands sailors. I was brought up with boats and can handle rudders and oars. I suppose you are going to wait till night to steal the lumber?" At Gaspar's nod, he continued, "Let's use the time to write up what we've seen. Rome runs on paper like a horse runs on hay."

An idea came to Mikail, and he dug in his pack for the epaulet. "You're a soldier, Gaspar. Can you tell what rank this is?"

Gaspar looked at it and whistled. "See them little gold suns. Senior colonel. Special rank for special people. Kind of a general-in-training."

After nightfall Gaspar went out and returned carrying two pieces of lumber. They quickly shaped two paddles, and Gaspar led Mikail to a shed built over a creek to where a rowboat, bobbing up and down, was tied to a sapling. Mikail thought it was the most beautiful thing he had ever seen. They cast off and quietly paddled down the creek. Dogs barked but nobody followed them. In a few minutes, they were in the Pruj, putting their backs into paddling against a strong current. After all Mikail's worry, the crossing proved uneventful.

Once across, Gaspar insisted they hide the boat. "If the Mongols see a boat in the morning that wasn't there the night before, they'll send a search party. There's a village over there, but the dogs will wake everyone. It's a nice cool night, so we walk."

Trudging along, they fell into conversation. Gaspar wanted to talk about smuggling. "Everyone in Imponza knows about the smuggling. Most of the town is in it one way or another. It's mostly silk. The rest is coral, perfumes, diamonds, and precious stones, pearls, all luxury goods. Be a good market for carpets, but they're too heavy.

"Now you take silk. Perfect for smuggling. It's light. If the Mongol merchants had their way, they'd ship it directly to Imponza, pay customs, and make a whopping profit selling it in Rome. But the Mongol Khan has a deal with the Greeks. Luxury goods that cross Mongolia have to go to the Greek Emperor's city of Constantinople first. That way the Greek Emperor gets his customs, and the Greek merchants mark it up before they sell to us. Mongol merchant gets no profit. So, instead, he smuggles. Sells the silk in the Zone to a smuggler, smuggler resells it on our side of the border, and still it costs less than if it went through Constantinople, even after paying the required bribes. If the Mongol merchant—he's usually a Chinese—could sell directly, the smuggler would become an honest merchant and silk would cost less."

"How did you get into the business?" Mikail asked.

"Honestly at first," Gaspar replied. "Well, honestly as anyone else. When I was still in the Army, I used to make extra money helping a smuggler unpack his goods and prepare 'em for sale. I was just working an outside job on my own time for a couple of good ones. My wife's from Imponza with family in the business. Nobody ever told me the goods I was packing and sorting were smuggled. 'Course they didn't have to, did they? It was good money and half the army was doing it. Later on I got to be drinking friends with a couple of the smugglers and learned the business. I like to drink." Mikail grimaced, remembering that fact. "One day somebody got sick when goods were coming in, and my buddies asked if I could lend a hand on the other side of the river. When I did a good job, I got to be a regular. I learned to handle a boat and met the Mongol merchants. It was good money, but I spent too much time away, and my woman got too friendly with my Sergeant Major. He's in the game too. He keeps the duty roster. He puts your friends on duty when your goods are coming in. No messing around with boats or shipping or packing for Sergeant Major Sodermann. No chance of being caught by border guards. What he sells is in his head, and he gave my woman presents with the money he got.

"Naturally, I didn't like it. I did something stupid. I threatened to tell my battalion commanding officer. I should have realized he was taking his cut. Next thing I found myself in the stockade. I never did talk to my C.O. He talked to me. Visited me in stockade to say I could be court-martialed and cashiered but without jail time maybe, if I made no fuss. If I kept up my commotion, they would kill me. So I took the court-martial like a lamb and moved across the river when it was done, to become a smuggler myself. The army gives good training. Teaches you to work hard, be careful, acknowledge danger, and take responsibility for yourself."

"Why doesn't the Khan just allow the merchants to sell in Rome?"

"Because, like I said, the Greeks pay him, stupid," Gaspar said. "They pay openly. Story goes round Greeks also bribe high officials and members of the Khan's family secretly, but I wouldn't know about that. That's what was so odd about George cracking down on the smugglers. We all thought he'd been bribed by the Greeks. Anyhow, tell me about yourself, Mikail. It's still a ways to Imponza."

The night was starting to lighten. Mikail's feet hurt and he was thirsty. Ever the old soldier, Gaspar had taken a canteen. "I'll tell you anything you want to know," he said, "if you give me a shot at that canteen and fifteen minutes on the grass."

Gaspar handed over the canteen, and they rested. After a long drink, Mikail started to talk. "It's Mikail Adrianus de Ruyter. I'm twenty-eight years old. All my people are sailors and merchants, real water rats from Flushing. My father was captain of the port until a crane fell on him while he was supervising repairs. When he died, I was two years old. My older sisters, Nellie and Miepie, both married sailors; they're still living in Flushing. The head of the family is Lucas, my older brother, the governor of Pomerania. He's sixteen years older than I am and talks to me as if he were my uncle. His wife's father was an aristocrat who used to be governor of a six-province diocese before the Emperor abolished them, so Lucas got to be governor of Pomerania and still is. Then his father-in-law died. Now Lucas is on the wrong side of important people in Aachen.

"The only famous member of the family was my great-grandfather. I'm named after him and everyone says I look just like his portrait. He started as a privateer, became a captain in the navy during the war with the Caliphate, and helped conquer Tunisia. He fought pirates off Africa and mapped its east coast. He was vice-admiral of the fleet that conquered Cuba seventy-five years ago and died out there when he lost his leg. He's buried back home in Flushing.

"When I got out of university five years ago, Lucas got me into the Political Department. I had a year of training in Trier, and I've been out here ever since. Being a political officer is no life. The closest I've gotten to any kind of relationship is a girl in Sapoda. I like her a lot, but I can't see how it has any future. Nothing in my life had been exciting before. Even if this is dangerous, it's exciting. I'm starting to enjoy it."

"I heard about the girl," Gaspar nodded, "from George. You make him nervous. But as an old soldier, let me tell you this sort of thing's only fun the first time."

By this time the sun was up. A cart came by with a load of sweet-smelling lumber. When the driver said he didn't take passengers, Gaspar dug into his pocket for a handful of coins, and the driver changed his mind. The freshly cut wood smelled like spring, the birds sang, the sun came out, and Mikail felt the world had just slid off his shoulders. In no time the towers of Imponza, with their crowns of moving semaphores, were visible. The driver let them off at the main gate, and the two men brushed themselves off, trying to look presentable. Mikail produced his silver card and told the guard on duty that they were on important state business and needed to speak to the duty officer immediately.

Chapter III

Castles

ONLY ITS CASTLE AND bridge made Imponza a city. Without them, Imponza-on-Pruj, to give the town its proper name, which no one ever used, would have been only a small market town for local farmers, craftsmen, and river fishermen. The castle was sited on a huge hill. It loomed over everything in the town below and dwarfed even the cathedral.

Just below the castle hill, carefully placed to be dominated by the guns visible on the castle's aggressive gray walls, stood the bridge over the Pruj that gave the city its name. Imponza was the only authorized point of entry from the Zone for dutiable goods for more than a hundred miles. Left of the bridge, the city sprawled in the shadow of Castle Hill, leaving the customs station and its warehouses squatting in the confined space between castle and bridge. To the bridge's right, a small walled port served river traffic and the few military vessels sarcastically called the Imponza Navy. The castle guarded the river and protected the road to Saint George's Castle, the Proconsuls' summer capital. Once the flowers started to bloom, the Proconsul moved down from Cluchia [modern Cluj] to reside at Saint George's to be closer to the Empire's borders for whose protection his Commandery existed, He lived there until September when the campaigning season ended. His Dacia Commandery ran from the Black Sea to the great Hungarian plain. Within it Aetius Da Costa (who everyone called "the Paladin") was Proconsul, military commander and civil governor. His word and writ were final, except for any citizen's right to appeal to the Emperor.

Even that was more theoretical than real. The Emperor was his friend and, rumor had it, his half-brother as well.

Within the main gate, Mikail and Gaspar awaited the duty officer. A smartly uniformed young captain soon appeared. He was not impressed by the two vagabond civilians until Mikail presented his silver card and introduced himself in his most official voice, "Political officer Mikail de Ruyter on the most important possible business. We must see the Vice-Commander at once; he will know me."

The duty officer maintained his sangfroid and asked, "What is this all about?"

"Just take us to the Vice-Commander," Mikail barked and, surprisingly, the duty officer replied, "Please come with me," as if he dealt with Imperial emergencies daily.

Colonel Christopher D'Hagen, the Vice-Commander, was the man who kept Imponza running smoothly. He was short and broad with a ruddy face, a resonant voice, a down-to-earth manner and the appearance of a friendly disposition, unless you knew him better. When the duty officer brought the two visitors into his office, he waved off introductions and greeted them with a roar of laughter, "By God, it's young De Ruyter and old Gaspar Nodiameau! As ugly and mismatched a pair of tramps as ever I saw. What grand Imperial emergency brings you to me, gentlemen?" He grinned as he drew out the last word.

Mikail stared directly into his eyes. "The worst you've ever seen, Colonel," he blurted. "Treason and invasion! The Mongol wars are about to start again. The Mongols have an army on Roman soil just on the other side of the Pruj. George Hoffman is a traitor. I don't know who else might be. I have documents and papers. Both of us have seen a Mongol army deploying on Roman soil with our own eyes." He added, "Sir, you may want to bring in the general."

"You talk to me," D'Hagen replied. "The general's in Saint George."

Mikail told his story and brought Gaspar into his presentation to describe the Mongol installations with more precision. He displayed the Mongol documents, the dead Mongol's identification papers and epaulet, the fan and the oddly shaped piece of metal and finally, handed over the notes he and Gaspar had written in the dugout. D'Hagen read them, and then let Mikail finish, asking only a few questions. What he did next was a surprise. He hefted the token carefully, examined it for a minute, and tried to bite it. Finally, he put it down and spoke, "I've heard of these things but never expected to see one in my own office. This is the Khan's tally, Mikail. This kind is given to show special confidence. No more than thirty are ever outstanding. That metal fan is a battle fan, an emblem of command. Senior Mongol commanders use them to give orders. The holder's name is cast into it, which again suggests it was the Khan's gift. Your senior colonel might have been a member of the royal family. Don't ever let a Mongol know you were the one who killed him. It would be very dangerous to brag about it."

D'Hagen took a breath before saying, "All right. I believe you. Or at least I believe those things. An attack on this castle is about to happen.". He told his secretary to call in the duty officer and when he came, told him in a calm voice, "Porshotz, get my aides, the signals officer and his clerk immediately. Find the general's secretary and any of his aides who haven't gone to Saint George and bring them here at once. Then follow the procedure to announce the general alert. It's all urgent."

For the next two hours Mikail and Gaspar sat in D'Hagen's office, answering his occasional questions and watching him put Imponza on a war footing. Nothing broke his concentration. He never raised his voice nor displayed nervousness, except by scribbling endless lists and notes to himself. Mikail and Gaspar's written notes were flying to Saint George by carrier pigeon when D'Hagen told the Duty Officer, "Put these gentlemen up in my own quarters. Set a guard at the door and get them riding clothes."

As they were leaving, he added, "One more thing, Nodiameau, I looked into your situation after Mikail talked to me. Sodermann always had a reputation for cutting corners, but people liked him, and I was fool enough to be one of them. We thought he was a merry, old-fashioned Sergeant Major. No patience for rules, but a good soldier who got things done. And get things done he did, by God! He corrupted half this place. I've got him in the stockade with half a dozen men. You'll be cleared when I get around to the paperwork. Now, Mikail, listen to me: Sodermann had something going on with George Hoffman, but he's too scared to come clean yet. Tell the Paladin that I'll get it out of him."

Mikail and Gaspar were given a bath, a meal, and a few hours to rest before being brought downstairs. D'Hagen was waiting for them with the duty officer, who was already mounted, as was a platoon of cavalry, and with a small open carriage. D'Hagen said, "The Paladin will want to talk to you. Porshotz, get these men to Saint George as fast as you can. Don't worry about the horses."

Porshotz kept his detail moving at full speed, but early next morning a cavalry detachment of the Proconsul's personal guard from Saint George was already waiting for them at a crossroad. Its commander and a civilian in ordinary riding dress were sitting on their horses in the middle of the road. The civilian greeted Porshotz, whom he seemed to know, dismounted and walked his horse back to the carriage. He stuck out his hand and said, "Hugh Pannonius. The Proconsul sent me to meet you. Would one of you fellows like to chat with me in that carriage after I've had a few words with captain Porshotz? Then I'd like to talk with the other."

Mikail offered his hand and said, "Mikail de Ruyter. I've heard so much about you," and immediately regretted his choice of words.

Pannonius grinned. "From George Hoffman? Oh, what George must have said! Snoop, henchman, hatchet man, and the man who does the Man's dirty work. It's all true, and George should know. You seem to have had a couple of lively days, de Ruyter, and still managed to get out alive. You're causing all kinds of excitement in our quiet lives in this quaint place. Oh, and I think I've met your father." He climbed into the carriage and, with a theatrical gesture, offered Gaspar his own horse.

"That must have been Lucas, my brother," Mikail said. "My father's dead. Lucas is much older than I."

Pannonius had come out from Aachen to work for the Proconsul two or three years before. Although he clearly was an important person—the grapevine even said he had been a senior aide to the Emperor himself, but that was absurd—somehow he was always "that oddball." Mikail had never met him before. George feared and hated him, but talked about Pannonius all the time. He called him "the double bastard," implying he was the Paladin's illegitimate son. No one else thought so.

Mikail saw a man of middling size, just a little on the plump side, with a high receding hairline, sad eyes, a well-barbered mustache and a touch of upper-class smugness in his face. He was probably in his middle or late thirties. When he spoke, one noticed his high-pitched voice and his politesse. His Latin had a plummy court accent that made him sound as if he were taking chocolate with the Empress. But his laugh was a loud cackle and his face clownish when he grinned.

For the next two hours, Pannonius pleasantly and informally walked Mikail through the most thorough debriefing of his life. When he finished, he thanked Mikail and congratulated him again on his initiative and ability. Then he called for Gaspar and asked Mikail to ride alongside the carriage while he debriefed the other witness. Mikail was impressed by how much precise military information Gaspar had gathered and how well this polite civilian understood it. The task complete, Pannonius complimented Gaspar and then, to Mikail's surprise, they talked army gossip about back pay, reinstatement, and pensions. Finally, Pannonius returned to the topic of George Hoffman, asking many questions, but getting few answers. It all ended with yet another round of elaborate thanks and effusive congratulations. Pannonius then broke the seals on the oilskin packets and started to examine the documents—apparently he read Mongolian. When he finished, he put the documents back into their packets and leaned out of the carriage to say, "You wouldn't believe what's in those documents. Now let me tell you a little about what's waiting for you at Saint George. You'll be in segregation for your own safety, and you will meet with some military people, who will go over the same ground until they understand it perfectly. I'll be in and out of the room. I have to report in to the Paladin, and he wants me to do the translations. He will talk to each of you himself. Hold nothing back. I don't expect it will take much more than a day, because he was in a tearing hurry when I left."

By early morning of the next day, they were turning onto the entry road to Saint George, or, to give the fort its official title, The Great Imperial Castle of Saint George the Warrior. The Castle had been designed and built shortly after Rome had acquired Dacia two hundred and fifty years ago and rebuilt and expanded many times. It was designed to project the overwhelming power and authority of the New Roman Empire and its Proconsul, particularly to the Mongolian and Byzantine Empires. Often besieged, it had never been taken. It was a self-contained walled city with endless armories, stables, workshops, storerooms, and barracks that could house many thousand soldiers. It even boasted a small palace, built to house the Emperor should he visit.

Visitors reached Saint George on a well-built, straight stone road, running over more than two miles of gradually rising open ground to the main gate. The visitor felt the eyes of the watchers in its high towers on him throughout the long approach. An immense treeless meadow surrounded the walls. In front of the walls was a wide dry moat with spears embedded in its bottom. The walls ran for more than a mile in either direction from the main gate. Behind the castle, the cliff dropped two hundred feet.

No familiarity with the castle diluted Mikail's astonishment, because George Hoffman did not allow his juniors to visit it. He was candid, "No visits, I don't want anyone going over my head." George reported to Andrew Kloffheim, Chief of the Political Department in the East, who resided in the castle. Kloffheim was George's old friend, and George made sure everyone knew it. Mikail had only met him at his annual inspection tour, where Kloffheim was friendly, but George monopolized his time.

Two large, unsmiling civilians awaited them at the main gate. After talking to them, Pannonius told Mikail and Gaspar, "You have quarters in the Keep near the Proconsul's office. Please stay there. We find surprises upsetting at times like these." Two processions formed, as one civilian fell in alongside Mikail and the other beside Gaspar, and soldiers joined them. One soldier walked in front of Mikail and the other behind him. They came out of the tower, blinking in the sunlight, into an immense cobblestone courtyard. Pannonius led them diagonally across the plaza to the Keep, a group of connected towers. Far away on the other side of the courtyard was the palace, looking dowdy and in need of a good paint job. The visitors were ushered into a reception room at the Keep to sign a ledger. No one spoke, Mikail felt as if he were being arrested. Pannonius must have sensed his feelings, because he turned around with his wide grin to say, "Grim ain't it? Makes you feel like you were caught stealing from your mother's purse. This is how we treat our friends, Mikail. We serve our enemies wine and cheese."

The civilian led Mikail and his escorts to one of the larger towers, up two flights of stairs and then into a suite off the second floor landing. He locked the door behind them and walked Mikail through an antechamber, past a pair of meeting rooms facing each other across the corridor and into a brightly lit room overlooking the Keep's inner courtyard. Mikail was surprised to see a lovely flower garden in the courtyard between the towers, giving a touch of grace to the castle's pervasive grimness.

At last, the civilian spoke, "I'm Willem. I've been assigned to keep you safe and comfortable. Mister Pannonius will be working in one of the meeting rooms, and people will talk with you in the other. There will be a guard outside the suite at all times."

"I couldn't help noticing the garden," Mikail said. "It looks so unlike everything else here."

Unexpectedly, Willem smiled. "The Proconsul's wife made the garden. He keeps it the way it was when she died and won't allow any changes at all. We have the same flowers in the same beds at the same seasons. And when his children visit, we keep holiday hours. Standing orders."

Mikail was left alone, except for Willem, for an hour, He felt alone and abandoned. When Pannonius returned, he sat down in his meeting room, spread out his documents, and set up a peculiar copying device that looked like a spider made of wooden and metal rods, with a pen at the end of each leg. He looked up at Mikail's woebegone face and grinned, "Would you like to see how this gadget works?" Mikail said, "No, thank you," and sat hunched up, feeling like a condemned man waiting to hear sentence pronounced. Pannonius stepped out for a minute and came back.

In few minutes, Willem knocked on the door to say, "I thought you might be hungry." He placed a platter of cheese and bread, and a carafe of wine on the table in front of Mikail. Mikail was startled. Pannonius began to chuckle, and Willem looked confused. Finally, Mikail understood. "You set me up!" Pannonius went off into his cackling laugh, as a general and two colonels walked into the room with a much younger captain bobbing in their wake.

The senior officers sat down at the table facing Mikail, while the captain went to the end of the table and opened a notebook. "Would you set your goddamn contraption up in the next room, Hugh?" the general said in a biting tone. "Later perhaps, you might tell us what's so funny." But Mikail found his nervousness was gone.

The general informally introduced himself as Dan Lauzac. A cavalry officer from his boots and britches, he was a small man, muscular, thin and nervous, with eyes that gave nothing away. He began, "Before we start I have to ask one question. Is there any chance, any possibility at all, that all this has all been staged to deceive us or is a scheme to force us into some foolish action? This information looks so good I have to worry if it's too good to be true. I don't mean to suggest you have any involvement or are telling us anything except what you have seen. But think about it."

A bubble of anger rose in Mikail. He snapped, "They could have fooled me with a lot less. I got those documents by killing a man. And Gaspar has seen the same things."

The general nodded. "Of course, but bear with me. You walked through an army looking for you straight to a boat over the river. If it's true, you are the luckiest man alive. Can you remember the face of the man you killed?"

Mikail called up the Mongol's face. "What sticks in my mind," he replied, "is his nose, a hook nose, twisted to the left. Perhaps he broke it, and it didn't heal the right way."

The captain at the end of the table broke in, "That's him all right," he said cheerfully. "Odsetag's son, Prince Subatai. He broke his nose playing polo. Odsetag is the older sister of the Khan's first wife. The ruling family is part Turcoman. They all have eagle beak noses. Kaidu is his uncle."

"That settles authenticity," the General said. "As if any of us really doubted it. Young man, you have just thrust a burning spear into a hornets' nest. You killed the Great Khan's favorite nephew. He will take it personally." Turning to one of the colonels, he said, "He was carrying movement orders to Osorian. His death gives us an extra day, maybe even two or three. Get that thing we talked about at breakfast started immediately. *Now*, Paul! *Now!*" The colonel leaped up and rushed out.

Lauzac continued, "Young man, I want you to tell me everything about the troops you have seen and their equipment. Start with the first time you saw a Mongol. When we are finished, Colonel Percolo will want to know about roads, bridges and such. He's an engineer. Then this young sprout (he gestured at the captain) who does the kind of thing we are not supposed to talk about, will want to know everything you can remember about that arch-devil George Hoffman and his evil works. I probably shouldn't tell you this, but the fellow Hoffman reported to here at the castle has gone missing too. Eventually, we'll have to begin a witch-hunt for spies and traitors, but right now we have more urgent things to do. Wait a second, I want to get Pannonius in for this."

The general had a ravenous appetite for detail and a talent for cross-examination. He had read the descriptions written in Gaspar's hideaway and brought in a map to check them against it. The examination was systematic; he kept a mental checklist of topics and continued asking questions about each topic until Mikail could not give any further information. It was a long time before the general declared himself satisfied. Then he told Mikail, "You have saved many Roman lives. You cannot imagine how much help you have provided." He left, and the engineer colonel took over. He had Gaspar brought in and worked his way through his list of questions. By the end, he and Gaspar were conducting a dialogue; they seemed to share a common language.

The young captain who had avoided giving his name took over next. He went looking for Pannonius, and because no one had eaten since early in the morning, sent Willem out for food. Then he and Pannonius spent two exhausting hours trying to pull out every detail of George's life. When Mikail finally objected to the repetition of the same questions, there was an ugly silence until the captain sighed, "The fellow he reported to hasn't been seen for a week. We don't know if he took any documents and can't trust what he left. Hoffman did his best to tell you nothing, but you are our only source."

It was dark when they finished. Willem had made up a bed, and Mikail fell into it, too weary to dream.

CHAPTER **IV**

A Long Conversation in A Round Room

THEY BROUGHT MIKAIL TO the Proconsul the next afternoon. Willem and his guards walked him down to the flower garden where crocuses and silver bells were already in bloom and then around it, and then up endless stairs to a waiting room at the top of the opposite tower. A sergeant behind a desk told Mikail, "The Proconsul will see you now. Go up the stairs and knock."

The sergeant opened a door behind him, disclosing a narrow, well-lit stairwell with smooth walls. The man at the top would have a clear view of anyone coming up, together with a clear shot. A small landing at the top of the stairs ended at a door. The light was arranged to fall on the face of any person who stood before the door. Mikail went up and knocked.

A well-built big man with a cheerful, clean-shaven face opened the door. The Paladin stood at six foot three and looked to be in robust middle age. His well-cut, reddish brown hair was salted with white. Honest gray eyes looked directly into Mikail's face The noble effect of the Paladin's face and height was a little diminished by his dress, old, faded pants, a well-worn comfortable shirt and scuffed shoes, and by his ink-stained hands. The man projected informality. He looked more like a dignified chief gardener than the commander of the eastern Roman frontier. His cheerful open appearance contradicted his reputation for deviousness. Mikail could not miss how the man's profile resembled the image on every coin, except that he wore no beard. The whispered rumors that he was the Emperor's illegitimate half-brother seemed credible.

"Come in, youngster!" he boomed. "You have no idea of the trouble you're causing." His voice was friendly, more tenor than bass, and he glanced at the long table in the middle of the enormous room where Mikail's maps and documents were spread out. A quire of paper and an open inkwell sat at the head of the long table. There were crumpled pages in the basket under the table. Although the day was not cool, one fireplace was lit.

The entire top floor of the tower was his workroom, a forty-five foot circle broken only by an enclosure that contained the stairs to the roof. The room was bright with light; its ceiling and the outside of the stairwell were whitewashed. From waist height to ceiling, windows encircled the room, interspersed with metal war shutters on rollers. If the castle were besieged the windows could be closed and shuttered, or opened and the room packed with snipers who would have clean shots over a long, uninterrupted field of fire. Tables were placed around the circumference near the window seats. Comfortable chairs and office tools and furniture were scattered around the room. Mikail noticed a cot with blankets neatly folded. The room's only decorations were an inscribed etching hanging on the wall of the stairwell of a young Emperor and Empress, and two small framed miniatures on a desk near the head of the table. One was of a pretty woman with three young children, and the other of the same woman in later years. Chessmen had been set up on a small table next to an open book of chess problems. The Paladin was a famous chess player. Next to the documents on the table toward which the Paladin had gestured were maps held down by stones at the corners. Obviously, they had just been in use.

From the windows you could see endlessly in any direction. Following Mikail's eyes, the Paladin smiled and told him to enjoy the view. "Everyone does," he said. "I wanted to talk to you yesterday but I was very busy." Mikail walked around the room, drinking in the fresh green countryside. As he did so, his host picked up the waste paper basket and walked over to the fire to feed its rumpled pages to the flames. The front and sides of the castle looked out over an immense lawn gently sloping down for hundreds of yards. Every irregularity or dead space had been filled in, leaving no hiding space invisible from the tower. Beyond the lawn was an almost treeless open landscape. The back of the castle looked down upon a sharp, rocky cliff. One might easily forget why the grounds had been so artfully built.

"It's beautiful," Mikail said.

"Yes, but it's cavalry country. A sudden attack in front might surprise the fortress. I gave orders to man the walls once the first semaphore came from Imponza. They won't catch us this time. Are you Lucas de Ruyter's son?"

"No, sir," Mikail replied. "Lucas is my older brother and head of the family. Do you know him?"

"Met him twice when he was at court years ago, and once again when they sent him to do a job for me. Nice fellow, not very flexible. A bit stuffy, in fact, if you don't mind my saying so, but very able once you get him concentrated on your problem. He fell out of favor with those who are 'in' at court. Has it blown over yet?"

Impressed, Mikail picked his words with care. "He says he's no longer at the top of the Chancellor's black list or likely to lose his governorship, but he's not in the way of promotion either. He's got a province to govern, but he complains that Pomerania's not a good one."

"So much for the gossip," the Paladin said. "It's always useful to place people. Now let's get to work." He gestured at a pair of chairs before stopping to say, "You must be starving. Wouldn't you like something to eat?" Mikail thanked him and said he had eaten.

"Have you ever had chocolate? The Danes and Icelanders bring it in from Mexico. We can't seem to grow it ourselves. Tried to do it in Cuba, but they wanted to use slaves and the Pope forbade it. It's supposed to be only for the court. My daughter sends it to me."

Mikail had heard of chocolate, but had never tasted it.

The Paladin surprised him. He walked over to a table Mikail had not noticed where water was bubbling over a small brazier and prepared the drink with his own hands, expertly grinding and mixing the ingredients. He made two large cups and set them down on the big table, along with a few pieces of a sweetened hard toast taken from a ceramic jar.

Sitting, he gestured Mikail to a nearby chair, and let his voice settle into a businesslike tone, "I'm going to entrust you with matters of great importance. I dare not tell the Emperor what I want to say through the semaphore system. At most I can give him a few hints, so I'm sending you to Aachen as my messenger with the materials you've collected and a letter. You are the natural person to deliver them, and he'll want to ask you questions. Pannonius will go with you. The Emperor sent him to me to learn, and now he needs him to help conduct his defense He has remarkable experience for his age. He comes from a courtier family and understands Aachen. My letter will suggest that the Emperor select you as Hugh's assistant. There are also two backup letters, one for the Empress and the other for my daughter, Dorcas. If anyone challenges your story, produce the token, the battle fan, and the officer's epaulet. They've told you what that token is, haven't they?

At Mikail's nod he added, "Don't flash it. It's solid gold." They hadn't told him that. "A warning, young man. The court will not look or feel dangerous, but don't be deceived. That letter threatens the lives of important people. Aachen will be as dangerous as Sapoda. They may try to kill you—maybe more than once—and would consider it self-defense if they succeeded. Women there are as dangerous as the men. Watch your tongue and suspect everyone. Take care with what you eat and drink, and even more care with whom you eat and drink. There are plenty of people in Aachen as false as George Hoffman, and not so incidentally, your friends working for him are dead."

Fear gripped Mikail. He managed to ask, "Are you sure?"

"Hoffman would be a fool to leave them alive," the older man replied, "and he won't."

Feeling so out of place that he was almost dizzy, Mikail tried to get his thoughts together. "I can understand why you are sending me to Aachen, but why are placing these responsibilities on me and treating me as if I were someone experienced and important. Why should anyone even listen to me?"

"If the Emperor sends you, people will listen. No one who hasn't faced down a coup has any useful experience. I know. I was part of such a defense a long time ago. However unlikely it seems, you are the right person for the work. You won't be alone; you'll be working with Pannonius who will be reporting to Louis Duval. If you need help, ask one of them. Why are you the right person? In the first place, you're *here*. In the week it will take you and Pannonius to travel to Aachen, the two of you will become a working team. It would take another week to get others to that point, and that's time we don't have. You're young enough to adjust to new conditions, and you managed to survive under impossible conditions. Above everything else, we can trust you, and right now we don't know whom we can trust in Aachen. There's a plot that hasn't declared itself. You see, the Emperor can't be sure whom he can trust."

Mikail thought, *So this is how it feels like to be at the center of things. Like standing in deep fog on top of a cliff when you don't know where you can safely place your feet.*

The Paladin paid no attention to his visitor's discomfort. He went on, "I am only going to tell you what you must know. The documents you brought consist of a set of movement orders for the Mongol army and a personal letter from its commander, Kaidu, to Osorian, one of his generals. Osorian's two double tumans—about eight thousand cavalrymen, approximately a third of Kaidu's army—are to cross the border into Roman territory on a special mission. Subatai, whom you killed, was carrying the orders directing Osorian to commence that invasion. His death probably gave us a couple of extra days to respond— yet another gift for which I am very grateful. Nevertheless, Osorian may already be over the border. I don't know what arrangements the Mongols made after Subatai's death. I have already started to do something about Osorian, but I'm not ready to talk about it."

"The main body of Kaidu's army—remember, that does not include Osorian's tumans—will cross the Pruj when directed and move on this castle, or go north to support another force on our side of the border. Either way they will try to seize Imponza by surprise first, but, again, thanks to you, Imponza will be ready for them. Kaidu himself will also move soon. His plan is for Osorian to move a few days before the main body.

"All this is important. Indeed, it's life and death to many soldiers yet what's most important is that letter. Kaidu writes his subordinate to set out his intentions at the beginning of the campaign and to give certain specific directions. I knew Kaidu when I was deputy to our ambassador at the Khan's court in Sarai. We were your age and played a lot of chess. A very able man is Kaidu, untrustworthy but imaginative, and tricky, fond of a risk.

"To understand what follows you must know that two years ago I unwillingly lent five thousand of my best cavalry to the Magister Militium for service in Tunisia. He promised to return them as soon as our difficulties there were over. The Magister stalled on his promise, and I had to go to the Emperor before he grudgingly agreed to send them back. In this letter [he tapped the paper], Kaidu tells Osorian to ambush those five thousand men deep in our country while they are *en route* to Saint George before any declaration of war. He describes them as half cavalry and half infantry. He knows the exact route they will be taking and tells Osorian where to lay his ambush. But, I only found out that the Magister was finally sending my men back and that only half would be cavalry, by a semaphore message from Aachen three days ago. Kaidu knew what troops Aachen was sending and the route they would take long before I did! Someone in Aachen told him. Worse, the letter hints that the assassination of the Emperor or a coup against him is being planned. It's treason, the deepest and blackest of treason.

"Now, back to you. The Emperor needs people he can trust now. He knows Pannonius and trusts him, but doesn't know you. I want him to understand that you are trustworthy. The best way to do that quickly is to tell you family secrets neither he nor I would tell anyone we did not trust."

The Paladin paused and asked Mikail if he had any questions. Mikail was too astonished to reply. "Then let me answer the question you are too polite to ask," the Paladin went on. "Of course, I am the Emperor's brother. Isn't it obvious? Father even insisted that my brother and I shed drops of blood and mix them in wine to drink while swearing the brotherhood oath. It's an open secret, but publicly I am never acknowledged. There are strong reasons for this peculiar arrangement, which Father gave to us when he made us take the oath, and I will share them with you.

"Father said that opposition to the Emperor coalesces naturally around his brother. Once that process starts, the brothers can never trust each other again. Every Emperor always tries to force his brother out of the political mainstream. Inevitably, the brother fights back. It's impossible to resist. Look at your Uncle Clovis and myself. 'I do not want my sons to hate each other,' our father said. 'I want you to have a career and a good life, Aetius, and I want Martin to have a brother who will always be on his side. The only way we three can get away with that is for you to go on being Da Costa's son. Then your brother can safely promote and trust you and your children. For safety's sake, your children had best be born out of wedlock too.' He told my brother he must keep his half of the bargain and, regardless of whatever I said or did, always behave as my brother.

"I had better explain the technicalities. Under the law—and for two hundred years every Emperor has sworn in his coronation oath never to change it—only 'true successors to Charlemagne' are eligible for the throne. That includes every descendant, male or female, of the twelve Carolinian Emperors. Presently, there are about four thousand. There are always enough candidates available so that the Emperor cannot be forced to designate a Nero or Caligula just because there is no one else. It also helps prevent the curse of the old Roman Empire, usurpation by successful generals not related to the throne, by creating a whole clan with interest and influence as a counterbalance. The Emperor himself must be legitimate, but the true successors include descendants of *acknowledged* illegitimate children. Therefore, I am not acknowledged, and I could never marry my children's mother, although Donna was my wife in every real sense. Do you understand this?"

"Yes," Mikail said. "Only someone who is not legally the Emperor's brother can be trusted as his brother. It's strange."

"Exactly," the Paladin continued, "My mother, Adela Da Costa, was a lady in waiting to Clara, father's favorite sister. It was the old story— it's hard for any woman to say no to an infatuated Emperor. My father was handsome, virile, and needed women. He liked their company and knew how to make them enjoy his. Erich Da Costa was a dry stick, twenty years older than his wife, away for months at a time, and he had not given her any children. So I came into the world as the son of Erich and Adela Da Costa. Erich Da Costa was not happy, but what could he do? He was honorable. He treated me well, kept his mouth shut, and never asked the Emperor for anything. He taught me to ride, swim, and play chess. I cried harder at his funeral than my mother.

"There are schools for boys and girls in the palace. I was always one of my brother's playmates. The Emperor used to come to see the children two or three times a week, and I was easily integrated into the family group. Da Costa of all people told me the truth when I was about nine. By twelve I was living in the palace at the school dormitory, and Martin was living down the hall. Father told Martin at about the same time Da Costa told me. He had already figured it out.

"When Martin graduated he went into the army for three years, as the Crown Prince always does, but Father sent me to Constantinople to learn court manners and court style. After two years, I was sent to Mongolia to get real responsibility for the first time by working with our ambassador in difficult negotiations. That's how I met Kaidu. Then father brought me home. Martin had been busy trying to find out how the army worked and in making friends. He was only a year away from twenty-five when his position in the succession would be official, but the first few years can be dangerous for a young Crown Prince

"For the next few years I was a busy and important young string-puller, manager, and man-about-town. A ladies man but never serious. Jenny was twenty-two when I met her." It took Mikail a few seconds to grasp that 'Jenny' must be Genvira Horatia, the Empress. "My brother and I met her at the same party. She liked us both. Then father had a stroke when Martin was twenty-six, old enough to succeed, young enough to be vulnerable.

"Uncle Clovis decided to attempt a coup. His wife was foolish enough to patronize Aunt Clara, who drew the right conclusions and warned Martin. We struck first and gave Clovis the choice of public disgrace or having a 'heart attack,' with Martin's promise that his wife and family wouldn't suffer. Clovis chose the heart attack. We gave him a state funeral. With no candidate, the conspiracy dissolved. Is all this clear?"

"Yes," Mikail said. "It's not exactly what they taught us at school."

"Never put them right," the Paladin said with a laugh. "If people only knew . . . Soon after his elevation, Martin decided that he needed Jenny for his Empress. He told her all the things no woman can resist: that he wouldn't and couldn't go on without her, that he loved her more than his life, and he appealed to her sense of duty. Jenny couldn't resist it. I could not bear it and there was a scene. I called my own brother a thief, a conniver, and worse. Martin told me that I was the lucky one, 'The Emperor's purple robe is a winding sheet. It wasn't you, Aetius, our uncle wanted to kill.' One of the servants ran and got the Old Empress. She told Martin he was Emperor now and had better learn to control his temper and mouth and reminded me of my oath. 'Aetius,' she said, 'my heart bleeds for you, but there is nothing you can do about this.' We made up, and for two years I helped Martin get his government in order. But it did not help me to see that Jenny was happy and the marriage a good one. So I went to my brother and told him, 'You need someone in Dacia you can trust to protect the borders and I need to get away from Aachen.' When he couldn't talk me out of it, he sent me here.

"When I got here I worked ten hours a day and played Don Juan afterwards. I earned a well-deserved reputation for being a roué and predatory womanizer. The Emperor wrote brotherly letters; the Old Empress wrote gentle letters; and my own mother wrote one I found painful to read. Nothing changed me. Eventually, I met the daughter of a local landowner and sang her my arias from *Don Juan*. We liked each other from the first minute, but finally she told me to go away. A month later, when her refusal and the letters had sunk in, I was back. I told her, 'A Proconsul's marriage needs the Emperor's approval. He won't give it, and I don't intend to resign my Commandery. So I cannot marry you.' Donna had been thinking too. She told me she wanted me 'in marriage or out of it' and would take my vow to treat her well and never hurt her in lieu of a ring, but I must understand that if ever I were false she would be ruined. I made the vow, and she settled in as my open mistress. Her parents disowned her. I stopped being Don Juan. We were very happy, and a year later she was pregnant, which changed things.

"I wrote my brother that I would go back to private life if he didn't consent to the marriage. Instead of an answer, I received a letter in the purple ink the Emperor uses to give a direct order ordering me to present myself at once in Aachen *alone,* underlined twice, without delay. Failure to obey would be a crime. Donna said, 'Go. I'm not going to ruin your life.' I went.

"When my brother made no concessions, I lost my temper. Then he lost his. He said he was still Emperor, and I knew perfectly well he could not permit the marriage. He called me an envious brother and a probable future traitor. I accused him of a perpetual desire to destroy my life. We were not dignified. We were not quiet either, and the noise brought Jenny. Martin had told her nothing about Donna. When I told her, Martin turned red. There was silence, and Jenny asked us to calm down while she talked to the Old Empress, and the women tried to work something out.

"When the women came back the Old Empress said, 'We have a suggestion.'

"Martin said, 'Never mind, I have a solution. The family will send a personal representative to the christening. Imperial christening gifts will be made directly to Donna and publicly displayed to show approval. While in the Commandery, Donna will be treated as if she were Aetius' wife, but there can be no marriage.'

"To my surprise, the women thought it wasn't enough. Jenny said she would stand godmother herself, but my jaw dropped when the Old Empress told Martin to apologize. 'I know what my Karl wanted,' she said. 'He wanted Aetius happy and settled the way you are. Martin, you had no right to push him this far.' Martin apologized. We have not quarreled since.

"In my letter I tell the Emperor that I have entrusted you with these family secrets. He will know that if I am willing to do that, I would trust you with my life. Tell no one, no one at all, not even Pannonius, any of this. Never trust Clovis' son, Frederick. He knows how his father died. Don't trust anyone connected with him either and that includes my own son David He is on Frederick's staff. We have quarreled—that never would have happened if his mother had lived, but he's too old for me to control. On the other hand, you can trust his sister, my daughter Dorcas.

"Now put it all together and repeat the instructions I have given you."

Mikail did so, adding that he would not fail through negligence or lack of attention. An obscure emotion made him stand up and salute, something he had never done before.

The two men had been sitting facing each other. The Paladin stood up, stretched, came to a conclusion, and started again. "One last thing," he said, "when you see the Emperor tell him that I don't want to spend the rest of my life as his Proconsul. I don't like this place without my wife. I'll buy some land down the river near my older daughter, make wine, play with my grandchildren, and be an ordinary man. I'll come to court twice a year to see my son, with whom I will make peace somehow. I'll have done my duty."

Astonished, Mikail blurted out, "'Shouldn't it be you to tell him that yourself, sir?"

"Tell him what I said," the Paladin instructed.

He turned back to Mikail and finished in a businesslike tone, "You'll leave tomorrow at sunrise. Destroy everything if you are going to fall into enemy hands. If there's trouble before you get well away— by now they will be very upset and thinking about out how to stop a messenger—worry about yourself first, Pannonius next, and your escorts not at all. The important thing is that those documents get through. A cavalry escort of a full Wing—that's about twenty-five hundred men—will see you to a safe point. Thereafter, I have use for that Wing, and Dan Lauzac has his orders. Good luck and, absurd though it sounds, take an old soldier's advice and try to get a good night's sleep. Tell the guard downstairs to send up Pannonius and General Lauzac." He put out his hand and Mikail shook it. There was no arm-to-arm Roman handshake as Mikail had half expected, nor any appeal to his patriotism.

The talk of marriage and a good wife had made him think yet again of Karita. He wished she were with him.

Halfway down the stairs, it occurred to Mikail that if he hadn't already done so, the Paladin would order Pannonius and Lauzac to kill him before allowing him to fall into enemy hands. "For Christ's sake, what have you got yourself into?" he moaned to himself and shivered.

CHAPTER V

Knight takes Knight, Rook Castles.

THEY BROUGHT MIKAIL DOWN at dawn. He wore what they had provided: outsized riding boots and a cavalry officer's riding uniform with light britches so the horse could feel his thighs. He hardly recognized yesterday's great field now with twenty-five hundred cavalrymen and their horses deployed on it. In front of each of the Wing's squadrons its guidon pennant flapped in the light breeze. Behind each pennant the squadron's troopers were standing next to their saddled horses. The squadron's officers were clustered in groups, receiving final instructions. Cooks circulated, bearing cold meat, biscuits, and warm-watered wine.

Conspicuous in red and gold full dress and scarlet cloak, the Paladin dominated the group of senior officers surrounding him. Gaspar was not dressed to ride. Mikail overheard the Paladin say, "I have a job for him. He stays with me." He finished his orders to the generals by instructing them in an anxious voice, "Stop for nothing. Speed is everything. Keep in continuous touch with your scouts. By now Osorian could be well ahead of you. We know where he's headed, but have no idea where he is. I can scrape up another five hundred men when De La Tour comes back this afternoon. I'll send them right along, but don't wait. Go!"

A trooper had brought Mikail a magnificent brown stallion, and he was already in the saddle when the Paladin walked over to say farewell in a formal voice, "Good luck and Godspeed, de Ruyter. It was a good day when you came." He tugged at Mikail's saddlebags to reassure himself that they were well attached before looking at his generals and nodding. The second in command, General D'Atri, ran to his horse, leaped onto the saddle, and trotted toward the lead squadron. Seeing him coming, its troopers scrambled to mount their horses.

Lauzac mounted and shouted, "We sortie!" and pointed to his bugler. The bugler stood up in his saddle to sound the *Mount* and then, almost immediately, the *Forward*. Every bugler in the Wing repeated the calls, and the first squadron was in motion before the sound had ceased to resonate. Squadron by squadron the rest of the Wing followed, its pace accelerating as it reached the paved road.

Once he saw his Wing in motion, Lauzac galloped to the commander's position a third of the way down the column. A ragged gaggle of riders—aides, flag bearers, messengers, signalmen, and Pannonius and Mikail—followed him, all spurring their horses to keep up with their leader. As the general passed, each squadron's pennant dipped, and the squadron's troopers shouted, "*Lauzac!*" The weak first light made watery highlights shiver over their helmets and breastplates, the three-piece lances that seemed to spring out of the back of the troopers' heads, and all the metal on the horses and riders.

The acceleration was intoxicating. Accompanied by the thunder of ten thousand hooves, the cavalry broke into song. Swept along by patriotism and comradeship, Mikail raised his voice. He had sung the Cavalry Anthem in school where its banal words and crude rhymes always made him wince. Today the same words made his blood run faster. Intoxicated, he bellowed at the top of his voice along with the rest.

Hurrah for the man on a horse!
A man and a half is he.
Glorious and victorious we be.
Heroes of Roman Cavalry!

Elated, he sang all five verses over again when the Wing repeated the Anthem.

They continued to gain speed, stopping only for an hourly five-minute break to let the troopers dismount. After several hours, there was a half hour's pause to unsaddle and rest the horses. Mikail kept up, but by the end of the first day, his exhilaration was wearing off and pains in his back and thighs kept interrupting his noble thoughts. Though a good rider, he was unaccustomed to this pace, but he soon became used to it. Pannonius rode easily alongside him. He seemed thoughtful rather than exhilarated.

In the middle of the morning of the second day, the column suddenly slowed and then halted. Mikail saw dusty scouts galloping towards them. Lauzac immediately led his senior staff and squadron commanders into a field by the side of the road. On the road, his cavalrymen dismounted to keep their horses fresh and waited. The scouts galloped into the field to report, and an impromptu command conference began. Aides set up a varnished board, where Lauzac sketched out what he wanted done and spoke for a few minutes, pointing at various officers as he did so. After a few final questions, everyone nodded and rode back to station.

The troopers turned their horses around; Lauzac rode to the rear of the column and led it back at a gallop towards a ford they had crossed less than an hour ago. Crossing the ford, they emerged into a meadow between the water and a small wooded hill that overlooked both meadow and ford. The road, which had been interrupted by the water, began again in the meadow and continued for a hundred yards before circling the hill and straightening on the road at its far side. Lauzac halted his column behind the little hill, taking care to position men and horses where they would not be not visible from the ford. He left General D'Atri and seven hundred mounted men behind the hill.

The rest of the Wing dismounted. Every tenth man was told off and ordered to lead the horses further down the road and hold them there. Lauzac led his dismounted troopers over the wooded hill to the rear slope overlooking the stream and the meadow, there posting them carefully group by group just behind the tree line where they could see without being seen. Then he walked down to the ford and looked up at the hillside to assure himself that his troopers were invisible. Behind the tree line, the dismounted men formed a dense line two hundred yards long overlooking the area where they needed to step only a pace or two forward to be beyond the trees. Each trooper strung his bow and took a dozen arrows out of his quiver, pushing them into the ground to enable a continuous volley. Lauzac told them to sit and to rise to shoot only when they heard his command.

Behind the hill the men who had been detached to hold the dismounted archers' horses set about scuffling the ground to raise dust and create the sound of horsemen moving on the road. Buglers sounded cavalry calls that trailed off at the end to create an impression that the Imperial cavalry was moving away. Lauzac told Mikail, "Stay close to me whatever happens," and positioned himself further up the slope to have a clear view. A few yards away, a trooper detailed for the purpose, held the reins of Mikail's horse so that his saddlebags could be seen. Lauzac beckoned Mikail over and spoke quietly, "My guess is that they've found their dead man and worked out that we would send someone to Aachen with his documents. Two or three hundred Mongols—maybe a few more—will be coming this way within half an hour, according to our scouts. Once they're on this side of the water, we'll give them a surprise. Never get more than a few feet from your horse and always know exactly where those papers are."

They did not have long to wait. A dozen Mongol scouts on dusty horses rode down the road to the far side of the stream and sat on their horses patiently to mark the ford. Within minutes, hundreds of Mongols had gathered on the opposite bank. Following their commander, they swam across the stream. Once in the meadow, they started to regroup just below Lauzac's silent, hidden archers. As soon as he saw the Mongols assembled in the meadow, Lauzac blew a whistle, and his archers stepped out from behind the trees; the air vibrated with a continuous twanging sound of arrows flying and bowstrings being released. The volley was followed within seconds by five more. Most of the Mongols and their horses went down as the rest milled about in confusion. Another whistle, and the seven hundred Roman cavalry hidden behind the hill galloped around the hill and into the meadow charging the disorganized surviving enemy. Some kept their heads and rode into the water trying to get away, but they made good targets for the archers. Few escaped.

The slaughter was quick and efficient. Mikail remembered his exhilaration of yesterday and felt disgusted and ashamed. Suddenly, Lauzac was at his elbow speaking, "They were looking for *you* young man. For *you* personally, and no one else. They took an enormous, foolish risk. They risked a trap to save a few minutes, because they knew you were almost safe. In a few hours you will be leaving us. When you get to Aachen remember that keeping you away from Aachen was worth the lives of hundreds of men."

Lauzac and his aides rode down to survey the carnage and rummage for documents on the bodies of dead officers. It did not take long. Lauzac spurred his horse, his deportment showing his urgency. The Wing reformed back on the road and quickly moved on.

Turning to Pannonius, Lauzac told him, "They were a detachment from the main force, Hugh, not Osorian's rear guard, thank God. That's what I was looking for. You know what I'm doing next don't you?"

"Yes. Ambushing the ambushers by coming in behind Osorian's men."

Lauzac nodded. "The Mongols won't overrun our people. They have been warned and are building breastworks and ditches. That's what the Proconsul was organizing before he spoke to you. By this time tomorrow, we'll know if it worked."

The Wing had already started to move. Lauzac sped after them, leaving an officer and a platoon of horse to accompany Mikail and Pannonius to Cluchia, where a coach would take them on the next stage of their trip to Aachen.

Later, when they were nearing their destination, the news of Lauzac's victory at the Hormordul River caught up with them but by then their minds were set on Aachen.

Lauzac reported his victory over Osorian by carrier pigeon, but he knew the Paladin would be anxious to talk with him. Three days later he was back at Saint George. When the Paladin congratulated him, Lauzac was not entirely happy. "You are a crafty old devil, Aetius," he said, "and you judged all the angles and played it like a perfect pool player. You knew just what they were going to do, and you had our people right where they should have been, but if I had arrived a few hours later it would still have been a disaster. They must have done better than forty miles a day carrying the parts for a pontoon bridge while using mountain passes for surprise. Who ever imagined they could move that fast in our country?"

"I think they spent years scouting their routes," the Paladin said. "They took plenty of remounts, and it wouldn't surprise me if they stocked fodder on our land at one-day intervals to move at full speed day and night. They kept no reserves and held nothing back from the attack. So when you came in behind them, they were lost. How badly did they hurt us?"

"It could have been worse," Lauzac said. "It only cost us three hundred men."

"Only three hundred men!" exclaimed The Paladin and he quoted Erasmus, 'Sweet is war to those who do not know it.'"

Lauzac went on, "There's worse. De La Tour took an arrow in his throat and died."

"A good friend gone. The older I get, the less stomach I have for this business," the Paladin said. "How badly did you hurt them?"

Lauzac's face cleared. "Oh, I hurt them all right. In fact, I wrecked them. When I came up they had split into left and right flank forces, which were almost separate armies. All their reserves were engaged, and there was only a scrim of cavalry in the middle to connect the two flank forces. And they were tired. Their right flank was dismounted, arrow-dueling with our infantry, which was dug in behind earthworks and doing very well. My scouts brought us in right behind that Mongol right flank, and when my people unexpectedly charged them from behind, they were fully engaged with our infantry. Poor dismounted devils, they had no horses and no place to run. We rode right through them. Nice ground too, absolutely nothing to slow us up. Then we turned around and hacked our way back through the survivors, leaving our infantry to finish them. There won't be much left of that right flank, and it must have been a good half of everything Osorian had.

"Then I moved over to take care of their left flank. We caught them out in the open, showered them with arrows, and charged. Even so, they managed to pull themselves together and started to make a fight of it. They really are very good, Aetius. But when those last five hundred men you scraped up arrived, D'Atri sent them in with fixed lances. He got the point of impact exactly right, but it still was a fight for a while. That's when De La Tour was killed. Finally Osorian's forces were demoralized. It took him a while to get what was left organized enough to run off. I left D'Atri behind to clean up and pursue them. Whatever's left will get away over that underwater bridge."

The Paladin grinned wolfishly. "That they will not," he said. "I sent forces on boats to destroy the bridges and works at the crossings. Kaidu left almost nobody behind to protect the works. I put two hundred men with torches, axes, and crowbars on the Imponza 'navy.' They picked up Gaspar. He knows that river like his own living room and we caught them by surprise at daybreak and destroyed the bridges. With a little luck, D'Atri will catch whatever is left with their backs against the river, and they'll have to swim for it.

"Now, Kaidu doesn't have enough left to push his raid in force, and he'll have to make uncomfortable explanations to his Khan. We can concentrate on the Byzantines. If this was designed to get us to commit to the north before the real blow came in the south from the Greeks, then we have done the job on them. We will concentrate further back and further south and wait. Don't look so glum, friend. You and I are heroes. You know where I keep the good Rhine wine. Pour two glasses so we can toast our mutual brilliance and that false bitch, Victory."

Lauzac did as he was asked. When he sat down again he said, "All right, now what?"

"You have to get some infantry into this castle. Don't overdo it. Take enough cavalry to cover Kaidu, but don't be drawn into a full engagement. We will move everyone else back and concentrate around Cluchia. When they do something, we'll know what happens next. If we're lucky, nothing happens."

"That doesn't seem likely," Lauzac said. "Not if they have been scouting us for so long and have set up for dirty work in Aachen. It's too important for them—whoever *they* turn out to be. I wish I knew what Mikail was going to find in Aachen. Why didn't you go there yourself?"

"Couldn't, we need someone here in Dacia who doesn't have to ask Aachen before he takes action. Nothing wrong with the boy, but he's not yet up to this kind of job, so I sent Hugh too. To soften Martin up for later, I told Mikail to tell him that when this is over I want to retire. Do you want my job? You can do it, and D'Atri can do your job. If I can't give D'Atri what he's entitled to, I'll have to send him on to Tunisia. I think the man in purple will take my advice."

Lauzac took a mouthful of wine, chewed it, rolled it around his mouth, grinned, and then looked straight into his Proconsul's eyes before he responded, "And spend the rest of my life being a fucking civilian dealing with the other fucking civilians, not to mention the snakes in Aachen to whom you've just thrown that nice boy? On whom may God in His infinite mercy have pity. No, Aetius, no! No, thank you."

BOOK II

Mikail and Pannonius

May and June 1812

CHAPTER VI

Wonderful Speed

THE JOURNEY TO AACHEN took eight days. It began with two days of hard riding on mountain roads through the Carpathians. By the time their horses stumbled up to the front door of the Paladin's palace in Cluchia, riders and mounts were exhausted. The Paladin had sent instructions by carrier pigeon, so changes of clothing, hot baths, and hot meals were waiting, but they were allowed only two hours rest. Pannonius complained, but he was told, "Sleep on the coach. Proconsul's orders." Two hours later, when they stumbled into the courtyard, a coach was waiting with a soldier coachman on the high seat and four muscular horses harnessed in the shafts. The Paladin's representative had handpicked the four strongest beasts in all Dacia and a madman with a whip for coachman, but he had not been wholly without mercy; the coach had springs.

It carried them over the hilly foothills at the back of the Carpathians onto a straight-edged highway over the great Hungarian plain. Changing horses at each post stop, the coachman kept his team running as if they heard a pack of mountain wolves howling in pursuit. They saw nothing through the windows, except an immense prairie landscape of earth and sky, with endless grass dancing in the wind all the way to a flat, distant horizon, punctuated only by an occasional tree, the tall poles of the Hungarian well hoists and now, and then, a distant church steeple. Though they passed through flocks of sheep and herds of long-horned Hungarian cattle, they rarely saw a person, even when their horses charged through a small town, other than a passing rider on an unknown errand, a herdsman leading his cattle, or a shepherd with his crook. It was an event when they crossed the river Tirza over a well-made stone bridge.

Spring was wet and stormy. Vast banks of dark low clouds loomed above the plain, and they moved quickly. When they reached the coach, the hard rain came suddenly, announcing itself with a drum roll of big drops on the coach's metal roof that quickly changed into a sustained pounding by a thousand mad drummers. The howling scream of the wind that continuously rocked the coach provided the wind accompaniment appropriate to the percussion of the rain. The noise was too loud for talking. Despite the coach springs, the travelers spent two days being shaken like dice in a box until they breasted the last hill before the river to find below them, sparkling in the smiling noonday sun, the beautiful cathedral at Esztergom and the grand curve of the Danube. The demon coachman drove directly to a pier where a chartered steamer was waiting for them, steam already up. It cast off as soon as the travelers crossed the gangplank and headed upstream toward Vienna; a day's run away.

The coach had been too noisy for conversation. Now, sitting at ease on the deck with their legs stretched out on folding wooden chairs, they could talk. Mikail told Pannonius pretty much what he had told Gaspar about his background, adding a great deal more detail about his work in the Political Department. They even discovered they had something in common: Pannonius had been a regular visitor to Trier, where his father had been a professor of mathematics while Mikail was studying there. They must have just missed meeting several times.

On deck Pannonius held school.

Mikail asked, "You wanted to get rid of George. What did he do?"

"I caught him making the wrong friends. Money was moving between him and the Imponza smugglers. It was never clear whether they were bribing him or he was financing them. Either way, his conduct was criminal, though no one suspected treason. The man he reported to thought that public disgrace for a man of George's long service would be bad for his service's morale, so the Paladin decided to send him where he couldn't do much harm. That's how we transferred him to the place where the Mongols chose to invade, but the Paladin thinks they shifted their impact point when they saw they had a man in place. He says Mongol soldiers are taught that the first principle of war is taking advantage of unforeseen accidents. As things played out, you provided the unexpected chance that gave him the opportunity to teach the Mongols their own lesson. He's very pleased with himself, and with you."

"George kept me away from you," Mikail said. "You're obviously some kind of aristocrat. He liked to suggest you were the Paladin's bastard son."

Pannonius' raucous laughter broke the air. "No such luck. The Paladin's rich, and I'm not. As for being an aristocrat, aren't we all plain citizens nowadays? The great reforms of Karl VII made all titles mere names. We don't even maintain the old Roman distinction between the honest and the humble.

"Yes, my family is large and distinguished, and the right line of Charlemagne too—like four thousand other people. My father is now Rector of Strasbourg University. My aunts and sisters married important people. You'll meet my only surviving grandaunt, the widow of a general, almost my second mother, and much livelier than the real one. My brother's the brightest of us all, but he chose to be a parish priest. Best of all, the Empress herself is a cousin on my mother's side. Not a close cousin but she acknowledges the relationship."

"Nobody's going to call your family plain folks."

"We aren't. But money? No," Pannonius said, "none whatever. I have to work for a living. Real money is in land or sometimes in banking. We don't own land, lend money, or buy and sell things The rich landowners who used to be kings, margraves, archdukes, and dukes before Karl VII reduced them to ordinary citizenship—not it has ever made the slightest difference in their superior social standing, because we Romans are all snobs—are aristocrats. They own thousands of acres, a palace in the city and a great house in the country. We have a comfortable house in the city and, maybe, a few acres in the country. Grandees marry each other, not the likes of us."

He leaned forward to emphasize his point, "We are *temporary* aristocrats. We serve in offices that are at the Emperor's pleasure. We depend on him. Politics always follows the money, so naturally we support him unless he's a despot. Then it takes real courage to oppose him. The Grandees don't need the Emperor and think they are as good as he is. So they tend to go into opposition. Their natural habitat is the Witanagemot.

"Mrs. DeHaavan taught me in the third form that 'a Witan's a wise man and the Witanagemot's the meeting of the wise men,'" Mikail recited in a schoolboy's singsong. "The Witanagemot is only a costume show. It hasn't any real power except to censure the Emperor for despotism. Doing that practically calls for rebellion and hasn't happened since they censured Otto VI for running a brothel in the palace and murdering his brother and his Chancellor when he was drunk."

"You haven't been listening," Pannonius said. "There are two kinds of power. One is the Emperor's, which lies in his prestige and in his men, like you and me."

"Hardly the likes of me."

"You, me, and the many thousands of civil and military men serving him. What's the Emperor to us? Our job, our career, our oath of loyalty. But the Grandees *own* whole provinces. They have enormous social prestige, the habit of command, and bonds of blood and marriage. To them the Emperor's the only reason they aren't absolute rulers in their own domains. When the Witanagemot meets, the Grandee party is all gathered in Aachen. The Witanagemot's a confrontation, an annual bomb that the Emperor must defuse. Most years it's not hard, but the Paladin thinks there's going to be trouble this year. Didn't he warn you?"

"He did say it would be dangerous. But who would dare to even think of trying to set aside the Emperor?"

"An able, well-connected, ambitious man with broad experience, great resources and a high opinion of himself, who thinks he's as good as the Emperor. There'll be quite a few of those in Witanagemot Hall. The Emperor's cousin Fredrick is the most obvious. Nobody can figure out his behavior toward the Emperor. The Emperor acts as if he owed him something which isn't natural. The prince presumes upon it and gets away with his presumption. He should be grateful, but he isn't and he doesn't show proper respect. Louie Duval thinks it hides a secret."

"Why are those people so ambitious? They have everything."

"It's not just ambition. The Grandees have real disputes with the Emperor, mostly about money of course, but they see them as questions of honor and prestige. They hate his panRoman policies and recently they have been pushing the Emperor about them at the Witanagemot every year. Duval blames Frederick for stirring them up."

They talked late into the night and started again at breakfast. When the steamer docked at Vienna late the next morning, a fidgety colonel was on the pier to deliver them to a steel railroad car, fully guarded and provisioned for the journey. "Food and water are in place with a guard watching them," the colonel recited. "I personally watched them brought in. Proconsul's orders."

The train took them on an uneventful two-day trip through the fields and hills of western Germany, a built-up country stuffed with busy towns. The countryside was green with grain, fruit trees, and grape vines and they saw many people working in the fields. They did not see the half-wild cattle and the flocks of sheep they had seen in Hungary, nor the goats they would have expected to see in Dacia, but every farmer seemed to have a cow. There was no visible military presence, except for an occasional uniform on a station platform. Old castles nested on the hills, but they were retired soldiers. Their defensive walls and outworks had been removed, moats had become ornamental ponds, and doors and windows cut into tower walls. The rounded, peaceable landscape grew ever richer and smoother as they approached the capital. When they detrained they congratulated themselves that even counting unavoidable delays, their journey had only taken them eight days, three hours and seven minutes. Incredible time!

Of course, that time would have been cut in half had the railroad tracks reached Cluchia. Railroads were a hundred years old, and the idea of a rail connection from Vienna to the Commandery had been bruited about for decades without a single mile of track being laid. Nor was it likely to be. Officially, the reason was the difficulty of building double track over wild country and driving tunnels through mountains. In fact, construction would have encountered no engineering problem not long since solved. The reality was that the Emperor did not want to spend the money and would not let anyone else spend it. To his mind, a privately owned railroad was a private tariff on a public road. The Empire's reconstruction and reunification by Karl VII in the Sixteenth century had been based on the prohibition of private armies, titles, fortifications, rights to coin money, and the elimination of tariffs, tolls and fees to robber barons and all other private impediments to travel, trade, and communication within the Empire.

In principle the Emperor was equally unyielding against private ownership of roads, canals, and railroads alike, but in practice the problem came down to the railroads. The Emperor followed good old Roman tradition and was a mighty builder of roads. He made sure his Counts kept them well paved and built feeder roads for farmers and artisans to get their goods to market. He believed in canals and laid out good money for their construction, knowing he would be repaid out of tolls. But he steadfastly refused to apply the same reasoning to railroads, whether because the initial outlay was so great, or because running a railroad required so much supervision, or simply because he was stubborn. Of course, a railroad to Dacia was an excellent idea. He would build it himself, he said, just as soon as funds were available, whenever that might be. Until then, nothing must be done. So nothing was done.

The length of the trip gave Mikail and Pannonius more time to talk about what awaited them in Aachen.

"Do you actually know the Emperor himself?" Mikail asked.

"Oh, yes, I was Louie Duval's second assistant. He is one of the Emperor's two chief aides and that put me mighty near the sun. I was in many meetings with the Emperor present, though I never met with him alone. Louie doesn't like that. I would have known him anyhow since the Empress is my cousin and I went to the palace school. The Emperor visits the school once or twice weekly and talks to the children. He knows them all by name. It's a tradition."

"With connections so good how did you get thrown out of Aachen?"

"Bad luck. I got caught between Louie and the Chancellor. Louie asked me to look at the Treasury's handling of military procurement costs, which were much too high. I suggested a special military treasury, being very careful not to blame the Chancellor, but he still took it personally and raised a storm. That turned out to be a terrible mistake on his part, because it led the Imperial Consistory and the Emperor to look into all Treasury functions. They took them all, military and civil alike, away from Sforza and gave them to a newly created Grand Treasurer. Louie got the new job for his first assistant, Roberto de Patrios. That automatically made me Louie's first assistant, a big promotion. The

Chancellor thought Louie, Roberto and I had planned it all to get promotions for Roberto and me. Like all the Sforzas, the Chancellor has a terrible temper. He demanded somebody's head as a public trophy. He couldn't get Louie's head, though he tried, and he couldn't get Roberto's either. But a head he would have, and since not only is the Chancellor the second man in the state, but Sforza is the Emperor's oldest friend, they had to find him one. Mine was the obvious choice."

Pannonius' voice had started to rise but he calmed himself before continuing, "The Emperor is not always kind with subordinates, but, since I am a relative, he gave me a private audience, the only one I ever had, and told me, 'The Chancellor says he needs a human sacrifice to protect his position, and I must oblige him. I know it's not your fault, and I have a better job for you. Aetius Da Costa, our Proconsul in Dacia, just lost his senior aide. You'll get to work with Aetius directly and learn a lot you'd never learn here.' How could I protest? He was being kind when he didn't have to be, and I suspected even then that he was right about Dacia being the right job for me. Being sent down unfairly hurt, but that sort of thing happens all the time in any court. What really mattered was that there was someone I deeply cared for in Aachen."

"The Paladin told me I'm supposed to learn how Aachen works from you."

"I just told you," Pannonius replied sullenly.

"How did you get the job in the first place?" Mikail asked.

"Oh, family connections. I had a good record at school, and my father's university position helped. As things worked out, I was good at the job and got promoted until I got someone important angry at me. Then I was fired. That's Aachen. To get in you need luck, friends, or family. You're in. Now you need good connections. The Paladin, who is never wrong about this sort of thing, thinks we make a good team. That's one connection. So work hard, let me know twice a day what you're doing, and come to me with any questions. You protect my back and come through on your assignments. In exchange, I will protect your back and see you get money and promotion. Try not to get any important people angry at you."

Mikail thought it best to change the subject.

"What's the Emperor like?"

"Naturally intelligent, understands people, has an endless appetite for facts and ideas, plus immense experience. Just like the Paladin, but he can be mean. He wants an independent mind, yet he demands a respectful tongue. Once he makes up his mind he's stubborn. His wife is his closest advisor. She brings him news and ideas he would never receive otherwise. She can talk to anyone about anything. He always listens to her, even if he doesn't always necessarily do what she suggests."

"Will I actually meet him?

"Oh, yes."

"Why did the Paladin give us a letter for his daughter?"

"To involve her so she could protect his interests. Dorcas is the most favored of the Empress' ladies-in-waiting. It's the tightest relationship you can imagine; even water can't seep between them. The Empress is Dorcas' mistress, her godmother, her best friend, and probably her aunt. Dorcas has a quick mind and knows everything going on in the palace, and what she finds out the Empress soon knows. God pity you if she doesn't like you."

"You don't much like her do you?"

"Why, no, I wouldn't say that," Pannonius murmured mildly. "I wouldn't say that at all." Perhaps it was nothing more than his soft, nostalgic smile, but Mikail thought of Karita.

Pannonius went on, "Now for the people around the Emperor. There is no prime minister; this Emperor won't have one. The closest thing we have is Giuseppe Sforza, the Chancellor. The machinery of civil government reports to him. He's the one your brother Lucas has to please."

"Do you know how Lucas got into trouble? He won't tell me."

Pannonius smiled. "He doesn't want little brother to know how stupid he was. The Chancellor wanted a favor that he shouldn't have had. Lucas rightly refused. Happens all the time. Sforza knows when he's in the wrong, not that it stops him from trying again next time. Your brother bragged how he had stood up to the mighty Chancellor and the story got back. Lucas is going to be staring at the Baltic Sea doing penance in Pomerania for a while longer."

"How does Lucas get back in the Chancellor's good graces?"

"By never repeating his mistake. Let's get back to Sforza. The Chancellor is more important than anyone else, but not more important than everyone else. Consequently, people gang up on him or run around him to the Emperor. Sforza doesn't ever take that in good grace. He retaliates where he can—don't I know it!—and his terrible temper, his relationship with the Emperor, and his enormous intelligence means we all step lively at court. He and Duval are at each other's throat more often than not. Louie's a lot of fun but twisty as a corkscrew. There's another other senior aide, Albrecht Desle; he's older and honest, totally reliable. These relationships keep the Emperor in charge and all of us dependent on him. Which is what he wants."

"Who else is especially important?"

"The Emperor likes old friends. One of them, the Mayor of the Palace, is responsible for provisioning the palace, keeping order, maintenance, arranging ceremonies—everything that goes on there. He's also in charge of the Emperor's spies. The Mayor's nasty. Another old friend is the Magister Militum, who commands the military. The Emperor's personal military aide is General Biakarione, a very talented fellow with some excellent people working for him. Which reminds me," he said as he opened the door, "Colonel Valla, would you join us please."

The colonel came into the room looking even more nervous than usual. Pannonius smiled and said, "Mikail, this is Colonel Raul Valla who has been avoiding me in the futile hope that I wouldn't remember him. As if I could forget. Raul used to work for Biakarione. He wrote the military part of my Treasury memorandum. We are talking about how things go wrong in Aachen, Raul."

"I can see why you would want me in that conversation," the colonel said dryly.

"Exactly," Pannonius said. "What were you doing in Vienna, you villain?"

"The same thing you were doing in Dacia, hiding from the wrath of Sforza. Biakarione sent me down there before Sforza could get me exiled as military attaché to the penguins. The Magister intends to send me to Dacia to replace De La Tour. He thinks the war there is going to wind down. What's Lauzac like to work for, Hugh?"

"I'll tell you later," Pannonius said and turned back to Mikail, "And there, Mikail, we end our two-denarii tour of Aachen. We look after our friends in the hope that they will look after us. Eventually, friends become connections. So you do your job and protect my back, and in exchange I will look after yours. You and I are going to be working for Louie, and if I'm lucky, he will look after mine."

"Louie? Don't count on it," the colonel said.

CHAPTER VII

The Great City of New Rome, Usually Called Aachen

MIKAIL HAD ASSUMED THEY would take the train into the city, but Pannonius had other ideas. They left the train ten miles outside the city. A carriage was waiting for them by the side of the track.

"This is safer." Pannonius said.

"Where are we going to stay?" Mikail asked.

"With my Aunt Luisa, the one I told you about who is the widow of a general. Since I'm named after him I'm still 'Young Hugh' there."

Aunt Luisa welcomed her favorite grandnephew with a shriek of joy. She was a tiny old woman with a sweet smile and hennaed hair. Her butler was another story. A dignified old man with ramrod posture and a pair of magnificent white operetta mustachios, he welcomed "Young Hugh" with dignity and asked him whether he was keeping up his fencing practice.

"Yes, and I will prove it to you whenever you like. Just bring money," Pannonius replied. "Now, Janos, this is important. There's a small chance we might have unwelcome visitors. Be careful to lock up, and we're not here if anyone asks. You might leave a real sword in my room, not a practice sword." Janos accepted what he heard as an ordinary request. Somehow that did not astonish Mikail. What did was how unsurprised sweet little Aunt Luisa was and how complacently she nodded her approval.

Then Pannonius and his aunt spent more than an hour catching up in a rambling conversation that mixed Aachen political gossip and family news. There didn't seem to be much difference between the two. She told him that the Imperial couple were visiting the Empress' sister and would not be back for two days. Pannonius decided to do nothing until they returned.

If this was a safe house, it was a peculiar one, albeit very comfortable. In the parlor Aunt Luisa did needlepoint and talked to Mikail as if he were a contemporary she had known for fifty years. She told him about the old Emperor's affair with "that Da Costa girl," who had become so snooty once she had an Emperor in her bed, and described two other Imperial affairs the Old Empress had never found out about. Then she added in an offhand way, "He made his sheep eyes at me too, but I would never have betrayed my dear Rudolph."

Upstairs, fencing swords clashed in the attic as her butler and nephew stamped on the floor and shouted at each other. Eventually, they came down, and Janos transformed himself from fencing coach back to butler. He served them chocolate and small cakes, while Aunt Luisa nibbled at chestnuts preserved in honey. She asked Janos if he had been drinking with Pannonius, and the butler admitted he had.

"Janos, some day your home-brewed brandy is going to kill someone."

"One drink never killed anyone," Janos responded, "and it's been years since I had the pleasure of working with my favorite pupil."

"Look, Mikail," Pannonius said, "I can't leave the house. Too many people would recognize me, but you should start to learn your way around the city. Janos, can you provide him with civilian clothing?"

"We do have some civilian clothing around that my wife can tailor. He will look a little old-fashioned, but he can say he just arrived from the provinces," Janos said. "Glasses would be better cover than a beard; his hair would have to be dyed to match."

The noise from upstairs continued for the rest ot the afternoon. Next morning breakfast was tense. Pannonius looked bone-weary and hung over. Elizabeth served. "My poor, good husband is in bed," she explained, "because you beat him up so badly fencing yesterday. Young Hugh, you shouldn't force him to drink."

"Your husband may be old, Elizabeth," Pannonius noted coolly, "but he is neither poor nor good. He insisted on toasting my return with two of his homemade potions. That super-concentrated explosive he distills has no more effect on him than water. He had me half drunk before the bout started. Then he tripped me, hit me below the belt, used the broad saber slash, and shouted *Hey-La* when he hadn't hit me. So much for fencing practice. We went on to the quarterstaff. He broke all the rules there too. He used the staff like a sword, jabbed for my eyes, and held my stick. Then he announced that I owed him forty denarii and somehow not only did he persuade me to pay, but he made me agree to celebrate with two more of his homemade fireballs. My arms hurt. My ribs hurt. My head hurts. My eyes do not focus, and I feel like a black and blue pincushion."

Elizabeth huffed, "Young Hugh, you shouldn't speak that way about a kind old man. It's nothing but good training to save your life some day."

"It's more likely his brandy will kill me first," Pannonius retorted.

Aunt Luisa put a prompt end to domestic disharmony, "Mikail, I'm sure Elizabeth has your clothing ready. Why don't you go out and see the city? But look out for pickpockets, dear. They're such a problem here in Aachen."

She realized what she was saying an instant too late, but when she turned to look at him, Pannonius was managing to keep a straight face.

Palace Square, the heart of Aachen, was an enormous cobblestone oblong half a mile long on two wide sides that faced each other and a quarter mile on its two shorter sides. In the middle stood an equestrian statue of the founder of the modern empire, Karl VII, "the second Charlemagne," leaning forward on a bronze steed, his grim eyes focused on the palace, as if to assure himself that his successors still followed his policies. The palace's front occupied one entire long side of the plaza. Within it, the gold-roofed imperial residences used only a small part of the compound. The walled compound also contained: the Garden Wing, an enormous, free-standing building, where the chief officers of state and their senior staff had their offices, a chapel the size of a small cathedral; a hospital, a prison, a music hall, a theater; schools for the palace's children and the chapel's choristers; barracks for guards and housing for their officers; quarters for resident staff, stables, an exercise ring for horses; innumerable service buildings, and a good-sized private park.

Mikail stood near the statue and looked around. The square's two short sides, to his left and right, were lined with public buildings and private palaces, but in the middle of each street a break opened into the start of a major artery. To his left, an Arch of Triumph announced the start of Witanagemot Avenue, a tree-lined grand boulevard used for parades and imperial processions that ran for more than a mile down to Witanagemot Hall. To his right was the beginning of Great Street, the city's main commercial and shopping center. The entrance was flanked by a pair of massive, semi-nude marble statues brought from Rome so long ago that nobody remembered what they were supposed to mean. The Aacheners had named the male statue "Work" and the female one "Play." It was a very Aachen thing to say "Let's play together" when you proposed to meet someone at the statue. It established you were not a provincial.

On the other long side, Church confronted State. The entire half-mile was the front of a vast leafy Cathedral Close. Within the Close were the Gothic façade and soaring tower-steeples of the Cathedral Church of Saint Michael the Archangel in New Rome and a suite of smaller buildings. The Archangel—no Aachener ever called his cathedral anything else—replaced a previous cathedral that burned down almost two hundred years ago. A strong-willed Archbishop had raised the money for its construction through public subscriptions throughout the Empire. Although Aachen's public buildings emphasized its heritage as New Rome by their classical or classical-based facades, the Archbishop had made his own personal statement about church and empire. The Archangel was the only large Gothic building in the city.

To supplement the Archangel, Fischer von Erlach had built a suite of lovely Baroque buildings all made from the same materials and sharing the same elements of design. The same design element might appear on the façade or as an entrance, in different sizes, in brick, stone, or stucco, or in red, yellow, brown, black or white. Endless lively and unexpected echoes and turns and changes, created lovely rhythms for the eye that harmonized like instruments playing a Baroque concerto. The Archangel towered over the smaller buildings like a great baritone who sometimes sings with his instrumentation and sometimes sings against it and both completed Fischer von Erlach's design and contrasted with it, thereby creating a second, greater harmony. The rest of the Close was so extensive that its broad lawns and leafy tree plantations composed the Aacheners' largest park.

Mikail had not come to the Archangel out of piety. He was there to see the most famous painting in the world, Peter Paul Rubens' *Christ and the Church Triumphant*. Like most men who had attended Trier or one of the other secular universities, he would have described himself as "enlightened." Many, perhaps most, Romans preferred to refer to themselves as "devout." During much of the Sixteenth and early Seventeenth centuries religious differences among Romans had led to recurrent civil war and rebellion. Five Emperors had been deposed or murdered, many cities burned, often more than once, and whole provinces devastated. Finally, Karl VII's "Refoundation" had enforced a rough compromise that his successors had managed to convert into a habit of tolerance. Karl's grandson Otto once explained it, "If a man prays for me in his church and toasts me in his tavern, I don't interfere with him." So the Emperor publicly displayed his personal piety to the established Church, but he maintained a strong garrison in Rome, held tightly on to his right to appoint bishops and brooked no political intervention from those he did appoint. His Counts discouraged heresy hunting, but they had no qualms about action against dissidents once they thought might threaten the public peace.

After entering the Archangel through the central door and passing though a small marble foyer, Mikail was blocked by a dark velvet curtain, which, when parted, revealed a vast, light-suffused nave. Sunlight surging through a double row of stained glass windows filled the room and made the polished marble and semiprecious stone set into its floors and walls shine like Brobdingnagian jewelry. The upper and the lower rows of stained glass windows were as bright and fresh as they had been on the day Raphael finished installing them. Four rows of mighty columns sprouted upward like thousand-year old trees until their tops flowered into multiple, stone-carved fan vaults to hold up the distant roof.

Putting everything else aside for later, Mikail walked down the nave toward the chancel where the picture he sought hung behind the high altar. So vast was the canvas on which *Christ and The Church Triumphant* was painted that the picture could only be hung by stretching it top and bottom with a pair of great wooden spars manufactured in a Rotterdam shipyard under Rubens' personal supervision—hence the picture's nickname, the Mainsail. Its colors blazed down the long nave to the narthex where Mikail stood. He walked toward it.

The top two-thirds of the painting centered around an immense Christ in Majesty, three times life size, with his hand raised in traditional blessing. The intense glowing light behind him was unexpectedly cooled by Christ's spring-green mantle that celebrated and declared his resurrection. The archangels Michael and Gabriel flanked the great central image. Next to Christ's right knee, Michael flew forward with his head down and his wings angled so far back that he seemed about to plunge into his own cathedral. On Christ's other side, at the level of his shoulder, Gabriel soared upward, leaning backward on outspread white wings, whose tips were fringed with rainbows. Surrounding the three giant central figures, the remainder of the upper portion of the masterpiece was a chorus of almost a hundred singing and rejoicing saints and angels in irregular curved rows. They were painted in all the warm, glorious colors of Rubens' palette. Included among them were images of Rubens' mother and his beloved older brother, who had predeceased him. Each face and figure was carefully individualized and appropriate. Rubens never repeated himself.

A band of cloudless blue sky separated heaven from the lower third of the painting that showed this world. There, Rubens had thanked the citizens of Aachen, whose subscriptions had paid for the work, by painting a procession of fifty-seven life-sized portraits marching upwards from the bottom of the canvas to the cathedral itself. The reigning Emperor was there. He was shown as an ordinary man (you had to look hard to find him) among the workmen who had helped build the edifice, the bishop, and an almost random selection of Aachen citizens. The cathedral's towers pierced the sky to align themselves with, and point at, the central figure of Christ. This established a strong vertical axis, but the left and right halves of the painting were slightly off balance. Michael's sharp dive drew the viewer's eye quickly down and forward and contrasted with Gabriel's slower upward soaring rise backward and away from the viewer, which was emphasized by his great outspread wings. Rubens' subtle placement of the groups of figures in heaven and at the cathedral reinforced the difference and subtly suggested that the picture itself rotated around Christ and his church. The imbalance was so gently suggested that a viewer unconsciously felt the motion long before he perceived it.

A friend asked Ruben why he had not signed the painting."

Who else could have painted it?" he had replied.

Mikail walked down the aisle to view the Mainsail more closely from the open space between the recessed choir stalls. Seen more closely, the painting still did not disappoint. Mikail rejoiced. Rubens was a national hero throughout the Lowlands, and Mikail was a Fleming. Most connoisseurs admitted only Michelangelo as his equal, although a few preferred Rembrandt. He could make up his mind without leaving the cathedral. Rembrandt's masterpiece, *The Mourning Virgin,* almost as famous as the Mainsail, was just behind the altar in the Lady Chapel.

Turning to walk back to the crossing, he found a brass plate in the floor that informed him he was standing on the bodies of Karl VII and Clara, "buried here in humility that visitors may forever walk over our graves."

When he turned around to view the painting again, its bold design, singing colors, and perfect execution still overwhelmed him.

Nearby, another of the Archangel's famous treasures, della Robbia's frieze of children making music and dancing, surrounded the Imperial pew. The carving was so perfect that the marble children seemed to actually frolic and you almost heard their music. After admiring it, Mikail went to see *The Mourning Virgin*, where Rembrandt's intense, human-hearted vision of the Virgin as a lonely and heartbroken old peasant woman moved him, though his heart remained with the Mainsail. Next, he climbed the five hundred eleven steps to the cathedral roof just to be able to say he had done it, and left.

When he left the cathedral, he turned into Great Street, eight lanes wide and bordered by broad sidewalks swept and cleaned regularly; elsewhere, Aacheners mostly had to ignore the natural consequences of a horse-powered city. Great Street also boasted its own corps of tall, well-built Watchmen. In their yellow and blue uniforms and plumed red shakos, they looked like a race of multicolored giants. To an Aachener, Great Street included not only the street itself but also the surrounding shopping district where crowds of people bought and sold every imaginable commodity. Except for an occasional old-fashioned shopkeeper still living above his store, there were few residents. When their work was done, people went home. Home might be a palace on Witanagemot Street with conservatories and large gardens if you were rich, or a crumbling tenement should you be poor, but the typical Aachener lived in a long, narrow brick house with a tiny garden at the back.

Mikail thought he understood cities, but he had never imagined anything like the miles of shops that lined Great Street and extended deep into its crooked side streets. As he passed, he could see every store's merchandise laid outdoors on its counters. If the weather turned, the shopkeeper simply unrolled the awnings above the doors to protect his merchandise

Suddenly, he heard birdsong. The sound led him to a crooked, unpaved side street where a dozen bird stores huddled together. Mikail had a always had a bird in his room when he lived at home. So ignoring the aristocratic establishments that sold falcons and falconry equipment, he went looking for one selling small songbirds. He soon found it. The proprietor showed him finches he had never seen before and all sorts of canaries—some red from beak to tail feathers, others with dramatic black heads and red or yellow bodies, and, strangest of all, some with heads crowned by strange and wonderful crests that did not even look like canaries. There was also a cage of talking mynahs, and, wonder of wonders, a walk-in aviary crowded with flying parakeets from the Americas. He had never seen parrots or parakeets before. The storekeeper gave him a handful of birdseed and sent him in. He spent more than an hour in the aviary, and when he left, he felt very differently about Aachen.

As he continued exploring, he came to a large, crowded district where the stores sold women's wear. The women of Aachen dressed well and shopped in groups while keeping up a blithe, cheerful chatter that reminded him of the flocks of tropical birds he had just seen. Their exhilaration was infectious. It occurred to Mikail that Karita would be happy here; she would fit in perfectly. He could not help noticing how attractive these cheery urban beauties were and how they made the women of Flushing he remembered seem dour and dowdy. Local patriotism tried to make him crush that traitorous comparison. It failed, completely.

It was time to look for an interesting tavern. Finding one, he sat down at the Strangers Table, the usual long table where anyone could sit. Strangers spoke easily to one another at the table, freed from any need for formality. You were expected to share in the conversation. If you wanted to drink alone, you could sit at a small table and endure sour looks from those who judged you an unsociable souse.

Mikail sat down next to a member of the city Watch spending his afternoon break nursing a beer. His hat perched on its own chair. The Watchman caught him eyeing it and greeted him with a cheery, "Stranger in Aachen? Don't be embarrassed. Everyone's curious about the hat. Look." He opened a row of buttons on the hat's right side that Mikail hadn't noticed and displayed a pen, a sealed container of ink, notebooks, and a pad of printed summonses, all neatly fitted into side pockets. "It can carry a lot more," the watchman said, "and it keeps your hands free and your belt uncluttered. You can use your hands or even reach for a weapon if you must. Your hat can't fall off." The hat had straps and fittings that would keep it on through any imaginable event. "Go ahead. Try to push the hat off," the Watchman urged, putting his hat on. Mikail tried but the hat stayed on. "Not so stupid as it looks is it?"

Mikail confessed to being green as fresh grass in Aachen and explained that he was on detached service without offering further explanation. He fell into conversation with the Watchman, a clerk from the Chancellor's office, and a salesman of women's boots. Standardized sizes were a novel idea, the salesman explained, but once it took hold in the capital, the provinces would follow

Ordering the next round of drinks, Mikail asked, "What do people in Aachen talk about?"

"Politics and gossip mostly," the clerk answered, "Old Sweetie wants one thing, and the Grandees in the Witanagemot want something else."

"Old Sweetie?" said Mikail, not quite believing what he had heard.

"It's what the Empress calls the Emperor, so Old Sweetie he is to everyone. But whatever's between him and the Grandees, it's no business of ours," the Watchman said. "For the likes of us, politics is a sport to watch. When it turns vicious, we get hurt. Right now the war in Dacia is the big thing."

Mikail blessed his lucky stars that he hadn't mentioned Dacia. "I don't remember either the Emperor or the Grandees asking for my opinion," he said.

"Everybody thinks the powers-that-be are headed for a fight," the clerk said, ignoring him. "We're afraid it's us that will pay for it."

The Watchman jumped in, "It's not right to want to depose him. He's not a despot," he said sharply.

"Not to you or me maybe," the clerk replied, "The Grandees think otherwise."

"I have to leave," Mikail said. "My mother told me never to talk politics or religion with strangers." He didn't get up. Everybody laughed, and the salesman said, "My turn," and rose to buy the next round.

BOOK III

The Emperor and His Men

May 1812

CHAPTER VIII

Enter Dorcas, Running

IN THE END, ALL they needed to do was to enter the palace through the public gate and walk over to the building housing the Empress' suite. The doorkeeper remembered Pannonius, who asked him to tell Dorcas DaCosta that she had a message from her father. In five minutes, they heard her shoes running down the hall. Dorcas lived her life on the run; she rarely walked and had to concentrate to slow her movements. The first thing you noticed about her was her striking russet hair which she wore long, curling, and falling on her shoulders to frame her face and minimize its long, angular shape. That face was forever in motion. All her movements were sparrow-quick. Her figure was shapely, her dark eyes handsome and her hands elegant, but they were harder to admire, because they were never still. Mikail remembered Pannonius telling him how much she loved to dance. Her personality followed her metabolism. Naturally warm and affectionate, she was too impulsive to always be kind or thoughtful.

She had expected only Pannonius. Mikail's presence did not please her. "Who's *he*, Hugh?"

Mikail answered for himself, "I have letters from your father for you, and for the Emperor and Empress. Your father insisted no one is to know of them before their Highnesses have read them. Pannonius thought it best we start with your letter."

Dorcas glared at Pannonius and took the envelope. She flowed into a chair in a single, graceful, liquid movement and read the letter. Then she turned back to reread it before looking at the documents. When she was finished, she said quietly, "Oh, my God," and then, "This will take a little time. Wait for me and please don't leave this room. I'll be back as soon as I can." She left the room as she had entered it, on the run. In twenty minutes, they heard her distinctive quick steps, and she was back to lead them at a flying pace down long empty corridors to an ordinary door. She took out a key and opened the door into a small foyer. In the next room, the Empress herself was pacing, the letter in her hand. Pannonius started to kneel, but the Empress said in an irritated voice, "Not now, Hugh."

Mikail handed her the packet with her name on it and placed the gold tally on the table. The Empress sat and read with care. When she finished, she turned to Pannonius to say, "Welcome back, Cousin Hugh. Please bring better news next time. Where are you staying?"

"With my Aunt Luisa, Ma'am. About a mile from here."

"That won't do," the Empress said. "We'll be needing to talk with you. Get them moved into the palace today, Dorcas. Mikail—it is Mikail, isn't it?—give Dorcas the Emperor's copy. All three copies and everything that relates to them go into my safe, Dorcas. I have a meeting where my absence would cause comment, but, gentlemen, the Emperor and I will most certainly see you later. In the meanwhile, Dorcas, get them settled in and find someone to brief them on what's going on in Dacia." With a wicked smile, she added, "If anyone asks why you came back, Hugh, why don't you tell them it was because you're so desperately in love with Dorcas you couldn't live without seeing her. That's close enough to the truth isn't it, cousin?"

Pannonius went red. Dorcas did not look unhappy. She smiled and said gently, "Everyone knows, Hugh. They always do. Don't let it bother you. Be back as soon as I can." She bobbed a graceful curtsey to the Empress at high speed and was running before she left the room. In the course of the next two hours, she had them moved into a suite, arranged for them to be admitted into the court mess for meals, had someone pick up their clothing and luggage from Pannonius's aunt, sent a tailor to have Mikail properly dressed for court, and found a few minutes to talk to Hugh about her father's health. Then she left to find someone from the Magister Militum's staff to brief them.

The officer she sent was a bespectacled, middle-aged staff brigadier with a small potbelly and a double row of decorations on his belt. "I prepare the Dacia morning report for the Magister Militum and the Emperor," he said. "I know whatever is known here about current events. Trouble is, what I know is mostly stale. We get daily reports on the semaphore, but they can't carry much detail. The Paladin's daily report is always days behind, though he sends it by pigeon. Same thing for Lauzac. Right now nothing seems to be happening. It's like a war in Sleeping Beauty's castle or, even better, a game of chess where both players sit staring at the board waiting for each other to move, because they've have forgotten whose turn it is. Mongols always try to keep the initiative. After their big raid went so poorly, we expected they'd send reinforcements for a prompt counterstroke, but we don't see reinforcement, and Kaidu shows no intention to seek battle. On the other hand, neither has he shown any sign of retreat. Most of his army is sitting dreamily in front of the walls of Imponza without a siege train and none on the way.

"After the raid failed, we chased Osorian back to the Pruj, but Kaidu managed to keep his raiders from being totally wiped out by using every boat he could scrounge and whatever was left of the bridge network. Osorian himself was killed leading a charge to cover the retreat. The Mongols escaped with an overall loss of more than half their men, a disaster if not the annihilation the Paladin hoped to achieve. Lauzac thinks they are waiting for instructions from their Khan in the Crimea, and that distance accounts for their slow pace. The Paladin disagrees. He thinks another shock is being prepared. If the Paladin has any idea of what it will be or from which direction it will come, he hasn't put it into dispatches. The Byzantines have said nothing and done nothing. That means whatever you want it to mean."

"What do you think the Paladin's thinking?" Pannonius asked.

"Well," the Brigadier said, "he has drained the nearby provinces of men to concentrate a large army far back near Cluchia. Now he could move safely in any direction, but he doesn't. He's usually much more aggressive. For that matter, the Magister himself would normally be in the field. I'd have been sent ahead long ago to set up a headquarters for him. This time he's in his office. All these aggressive and highly intelligent people are doing nothing. There has to be a reason, but I don't see it."

"Thank you," Pannonius said with sincerity, "Thank you very much. You've been very helpful."

"Have I?" the colonel said. "I'm glad you think so."

Eventually, Dorcas came to collect them for their audience in the Empress' sitting room. She told them that the Emperor usually had a drink and a chat with his wife before dinner, which they would forego tonight for their private audience. "This is special," she said, "you're going back stage to see the leading players."

She led them down private corridors, empty except for the occasional passing servant and out-sized storage cabinets lined against the wall. Eventually, she knocked on an inconspicuous door. An armed guard opened it. Four more were standing behind him. They were searched and passed through two empty receiving rooms before entering a pleasant, west-facing room full of comfortable furniture, with family miniatures on the walls and bibelots on a table. Large windows caught the late afternoon light, which mirrors amplified. The Imperial couple was sitting on one of the couches. The Empress had a piece of needlepoint in her hand that she laid aside when they entered. The Emperor was sitting in his stocking feet, in a slightly slouched position, He straightened up as soon as he saw them.

Tall, although not quite as tall as his brother, even seated he exuded self-assurance and authority. Dorcas hissed, "Kneel," before making her curtsey and whispered, "I'll talk to you outside when you're done." Then she retired to the far side of the room.

The Emperor waved Mikail and Pannonius to club chairs and pointed to the wine on the table. He welcomed Pannonius home, and immediately asked whether "my brother" was in good health and spirits. Then he asked Pannonius whether he carried any oral messages.

Pannonius answered, "My only express instructions were to make myself useful to you and to tutor Mikail. He said you could use people whose loyalty was beyond doubt and that we would work well together."

The Emperor steepled his hands and said, "Yet he certainly could use you right now. Is his sending you to me a message in itself, especially considering the circumstances under which you left me three years ago?"

Pannonius took time to answer. "He didn't say that to me. But if that is your question, yes, his mind does work that way."

Very quietly the Empress said, "You think the Chancellor may be a problem too, dear. What do you think Aetius is thinking, Hugh?"

Pannonius had been asking himself the same question and spoke slowly, thinking aloud, "He's built up his army but he's holding it well back from either the Mongols or the Byzantines. That way he is free to move in any direction. He must think that Kaidu's delay is caused by Mongols trying to renegotiate. Now that their raid has been so costly they'll want more from the Byzantines. In any case, he must suspect the next blow will not fall in Dacia. Perhaps he expects it to come here."

"Or Tunisia or Sicily," the Emperor said, "but for that we are strengthening our forces and stationing them further back in Spain, just as Aetius holds his army back. It's a risk. We are left somewhat open and vulnerable to surprise, especially here. My brother sent you to me because he thinks there's a problem here in Aachen. I already thought so and so did my wife. Now [he tapped the letter] Kaidu explicitly says so and the absconding of Kloffheim and Hoffman also suggests conspiracy by their superiors here. The difficulty is that our enemies won't declare themselves until they see a good prospect of success. If we wait for them, it may be too late."

Mikail had been studying the Emperor as he waited his turn to speak. As a man who could consider himself successor to Julius Caesar and Charlemagne, his mien suggested that he expected to be obeyed and might be unforgiving if he were not. Not that the face was hard-featured or brutal; on the contrary Emperor's features were more delicate than the ever-present profile on every coin would suggest. The brothers shared the same profile: brow, nose, and, insofar as the Emperor's beard did not conceal it, chin. The laugh lines prominent on his brother's face were absent from the Emperor's narrower face. His features suggested a predominating will, and he smiled only when he looked at his wife. Although he was the older brother there was no white in his glossy black hair. (*Does he dye it?* Mikail wondered. *He must.*) The burden of his responsibilities showed in a network of fine lines across his forehead and around his alert, ever-moving eyes, which were observant, suspicious, and not particularly sympathetic. There was little music in his voice. His diction was clear, but his tone was more courteous than kind, and his words went right to the point.

The Emperor turned finally to Mikail. "Aetius says some kind things about you and suggests that we will find you of use here. I'm sure he's right. He usually is, but he couldn't tell you everything or let you read

83

his letter to me. These two pages put our situation fairly." He folded the letter to leave one page showing and handed it to Mikail. As he did so, he pointed at the open page and said, "Read that page and the next one." Mikail read:

The Mongols must be acting in collusion with another power. Kiev and Moscow have bad relations with them, and the Caliphate is not ready for war. That leaves only the Byzantines, the foreign power most likely to be able to penetrate our military deeply enough to get the kind of information someone has given Kaidu.

Kaidu says 'Something will be attempted in Aachen,' presumably a coup or an assassination. Their chance of temporarily dislodging us from Aachen or even killing you—they will have to try—is better than their chance of making the coup successful, because I hold an army here. Your son will have another in Spain. But that would be little consolation if the coup succeeded only to be reversed later, or, worse, if you were assassinated. In any case, it would make a fine diversion for whoever wants to attack the Empire in Dacia or Tunisia.

So who will try the coup? If we see our foes as a combination of the opposition to you and the pro-Byzantine party, the Chancellor must be considered. He is tied to the Grandee clique of great landowners and may still be angry over having been divested of the treasury three years ago. The Byzantines usually work by bribery. If you can find the flow of their money, you will have a connection to the members of their party. Their charming ambassador and his staff are all spies.

Certainly someone has corrupted a significant part of the Political Department. Investigation is delicate. The Department reports to the Chancellor. He is himself a suspect, and he has armed men. Most of the public safety forces in Aachen and elsewhere report to him. Another natural suspect is Frederick, who has always been active in the Witanagemot as well as the Consistory. Directly and through his wife's family, Frederick is closely connected with the Grandee landholders in the Witanagemot, who fight your panRoman policies whenever they dare.

I will send everything I learn to you immediately through Hugh Pannonius if you appoint him your coordinator to receive all information from Dacia. The Chancellor won't be fooled, but it gives Hugh a legitimate interest in everything, aside from being good cover.

When Mikail looked up from his reading, the Emperor continued, "As you see we must be discreet in investigating Hoffman and Kloffheim. Hoffman comes from Rostock on the North Sea, and Kloffheim from a town nearby. That's interesting. So you're going to go to Rostock, young man. See if you can find out anything useful about the Chancellor or the deserters. I'll send someone to your quarters later tonight with instructions. You leave tomorrow."

Mikail had not expected to be thrown into water so far over his head this quickly. He thrashed about for something to say, but the Emperor was already speaking to Pannonius, "We need a small working group to organize our defense and oversee investigations. Since it can't be public, we need to find you a cover. The best cover is a real job. As Aetius suggests, we need someone to coordinate all of Aachen's responses to the problems in Dacia, including the traitors, and to act as a central clearinghouse for all messages from to and from Dacia. It gives you a reason to talk to almost anyone about anything."

"Personally," Pannonius said slyly, "I liked the Empress' ideas about cover."

The Emperor was not amused. "You woo on your own time, not mine."

The Empress (who *was* amused) changed the subject. "Whom do you want in the group?" she asked her husband, "The Magister and the Mayor of the Palace, of course. Who else?"

"Yourself naturally, Louie Duval and Albrecht Desle," her husband said. "They're so close to me, I couldn't hide this from them if I wanted to. Dorcas too. She knows everything going on the palace, and this is a conspiracy. She's family, and therefore safe. Besides, she has her father's brains. I'm not entirely sure about the Mayor, but we need his spies, and we can't keep this secret from him, so he's in.

"Now that's all for the present, gentlemen. My wife and I have to dress for a state dinner. Pannonius, you have a breakfast appointment with Louie and the Mayor tomorrow."

Dorcas took them back.

"I assume you overheard everything?" Pannonius teased her.

"You know I'm not supposed to listen!"

"Yes. Does the Empress know you listen?"

"Naturally," Dorcas explained, "she calls me her second memory. If she doesn't want me to listen, we have a signal. And I *don't* listen to her personal conversations with the Emperor."

Guards had been posted when they got back to their suite, where a small parcel awaited them. When Mikail broke its purple seal, he found it contained personnel files for Hoffman and Kloffheim, a few other documents, and a scribbled, unsigned note. The writer pointed out that the head of the Political Department was Thomas Marsalia, who reported directly to the Chancellor, and noted that three years ago a suggestion had been made to take the Political Department away from the Chancellor and give it to the Diplomatic Service. It was never done because of the Chancellor's vehement protests.

"Duval's handwriting," Pannonius said. "I had nothing to do with that bureaucratic mud-wrestling match. Louis thought that since the Political Department exists to provide information for the diplomats, it belonged there. He didn't think the Chancellor would mind; there was no money in it for him. But Sforza made a tremendous fuss, so Louie had to back down."

Three hours later a dark, elegant man, with piercing blue-green eyes under straight jet-black hair, walked into the room. Louis Duval had arrived. His step was still lively, although the hour was late. His elegant clothes showed that he had spent his evening at a formal event, presumably the one for which the Emperor and Empress had been preparing. He wore a formal jacket of red Chinese silk, embroidered with a pattern of clouds and blooming trees. An even deeper vermillion cravat emphasized the gold medallion of office hanging around his neck. His black court breeches were impeccably tailored, and evening dress slippers shone like a matched set of mirrors. Two lines of orders and medals were arrayed on his belt. It must have been a long night, but not a hair was out of place on his well-coiffed head. He carried a small traveling bag.

Pannonius greeted him breezily, "Hi Louie. Ain't you the beautiful one."

Unabashed, Duval replied, "I was at the Emperor's annual dinner and reception for the Consistory members; very formal. Introduce me to your young friend, Hugh."

"This dazzling vision of magnificence, my boy, is Louie Duval, most senior of all political aides to the Emperor. I would watch my pockets if I were you. Louie, Mikail de Ruyter."

Duval smoothly replied, "I am not only a vision of magnificence but a fountain of munificence, for I come not to pick the young man's pockets but to fill them." He opened his bag with a showman's sweeping flourish. "I bring him portraits of our Imperial lord in silver and gold. Or, in other words, five thousand denarii in big ones and good ones. Plus a letter of credit good for up to thirty thousand more in case he needs to do some serious bribery. Also a letter signed in purple ink by Caesar himself, commanding everyone to help him and do whatever he asks. Here is your identification DeRuyter, although strangely, your name seems to have become Adrianus van Hoogstraaten, a junior partner in the Ghent trading house of Hoogstraaten & Van Dam, looking for business in Rostock. I have a letter of instruction that tells you what to do and say, and what we need. It's in the bag with your tickets for tomorrow's one o'clock train.

"As befits your position, you have a manservant. Phil Ganz will meet you at the train. True, he is better at breaking people's bones than pressing their pants, but he knows how to valet, and he's your bodyguard. Phil studied for the priesthood, but his vocation doesn't seem to have taken, because he used to be a burglar before he came to us. You have a reservation at the Inn of the Western Wind. Best place in Rostock. Haven't been in the town for years, but Rostock has eleven breweries, and I remember the beer fondly. Evander Leiden will be waiting for you there. A tailor will be here shortly to fit you for proper travel clothing; Dorcas's idea. She thought you would need more appropriate garb for the part. It's all in your letter of instructions. Work fast. We need you back here."

Mikail, who hadn't been able to get a word in during Duval's monologue, was appalled. He blurted out, "Hoogstraaten and Van Dam is the biggest trading company in the Lowlands. They're ruthless. When they find out I've been impersonating a partner, they will ruin my entire family."

"Oh, I don't think so," Duval said casually. "We do this sort of thing all the time. Besides, the Treasury is a silent partner in Hoogstraaten." He turned to Pannonius. "Hugh, breakfast tomorrow morning at the usual time. Be fun to have you back. Think about who you'll need for staff." When Mikail looked again, he was gone.

Mikail turned to Pannonius. "These people seem to think I can work miracles!" he wailed.

"Why not?" Pannonius said with a shrug. "So far you have."

CHAPTER IX

Rostock

EASTERN STATION LOOKED so old and worn that visitors expected that it would soon be replaced. The dingy central hall needed a good cleaning, and its old-fashioned low ceilings and polished stone walls ensured it would be noisy. Traveling by railroad was uncomfortable and expensive. Travelers, expected to endure grime and smoke and usually wore old clothing. But a partner of Hoogstraaten and Van Dam would be expected to be well dressed whatever the circumstances. And so, wearing fashionable clothes and with traveling case for money and papers in hand Mikail processioned grandly to his expensive private compartment, preceded by a porter pushing his luggage on a squeaking hand truck.

Waiting for him on the platform was a sturdy, middle-aged man wearing a gray suit, an old-fashioned hat, and a humble air. His hands were folded and his head slightly bent. "I believe you were expecting me, sir," he said unctuously. "Phillip Ganz, Sir. Let me get that luggage on board."

Duval was right. The man knew how to valet.

Phil got the luggage into place in the compartment. He was carrying two cases, "one for me and one for me tools." The men took off their jackets and sat down. Along with his jacket, Phillip doffed his humility. In his shirtsleeves, he was another man entirely, burly and muscular, with an assertive look. His first words were, "Mr. Duval told me Ev Leiden is waiting for us in Rostock. Have you worked with him before, Sir?"

"No, I'm new to this business."

"I'm not," Phil said. "Nor is he. I can do almost anything except code, and he's good at that. Between us, Mr. D. gave you the full team. How are we fixed for grub?" This was an important question. Their trip to Rostock would take almost two days. No cooking was permitted on board because the coaches were made of painted or lacquered wood. Sometimes, you could purchase warm food on the platform when the train stopped, but more often you found nothing available. Experienced travelers carried their own food. When Mikail produced the palace's big hamper, Phil smiled.

"All right then," he said, "Mr. D. seems to think this is important. Can you tell me why?"

"No, it's an open search," Mikail responded. "We are supposed to find out everything we can about two members of the Political Department who have deserted to the Mongols."

That answer did not sit well with Phil. "I can't sit here for two days with my mouth stitched up. Let's use the time for me to teach you a little bit about the business." As a result, except for reading and rereading his letter of instructions until his eyes were grainy, Mikail spent the rest of the trip learning how to avoid tails, shadow suspects, break choke holds and the art and science of kicking men in the testicles. This last skill was difficult to practice in a moving railcar compartment and turned out to be much more complicated than Mikail would have supposed. Phil was a surprisingly good teacher. He also wielded a heavy fork. Even after Mikail had contributed his own substantial stash, the level of bread, cold sausage, and pickles in the hamper fell like the mercury in a barometer before an approaching hurricane.

Two days later after they had checked into the Western Wind, a pleasant inn in the heart of Rostock near Neuer Market Square, Mikail sent Phil off to find Ev. He soon returned, bringing with him, an oversized pitcher of beer no longer full, three glasses, and a platter of sausages. Ev himself was a non-descript man of middle height and age, so ordinary you would have been hard pressed to remember the color of his eyes or hair.

I'd better get this moving, Mikail thought. *They're already two drinks happy.* "What have you found out, Mr. Leiden?"

"Quite a lot. Let's start with Andrew Kloffheim, the Chancellor's cousin and godson."

"We knew that," Mikail retorted. "George always said so."

Well, don't you believe it," Ev said. "He's the Chancellor's natural-born son. Everybody here knows. His mother's a distant cousin of the Chancellor, who was teaching in a girl's school in Aachen. She had never been in Rostock before coming here, three months pregnant, to marry a small-time grain merchant named Kloffheim. Soon as he marries her, Kloffheim becomes rich on Army contracts."

"Hasn't the Chancellor other family here?"

"Not a one. The Sforzas come from Northern Italy. He's barely related to the mother but comes all the way from Aachen for the christening of this child of an obscure cousin. Even stands godfather to the baby. Then this son of two nobodies goes to St. Matthew's in Lucerne, where the swells educate their sons, and spends his vacations in Aachen with his godfather. When his mother died he was fifteen, and Andrew left Rostock, never to return."

Ev poured himself another glass of beer as a reward and looked for compliments. Phil provided them. Mikail let him cheerlead for a minute or two and then asked, "What's Andrew's relationship to George Hoffman?"

"I haven't had the time to find out much about George yet. I don't know who sponsored him. The Chancellor got Andrew into the Political Department."

"What's in George's public records and baptismal certificates? Didn't you get them?"

"I did. There isn't much there. George Hoffman went through this town like a fish through water. Perfectly at home but leaves no trail."

"He's still like that," Mikail said. "Go on."

Ev resumed, "George Stephen Parides Hoffman is the son of William Hoffman, a partner in the Parides Company. His father is one of the Syndics of the city. Very rich. George also went to Saint Matthew's. George's mother's not well; he used to come home to visit her more than he has recently."

"Concentrate on the Hoffmans, and. see what you can find out about the Parides company," Mikail said. "Have you made the acquaintance of the Count yet?" [The governor of a province was always "the Count."]

91

Ev nodded, "Mr. D. arranged it on the semaphore. He knows he's to cooperate."

"Good," Mikail said. "Please make an appointment with the Count for the day after tomorrow. Tell him I have a purple letter and warn him this is confidential."

So it was that Adrianus van Hoogstraaten appeared next morning at the shop of Parides and Company, groomed and dressed as befitted the scion of a great trading company and properly accompanied by his manservant. Phil had worked hard half the night pressing and brushing to create a shining spectacle of glorious aristocracy. Mr. van Hoogstraaten spent a half hour looking at jewelry and pricing it, while chatting with the young salesman and charming him with his easy, condescending way. In the course of their conversation, the salesman told him that the Parides Company was old, well-established wholesale and retail merchants of amber and jewelry. Mr. William Hoffman was the head of the company in Rostock, with offices above the factory.

"I've haven't much time here, but I've heard all sorts of good things about your company," Mikail said. "Would your chief—you said his name was Hoffman didn't you?—be available to talk to me this afternoon?"

"Anyone would be interested to talk business with Hoogstraaten & Van Dam, Sir," the young man said. "May I tell him that you will be at our factory this afternoon?"

"I would like that," Mikail said. Eventually he used the Emperor's money to purchase an exquisite, oversized cuff bracelet of Florentined gold with a large central inset of clear, sharply carved dark amber set off in the broad surround by a ring of diamonds. It was one of the most expensive pieces that he had been shown. Diamonds were rare and very expensive. Almost all came from India.

Mikail was about to say that he'd simply take the piece—which he intended to do in any case—until an instinct made him say, "Has Parides any other branches? Perhaps you could deliver my purchases."

"Our headquarters are in Aachen, and there's another branch in Vienna, sir. We could deliver your piece almost anywhere. Because our home office specializes in the transfer of money and precious metals, we have a network of correspondents to messenger and accept property, here and in the East. Asia loves amber, especially deep carved, dark yellow amber."

"My cousin whose husband is stationed at our branch in Constantinople has a birthday coming. Could you deliver to her?"

"Certainly, sir. It will take about three weeks. But foreign deliveries are expensive."

"Then I must think about it," Mikail said. He bought four smaller pieces as gifts for his "family" to keep the salesman comfortable.

Once they were in the street, Phil spoke up, "I think I can get in."

When Mikail returned to the West Wind, Ev had pulled together his notes about the Parides family and was ready to report.

"I found out a bit more about the Hoffmans. The Parides family has been in Rostock for over a century. There are four partners now, all great grandsons of the founder, the three Hoffman brothers, Stephen, Demetrius, and William, and their first cousin, Julian Parides. The Aachen office controls the others. It deals in precious metals, not amber, and specializes in the deposit and transmission of precious metals and money. Stephen Hoffman, the head of the firm, resides in Aachen. So does Demetrius, the youngest brother. William Hoffman, George's father, runs the Rostock branch. William is the oldest, but Stephen is head of the firm. Their cousin, Julian Parides, runs Vienna. William lives quietly, but is said to be very rich. There's another related Parides family in Constantinople doing much the same business. The two companies do business together out East."

That afternoon Mr. Hoogstraaten visited the factory. After a perfunctory tour of the first floor where fifteen men were making jewelry, the foreman brought them upstairs. William's office was nearly empty; there were no papers on the clean desktop. All that was in the room was a desk, a few chairs, a file cabinet, and a safe. The seat of the chair in which Mr. Hoffman seated Mikail was rock hard. Mr. Hoogstraaten's manservant stayed outside and made conversation with William's secretary. From time to time her laughter could be heard in the inner office.

Following his letter of instructions, Mikail began by saying that Hoogstraaten and Van Dam wanted to broaden its operations on the Baltic coast and was seeking partners and correspondents there.

Mr. Hoffman was flattered that so large and important a trader would approach his small company. What specifically, he asked, might Mr. Hoogstraaten have in mind?

Mikail suggested that Parides might be interested in acting as local representative for Hoogstraaten's bulk trading operations in Baltic lumber and dried fish. If that was too far from their usual business, then Hoogstraaten would like to be a supplier of gold and silver or to assist with transfers of money or specie. Alternatively, Hoogstraaten's many correspondents included any number of merchants involved with jewelry and he would be interested in introducing them to Parides on the usual terms.

Mr. Hoffman did not even ask what those usual terms might be. He courteously expressed complete dismissal, saying, "Parides has satisfactory and well established arrangements. Naturally, we would be delighted to consult the Hoogstraaten firm should anything of mutual interest develop."

Mikail tried again, "Could you suggest any way in which we might be able to assist each other? I'll listen to any proposal." But none was forthcoming and Mikail was soon out of the office and on the street. This was peculiar. Parides ought to be overjoyed to be offered affiliation with a major trading firm on its own terms, but William could hardly wait to be rid of Hoogstraaten's representative, and Mikail thought he heard something close to fear in his voice when he refused Mikail's offer of assistance with money transfers.

Once he was on the street, the sun's warmth and the smell of the sea made Mikail unwilling to return to the inn. Instead, Phil and he found a beer garden. Duval was right; Rostock's beer was wonderful. "All right," Mikail asked, "did that secretary tell you anything?"

"Time you asked," Phil replied. "To begin with, she doesn't much like her boss. Thinks he's cold, distant, and secretive. The place gives her the creeps. It's full of secrets."

"What about George?"

"George hadn't been home for two years, but he was here twice this year. The two of them spent a lot of time alone in that office. William was upset and sad for weeks after his son left. The secretary hates George. William isn't mean and even has streaks of kindness, but George is nasty. He doesn't like women. Another thing, William's afraid of his brother, Stephen. When Stephen's in town, he gives the orders in William's own branch. William hates that. By the way, he called in the clerk at the store and screamed at him. Said everybody knows the

Hoogstraaten people are spies, and the Emperor's a silent partner in the firm, but he didn't dare to avoid you."

Phil took a long swallow of beer and went on in a self-satisfied voice, "One very important thing she did say. William keeps a separate file for his important letters, writes them by hand and files his copy in a locked desk drawer. There's a special money transfer system among the Parides' branches, with messengers out of Aachen twice a month. William personally writes all directions for transfers of money and keeps them secret as well. I think I could break into Hoffman's office on the second floor and find out what's in that desk. Sunday morning would be best, then I can be finished in time for the last train."

❋

The next day was Friday. Since Mikail's appointment with the Count was not until eleven, it gave him time for a pleasant stroll. Rostock made Mikail homesick. When the wind was in the right quarter, it smelled just like Flushing. To the smell of the sea that permeated everything, the city added its own grace note odors of spilled salt water, fish, vinegar, and brewery yeast. The houses had the same orange-yellow brick facades, with staircase roofs on which the same black and white storks were standing on one leg. The harsh North German spoken on the streets even reminded him of the Flemish his family spoke at home. His mouth recollected its heavy, chewy taste and the gargling feelings at his back of his throat when he made the guttural sounds. It had been too long since he had seen his mother and sisters. He missed them. He did not miss Lucas.

He ended his excursion back at the Neuer Market, a cobblestoned plaza across which Rostock's Town Hall and the Count's palace faced one other. Both were large buildings fronted by stone arcades that sheltered pedestrians in inclement weather. The Town Hall was an old four-story Gothic red brick box onto whose front an elegant carved stone Baroque facade had been installed, thereby creating the disturbing effect of a sturdy old peasant woman with the face of a brittle young beauty. Above the entrance portal hung the city's emblem, the Golden Griffin. The Rostock Griffin had the head, shoulders, and talons of an eagle above the body of a golden lion with a snaky, lashing tail full of energy. Against a deep blue background that symbolized the sea, the Griffin strode forward. Its fierce eyes and beak showed that proud Rostock brooked neither affront nor impudence. Its golden color flaunted its wealth and its thrashing tail represented its energy.

The palace of the Count-governor of Mecklenburg Province was built in Modern Roman marble and brick style and faced the Town Hall. Tall marble Ionic columns, spaced like soldiers in close formation, fronted its façade, and larger-than-life bronze statutes of Charlemagne and Karl VII on either side of the entrance reminded every one who entered of t e power and glory of New Rome. Behind the colonnade, marble stairs swept up to a grand entrance hall. Mikail noticed that the Town Hall was slightly larger than the palace. The son of a maritime city himself, the visitor drew the inference he was supposed to draw: the Lord Mayor and his Syndics were boasting that *they* were the ones who really had the money.

A large fountain in the middle of the square was dedicated to Rostock sailors lost at sea. Inside a marble basin, four gilded, water-spouting griffons bore a ship's bow on their backs. On it, a bronze sea captain held his hand over his noble brow to shield eyes that eternally raked the horizon for survivors or, perhaps, for the rest of his ship. Perched atop the captain's head a sea gull searched the market in endless hope that an errant fish might drop from a passing cart.

A list of donors was chiseled on the fountain's base. Mikail noted the name of William Hoffman as well as the names of several Parides. The square was full of vendor's stalls and shopping housewives. He took deep breaths, enjoying the familiar, homely market odors of fish, freshly baked bread, cabbage, beer, vinegar, and pickled vegetables. He half expected to meet one of his sisters shopping there.

The balanced buildings neatly reflected the relationship between the Lord Mayor and his Syndics and the Count-Governor. On the one hand, Rostock was within the county of Mecklenburg and thus subject to the Count. On the other, it was a free and independent city with a four-hundred-year-old charter from the Emperor that contained many rights and privileges. These included the right to send a representative to the Witanagemot and the privilege of direct appeal from the Count's decisions to the Emperor himself. Like the good businessmen they were, the burgers of Rostock prized their capital and paid the Emperor a healthy yearly subvention to confirm their charter.

It was never in the Emperor's interest to disturb the Lord Mayor of Rostock and his thirty-three Syndics. Moreover, experience had taught Aachen that whatever it or its Count might command or forbid, when secret information came to the knowledge of one Syndic, it was secret no longer from the other thirty-two. The Emperor might be all-powerful, but like the Divinity, he was far away and busy with many other projects. So Syndic hand washed Syndic hand. It always had and always would. Mikail's instructions forbade him to talk to the Lord Mayor or to any Syndic, except William Hoffman. Lord Mayor and Count knew better than to surprise each other. Mikail knew all this too, without needing to be reminded; things were no different in Flushing.

It was time for his interview. Mikail passed between the bronze kings and up the grand stairs to where Ev waited for him. Together they went to meet Arturo Fidelibus, Count of Mecklenburg, a tall, thin aristocrat with prematurely white silky hair, exquisite manners and a poker face. His letter of instruction told Mikail that the Count was highly regarded in Aachen.

Mikail introduced himself by his real name and presented the Emperor's letter. Fidelibus studied him and said, "You look just like Lucas. I would have known you for his brother anywhere." This was not an auspicious beginning. Mikail did not think he looked like Lucas. The Count noticed his reaction but went on smoothly, "Saw him in Aachen last month at the Chancellor's meeting of provincial governors. He looks well. What can I do for you? It's not every day we lowly folk receive an Imperial agent with a purple letter."

Mikail explained his mission and asked about Andrew Kloffheim.

"Don't know anything about him, because he never comes here," the Count said. "Half the people in this town are certain he's the Chancellor's son, but it was all before my time."

Mikail went on to ask about William Hoffman and the Parides Company. "I do know something about them," the Count said, "but I've only been in Mecklenburg for three years. However, my chief clerk is a Rostocker through and through. He will know him and his family well. I'll tell you what I know first. Then we'll bring in Gustave.

"William Hoffman is a rich man from a rich family. He was Warden of the Jewelers Guild last year and usually pays for the annual Guild feast. That's a considerable expense but a great honor. And he's a Syndic, so he and his company can get away with a lot. Despite its façade of respectability, the Parides Company has a reputation for paying even more bribes than most, and the Customs people have repeatedly complained about it. Nothing ever comes of it, and nothing ever will. They're too well connected. These big Rostock merchants cover for each other. Furthermore, William's always been charitable, particularly to the fund for sailors' widows and children. That matters here. I've never been in his house, and his wife—I think she's his distant cousin—only comes to the most formal receptions. She's said to be in poor health. I did meet George Hoffman once. I ran into him and his father in the street a couple of months ago when he visited. We were introduced, but George didn't have much to say. I thought he was dull, but maybe he's just sly. I do remember that William looked very sad. Now for Mr. Kunstler."

Mr. Kunstler was duly sent for. The Count introduced Mikail as Adrianus van Hoogstraaten. The name registered at once. The Count went on, "Gustave, this is a matter of extreme confidence. We have a purple letter, meaning we have been directed by the Emperor himself to afford these gentlemen every assistance and to say nothing about it. So, nothing to anyone, not even your wife. The case involves treason by William Hoffman's son."

"That shouldn't be a complete surprise," Kunstler said. "George Hoffman is no good and never has been. My son used to talk about him. He thought young Hoffman very clever, but a liar and a sneak. He rarely comes home to see his family, though his mother's ill."

"You need a patron to get into the Political Department," Mikail said. "Who was his?"

"The Count himself. At the time, our Count was young Frederick, a member of the Imperial family. His father loves George and thinks he's wonderful, but I'm not sure the family completely agrees. So they bought him a good job. Everyone thought money changed hands."

"Was he a friend of Andrew Kloffheim?"

"Not here in Rostock. Andrew's too much older. I suppose you know who his real father is?"

Mikail gently moved him along. "Let's talk about the Parides Company and the Hoffman family."

Kunstler turned to the Count to ask, "Everything I say is in confidence, agreed?" The Count nodded.

"All right then," Kunstler said, "The Parides Company started here a long time ago. The founder was Greek, because east is where the best market for amber is. Good deep Baltic amber is like gold in Constantinople, but nowadays amber is a sideline. It is a steady income, but it wouldn't even surprise me if they use it to cover for what they really do. Headquarters are in New Rome, where their business is money and precious metals and money transfer. They're quiet, rich and very well connected. William is able and well paid—it's a family company after all—but his younger brothers in Aachen run the company. Nobody questions Parides' depth of capital or experience, but they'll do anything for a friend. William knows better, but it's not his to make decisions.

"He and his wife lost two girls, and my wife says Helen's never recovered; she sits alone at home doing nothing. With his daughters dead, his son away—perhaps gone forever—his wife depressed, and not much say in his own family business, William Hoffman is a bitter, unhappy man. It shows and people don't really like him, but he gets respect."

The Count had been listening attentively. He joined in the conversation, "Does Frederick have friends here, Gustave?"

"He was friendly with our prominent families when he was here, particularly Rupert von Moltke and Augustus Walsenburg. He used to come here to enjoy hunting wild boar with Walsenburg in the fall, but hasn't been back for years. Walsenburg boasts that he stays at the prince's palace when he goes to Aachen for the Witanagemot. If anyone from either family asked for anything, the Count gave us no peace until he had it. Otherwise, Frederick was sometimes difficult to work for but not a bad Count. He got along well with the Rostock merchants which I wouldn't have expected."

The Count turned to Mikail and said with emphasis, "Walsenburg is a member of the Grandee clique in the Witanagemot."

After some further conversation, Mikail and Ev expressed their thanks and left.

They were to return to Aachen the next day by the two o'clock train. The train already had steam up when a dignified elderly priest carrying an old clerical valise brushed past them and sat down in the compartment.

"Pardon me father, that's not your seat," said Mikail.

"'Course it is," Phil said, removing his collar. When the train pulled out, he was ready to report. "Not good, not good at all. I did get in but it was not easy. There was no back door, and the front door had the best lock I've seen in a long time. The windows were impossible to open from the outside without breaking them. I had to climb up to the second floor where somebody had left a window a bit open to air out a room over the weekend. Hoffman's office had another good lock on its door. When I got in the office was as clean as if they had expected me. But, as that secretary, God bless her, said, there was a locked drawer in the desk. I got it open and found a file of correspondence in cipher. I copied the top dozen pages, which was all I had time for. See if you can get anything out of this, Ev.

"Boss, did you have the sense to bring something to eat?"

Mikail had bought the West Wind's best hamper. Phil started to demolish its contents and was we along before he went to sleep. When they reached Aachen almost two days later, Ev was still working on the cipher without success.

CHAPTER X

The Chancellor

PANNONIUS SENT THE CHANCELLOR a message that he would come to discuss the Political Department and settled down to a long working breakfast with Duval and the Mayor of the Palace. The three men agreed that the Chancellor would be furious unless he was allowed to review his subordinates' misconduct, but that it could not be permitted. After breakfast, Pannonius walked over to the Chancellor's office in the Garden Wing with his shoulders squared for battle. He did not expect a pleasant interview. Giuseppe Sforza, the Chancellor, was famous for his passionate temper and keen intelligence. He was also notorious for his explosive reaction to any criticism.

There was no small talk. The Chancellor had primed himself to explode his own surprise. Speaking immediately, his agitated words came out so quickly they tumbled over each other.

"Hugh, I know you are here because Martin thinks there is a conspiracy against him and that I may be a party to it. All appearances are against me. George Hoffman and Andrew Kloffheim worked for me for years. They are my people. I had a high opinion of them both, especially Andrew, my godson and protégé. I personally sponsored him for the Department and pushed through every one of his promotions. Worse, if there is a conspiracy, the conspirators will include people close to me. There will be Grandees at its heart and head, and I am a Grandee. I know myself to be innocent, but isn't that just what I would say if I were guilty? However, I can do one thing to help persuade you that I haven't plotted against Martin. I will turn over the investigation of these

101

traitors to you without reservation. The entire Political Department will report to you or to whomever you designate until you are satisfied it is clean. I am going to bring Thomas Marsalia up here right now. Do what you will." The Chancellor always called the head of the Political Department "Thomas". Thomas Marsalia hated to be called Tom as much as he hated to be touched.

In five minutes the head of the Political Department was in the office. The Chancellor was straightforward. "Thomas Marsalia, this is Hugh Pannonius. He used to be with Louie Duval. More recently he was with our Proconsul in Dacia. He holds a commission from the Emperor to look into the treasonous acts of the two senior members of your Department who have disappeared. He can investigate anyone or anything he thinks relevant. Do whatever he tells you to do. Withhold nothing, protect nobody, including myself. If either of us catch you trying to hide anything or to protect anyone—including yourself, Thomas—*you* will be aiding and assisting traitors. Above all, don't try to protect Andrew. I have cut him off. Make sure you do the same."

Marsalia's doughy, round face looked stupefied. It took him a minute's thinking to stutter out, "What is it that you want, Mr. Pannonius?"

Pannonius was still adjusting to the Chancellor's uncharacteristic behavior. Ordinarily when Sforza was criticized, he noisily took umbrage and immediately counterattacked in force. Pannonius asked, "Have either of you have any reason to suspect any other member of the Department here or in the field of being too close to the Mongols or the Byzantines?"

Marsalia immediately replied, "No."

The Chancellor paused before answering carefully, "Not that I know of. But inevitably some connection of some kind will appear once you start to investigate. Please, Thomas, prepare lists of everyone who reported to George or to Andrew in the last two or three years. Make another list of both men's friends and enemies; a display of enmity is often a sham in these situations. Pull out every report and letter either of them has sent out for the last two years, and all correspondence and directives sent to them by anyone, including us. Put it all in a locked room with no windows and station guards there twenty-four hours a day. Mr. Pannonius may want his own people to do some or all of the work. Do whatever he says."

He turned back to Pannonius, "Hugh, you are going to need a team for the investigation. Let me know if you want my help, although I can see why you might not. I make no exception, Thomas and I are obvious suspects."

Marsalia was dumbfounded. His mouth opened and closed in his commonplace face, as if the idea he might be suspected of treason had never occurred to him.

"I'm still settling in," Pannonius said.

"Go and get it started now, Thomas," the Chancellor ordered. "I need to talk with Mr. Pannonius alone."

Once he was gone, the Chancellor turned back to Pannonius and said, "You will be thinking in terms of a broader conspiracy. I insist that you search my files and review all my personal financial records. The Mayor will be in a panic about the police and paramilitary forces over which I have some authority. I will be only too happy to have that authority transferred over to someone else until I am cleared."

Pannonius had to laugh. "You know the Mayor well," he said.

"More than thirty years," the Chancellor responded. "By the way, he wants my job. Always has."

"And what do you want?"

"To keep my neck out of the noose when all appearances are against me and to protect my grandchildren from further shame. With a traitor for a father they will have a difficult life. I know you suspect me, but when it's all over you'll find I'm with Martin. I helped him learn the ropes when he was Crown Prince and I owe him everything. I would be the vilest of men if I were a traitor. He chose me for my exalted office as second man in the State."

The Chancellor straightened up before he went on, "There's one thing more you should know. I intended to replace Marsalia with Andrew as chief of the Political Department next year. Andrew knew. I told him. Another mistake, but it makes his actions inexplicable as well as treasonable. He had everything he wanted. And Andrew was the reason I fought so hard against folding the Political Department into the Diplomatic Service. Emma and I have no sons. One of our girls has the vocation. She is a nun. As for the other, well, we don't particularly like our son-in-law, and they have not given us grandchildren. We have always treated Andrew as if he were our son and his children as our grandchildren. The final blow has been his treatment of Gloria and the children. Not a word of explanation or excuse! The children are old enough to understand that their father has abandoned them. Gloria is destroyed; she thought they were happy. I never saw the least reason to disbelieve their mutual devotion. Now nothing I can do can console her or their children."

"Is there anything more you want to tell me about your relationship to Andrew?"

"No, but when further questions occur to you I will answer them."

"Did you tell Marsalia your intention was to replace him?"

"No, but he might have guessed."

"What do you think about him?"

"Thomas looks stupid but he's not. He knows how every aspect of the Political Department works and how to get things done. He has made it clear that he wants to stay there. Most good officers eventually transfer to the diplomatic corps. That makes the Department peculiar; junior officers are often of higher quality than their seniors. I told Andrew to stay so that when he was transferred to the diplomatic corps he would be offered a position there at a much higher level. I thought I was being clever."

"Does Marsalia know what you think of him?"

"I don't know."

"Have you any question about his loyalty?"

"None. I have never had the least reason to question it and I'd vouch for him. He's middle class with no Grandee or foreign friends or connections so far as I know. He does play office politics and is quite good at it."

"How did you meet George Hoffman?"

"Initially through Andrew, who was one of his teachers at Trier. George was an excellent student, very clever. He courted Andrew for his connection to me. George was very respectful, in retrospect too much so. My impression is that they used to be closer than they had been recently."

Pannonius went back to report to the Emperor and Duval. "I can't make him out." he said, "He sounds absolutely sincere, but the evidence seems against him. We should do something, but I don't know what."

"We should do nothing," the Emperor said with emphasis. "Discharging a Chancellor without public evidence of crime would be tantamount to publicly declaring an emergency. That's the last thing I want to do."

"What about his armed men?" Duval asked. "He agreed to transfer their control to the Mayor. Shouldn't we at least do that?"

"Again, no," the Emperor replied. "My father taught me that you must never allow all the armed men in and around the capital to be under single control. He made me read Tacitus, and we discussed Sejanus. Put them under the command of someone else in whom you have absolute trust. Let Giuseppe make the official announcement. If he's innocent, it saves his face. If he's guilty, it pulls his teeth. Personally, I can't believe he's guilty. He'll take money and do favors for friends and think I won't find out. But I can't believe my old friend Giuseppe is a traitor even if I have to act as if he were."

"What do you suggest I do next?" Duval asked.

"Discover how the Mongols learned about the men we were sending to Dacia. That will give you a window into the conspiracy at work."

Duval went next to the Magister Militum. "We have an army of some 300,000 men to defend the empire," the Magister began, "not counting people available as a last resort—the military schools, auxiliaries, people raising horses in Ireland, permanent garrisons, border guards and the like. Maintaining real strength in Sicily and Tunisia at all times takes up almost half of them, and Spain takes up another 45,000. We always have 25,000 men facing the Byzantines in south Dacia, and the Paladin has first call on our troops in the Balkans. Under ordinary circumstances that gives him sufficient strength. What we need is reserves. When I borrowed the Paladin's 5,000 cavalry for Tunisia I didn't want to send them back. I thought they were better used as a reserve and made him go to the Emperor to retrieve them. I wouldn't have done that if I knew what the Mongols were up to but . . . well, no point in going down that road."

"Who knew that you eventually had to send troops back to Dacia?"

"Almost everyone. It wasn't particularly secret, and army people gossip. No one anticipated an attack inside our own country, although Aetius says the Mongols have been planning this for years. Logically, we should look for someone who knew the movement dates and routes early on. But that's a lot of people because there was no reason to treat this as top secret." The Magister started to tick the list off on his fingers. "I knew. So did the staff people with whom I discussed it and who wrote and cut the orders. The Order of Battle general is told of any expected change, plus the Emperor and the Military Committee of the Consistory and God only knows how many clerks. And the Mayor because he was acting as intermediary between Aetius and myself in the matter."

"Who are the committee?" Duval asked.

The Magister reeled off the list, "At the time? Feuerbach, Bluschili, Walsenburg, de Onis, Laporte, and Korzylasky. Their clerk is Godfrey Faure."

"All Grandees, except Bluschili, Laporte and the clerk," Duval observed.

"Too many to find out quickly who passed the information. Finding out how whoever-he-is managed to get details to the Mongols so quickly might be a better place to start. If we can discover how the message was sent, it might tell us the messenger."

In the end, Pannonius found the clue. Mikail was still in Rostock when a semaphore message arrived from D'Hagen. Pannonius signed for it and read:

"Mikail: Sodermann admitted accepting messages on the semaphore from someone in Aachen for George. Sender's identification in Aachen is BVO2398. The messages are strings of numbers and letters. Text follows. D'Hagen

The semaphore system would explain how George could hear so quickly from his source in Aachen. Pannonius asked the Mayor to send the transmittals to the code breakers, but they could not find an immediate way to break the cipher. BVO2398 turned out to be Ulrich Himmelfarb, a bald, elderly clerk near retirement who spent blameless days and nights scrutinizing construction plans and cost estimates for government buildings in Southern Italy and Spain. Himmelfarb didn't know who George Hoffman was, had never seen the transmittals before, couldn't guess at how to read them and had no idea why anyone should be using his identification number. He soon persuaded Pannonius of his innocence.

Pannonius asked the signals people for help. They suggested he look at the messages surrounding the transmittals. The Aachen semaphore system devoted an hour every day to sending hundreds of routine signals from all the Chancellor's departments. Each message to Hoffman had been neatly tucked into the total daily transmission to make it appear routine. Pannonius told Duval who only said sourly, "Fine. Now we know how the magician performed his trick. We just have no idea who the magician is." When Pannonius explained his discovery to Mikail after his return from Rostock, Mikail asked him why Hoffman had bothered to use an illegal conduit like the Sergeant Major to conceal the true recipient. Once illegal semaphore procedures were discovered, an investigation would automatically follow. It would have been simpler, safer, and even a bit faster to send the messages directly to Andrew Kloffheim in Saint George. Andrew could then seal them and forward them safely to his partner by regular departmental mail. Why had the conspirators chosen this unnecessarily complicated and dangerous way?

Pannonius agreed and added, "Something here doesn't add up. Andrew was in a position to do real mischief, but we have found no wrongdoing. Yet he must have done something very wrong to explain his decamping."

CHAPTER XI

Cloud Money and Outside Gold

MIKAIL ARRIVED AT THE palace around dinnertime only to be told that Pannonius was unavailable. So far he had not yet exercised his right to eat at the palace mess, and he proudly took Phil and Ev there. The mess dined in an elegantly proportioned wainscoted chamber in an ancient building. On three sides carved dark oak wainscoting rose to shoulder height, and on the fourth, full-length windows gave onto a garden. The service was as exquisite as the room. Dignified elderly waiters in uniforms with cascades of gold braid presented parchment menus as if they were medals for valor. Mikail, who had never enjoyed such luxury in his life, swelled with self-importance, until he and his guests cut into their meat. It was tough, the wine was plonk, and the rolls were stale.

As they were ordering dessert, a messenger tapped Mikail on the shoulder, calling them away to meet with Pannonius. His friend looked younger and happy sitting in his office with Dorcas. Mikail handed over his report, saying, "George Hoffman's family may be a channel for Byzantine money." The three worked through the possible ramifications for hours. The candles were burning low before Dorcas brought the discussion to an end with, "I wouldn't wait till the morning, Hugh. He works late." She was right. The Emperor saw them at once.

Pannonius began, "At last we may have something for immediate action. Mikail may have found a conduit that the Byzantines use to move their bribe money. Tell us about the Parides Company, Mikail." The Emperor listened attentively. When Mikail finished, he said,

"Good," and told his duty aide to summon the Empress and Pannonius' committee. Mikail repeated his report and answered questions for almost an hour.

It was midnight when the Emperor took over the meeting with, "This is our best lead so far. Arrest the Parides brothers tonight. Put them in the small prison here in the palace. In the morning arrest the staff and collect the office records. Mayor, pick your best men, go with them, and don't let them frighten the clerks. We will need their cooperation. Albrecht, talk to the prefect of the watch at his home tonight. I don't want any squabbles over jurisdiction."

Albrecht asked, "How do you want to handle the branches in Rostock and Vienna?"

The Emperor pointed at Pannonius. "Semaphore the Counts in Rostock and Vienna to arrest the resident Parides partners, search the premises and detain the employees. Everything they find comes here to Aachen. Orders go out by semaphore at first light. I'll talk to the Chancellor. If Giuseppe's not already my enemy, I don't want to make him one. Has anyone further suggestions?"

"William Hoffman has a bad conscience and might talk," Mikail suggested. "Bring him here."

"Do it," the Emperor said.

Phil had gone quiet, awestruck at meeting the Imperial couple. In a tentative voice he said, "I couldn't get into William Hoffman's safe. His codebook might be there. Someone should bring us the contents of the safe and that locked drawer, especially the correspondence."

"That too, Pannonius," the Emperor said, "and sit down with young Mikail and these two fine gentlemen"—he waved his hand at Phil and Ev, who had never been so described in their lives—"to see what other good ideas they may have. I am available all night. Don't worry about waking me. If I am too busy to help you, do what I do. Ask the Empress."

Last to leave was the Magister. Holding the door open, he said, "As one old man to another Martin, you're enjoying this."

"Yes. It makes me feel alive to know there are people trying to kill me."

The Empress was shocked. "Those people are trying to kill you and me and our son! Are you in your right mind?"

"Probably not," her husband replied, "but it's temporary. I'd be a criminal if I had started this. But I didn't and, yes, I am enjoying every minute."

Long before sunrise palace guards hammered on the doors of the homes of Stephen and Demetrius Hoffman. Demetrius tried to flee and succeeded only in running into the guards posted at his back door. When he tried to choke the arresting officer, his comrades were not gentle, and when he bit the sergeant the soldiers threw him headfirst into the waiting coach. and delivered him to the palace jail with a black eye and a bleeding nose, still noisy and full of fight.

Stephen Hoffman contributed a surprise: he wasn't there. His wife blandly told the Mayor he had left home two days ago without saying where he was going or when he would be back. The Mayor sarcastically asked if vanishing was her husband's usual behavior, and she calmly replied, "Oh, yes. He just says he will be away and off he goes for weeks at a time. I can't tell you why. We never talk business."

Parides opened for business at eight o'clock. The Mayor held back the raid for a few minutes to catch tardy employees and then led his soldiers, Pannonius, Mikail, Phil and an *ad hoc* group chosen from the tax and spy services into the building.

There they found more than thirty Parides employees as well as a few visitors. Amid screams of confusion, the soldiers assembled everyone in the counting house. The Mayor was a small man, but he had a forceful voice. As his soldiers loudly shouted *"SILENCE!"* he deftly hoisted himself on top of a table, and boomed, "Listen to me! The Parides brothers are traitors who have been serving the Emperor of the Greeks against our own Emperor! We need to find out how they worked their treason, so we're going to search this building. We are not here to punish you. No one here has a problem unless he was personally involved, and I'll protect even those of you who were involved in the mischief if you confess quickly and help us. We are going to interview everyone when the search is over. Meanwhile, we will ask some preliminary questions, mostly about your records."

"What are we going to do about work on hand?" someone shouted. "People owe us money today."

"Parides is closed today. Nobody comes in. Nobody goes out. The Grand Treasurer's people will be over later to figure out how to get affairs settled. Who's in charge when the partners are away?"

"I am. My name's Marinus Liebkind. I'm chief clerk," said a chubby, middle-aged man.

"Come walk with me and let's go through the building together,"

Meanwhile, Mikail and Phil had gone straight to Stephen's office, where Phil got the safe open. They found jewelry and other valuables, personal correspondence (including love letters from a woman not Stephen's wife), a considerable amount of money, weapons, and a large box of coded messages.

Mikail went to look for the Mayor and found him in the basement vault where he and Duval were leading an inventory of precious metals, valuables, and records. Mikhail "borrowed" Liebkind and took him upstairs to Stephen's office to show him the box of coded messages, and asked him to translate them. "I can't," Liebkind replied. "They're in a special partners' code. Nobody but the partners uses it or can read it. I had to stop whatever I was doing when anything in that code came in and bring it to Stephen immediately." Pannonius had come upstairs with the chief clerk. He had brought with him Victor Bibenda, a tax examiner with great experience in complicated matters. The two men stood quietly conversing while Mikail talked to the chief clerk.

Pannonius came over and asked Liebkind, "Tell me, Mr. Liebkind, was there anything unusual or obviously wrong about this business? Everything's going to come out, and you'd do well to cooperate with us quickly. Your position as chief clerk to traitors compromises you." Liebkind wiped his sweaty face with his hand and tried to look away. Pannonius pressed his advantage and stared directly into his eyes, "Mr. Liebkind, you are a Roman citizen. Your family lives here. Now there's a Parides company in Constantinople that's close to the Greek emperor, and there's this Parides Company here in Aachen that is under our Emperor's investigation right now. I'm sure you know where your loyalties are—and where they aren't."

Liebkind felt an invisible pair of giant hands wringing the air out of his lungs. He tried to look like a man of the world, but he had to catch his breath before he could answer, "We cut corners and cheat on imposts like everyone else. But that's not why you're here. Yes, there is part of the business has always bothered me, because I don't understand it. We call it the 'cloud money,' because it comes out of nowhere and vanishes into thin air. We deal in precious metals. When we buy and sell gold for our own account or on behalf of a client, we account for it fully on our books. But sometimes gold was deposited with us by an unidentified source. We called it 'outside gold.' We kept it off our books and sold it immediately for cash. After deducting our commission, we deposited the cash in Stephen's safe and showed the transaction on our books as 'money received and disbursed to special account,' with no reference to the gold itself. That way it looked like a legitimate money transfer, but the 'special account' was Stephen's safe. Stephen took the cloud money on his travels and came home without it. Then the 'special account' entry on our books was adjusted to show a withdrawal by delivery to client. The client was never specified on our records. I never dared ask Stephen about it. I slipped once and said 'cloud money' in his presence. He told me he would fire me if I ever used that expression again."

"Bull's-eye," said Mikail to Pannonius.

"Doesn't tell us what we really want to know," Pannonius muttered.

"Sometimes numbers talk," Bibenda said. He turned to the clerk and spoke in the ordinary tone of one numbers man talking to another, "Mr. Liebkind, could you prepare a simple five year chart with the date and weight of each deposit of outside gold, the cash you received from selling it, the date and the date and amount for each reduction or write-off of it through the special account. I also need to know the dates that Stephen was away."

"Yes, it's all in the records."

Carefully keeping his voice friendly, Pannonius asked, "What do you know about your company's relationship with its counterpart in Constantinople?"

"Very little. Stephen didn't want me involved. He made that clear, and he didn't talk about it to anyone but Demetrius. He usually destroyed communications from Constantinople after he read them. Stephen and Justin Parides, our resident partners in Vienna, control that relationship. The Vienna office is deeply involved with the Eastern trade. Vienna and Constantinople even exchange clerks. I wouldn't be surprised if Stephen met people from Constantinople when he visited the Vienna office."

Mikail asked, "How did you know outside gold was coming?"

"Stephen told me when it was coming and how much to expect. I weighed it and signed for it. A redheaded man brought it and helped with the unpacking, a very polite and gentlemanly fellow with a south German accent. Afterwards, we shared a brandy."

"Could the messages from Constantinople that Stephen burned have told him when to expect delivery?"

"Certainly."

In half an hour the chief clerk was back with a chart.

"Now," the tax examiner, explained "we match Stephen's travel dates with the dates that the cloud money was written off." He showed that while outside gold came in irregularly, almost all the cloud money was held in the special accountant and paid out in equal amounts every January, April, July, and October. The dates of payment matched almost perfectly with the times when Stephen Hoffman returned from his regular trips. There were only a few other cloud money transactions. The largest was shortly after the time that information about the five thousand soldiers must have been passed to the Mongols. The conclusion was inescapable: Parides was making enormous, regular cash distributions on behalf of the Byzantines and keeping all detail about it off its records.

Now the team was ready for Demetrius. At first he told Mikail that his brother took care of money transfers. Mikail called in Victor, who showed Demetrius his own signature on hundreds of transfers. Then Demetrius told obvious lies with a grin. Promises, threats, and continuous questioning did not affect him. In the end, he refused to answer any questions, and the frustrated interrogators sent him back to solitary confinement on a diet of bread and water. Roman law prohibited the torture of a Roman citizen. Detentions after arrest could be long, and Roman jails were very far from comfortable, but Demetrius was a very tough nut.

❋

So things went until William Hoffman and his documents arrived from Rostock. Until then the code breakers from the Diplomatic Service had made almost no progress. A professor of mathematics from

Alcuin University, a clever, opinionated man much given to sarcasm, was attached to the group. Pannonius disliked him, but the other mathematicians worshipped him.

William's desk and its contents contained routine clerical material, a well-thumbed Latin Bible, and the box of encoded letters. When they saw the Bible, the code breakers smiled. "It's a book code," the professor explained. "Book codes can't be broken without the book they're based on. Each group of letters and numbers refer to a specific word or page in the book." In three days the code breakers had translated "R-5-35-F" as the fourth word in line 30 of Chapter 14 of the Gospel of Saint John, "received," and started to read William and Stephen's letters.

William's file contained copies of both sides of his confidential correspondence with the other partners. Most were reports to Stephen in Aachen, often showing bribes to customs and tax officials, which were useless to the investigators, but eventually the cryptographers found references to cloud money transactions. One even acknowledged receipt of gold directly from Constantinople.

Now the team was ready to talk to William. Pannonius began by telling him, "We have broken your partners' personal code, and we can read your correspondence." William insisted on proof. When it was provided, he displayed an unexpected dignity, "I have been waiting for this day for a long time. It can't be worse than I anticipated, but my wife will be living in Hell. I won't give evidence against my son, but, otherwise I will help you if you treat her and my people in Rostock decently."

"You have a deal," Pannonius immediately said, "I will send the Count orders to reassure your wife. Let's start with the cloud gold. You've heard the expression?"

"Of course. Stephen hates it, but we all use it out of his hearing, even Demetrius. The gold originates in Constantinople. When I once asked Stephen who receives the proceeds, he told me it was better not to know. Obviously, there are a number of recipients. I pay one of them myself."

"Does Parides Company receive any benefits from the people who receive cloud money?"

"Only a three percent transmittal fee, less a forwarding fee paid to our sister company."

"How did you make payment to the one person you paid?"

"Always in cash, except once in gold."

"Who receives the payment?"

"His agent. I don't know the real recipient. Stephen set up the procedure and introduced me to the cut-off years ago."

"What was the procedure to make payment?"

"Stephen comes to my office to drop off the money, which I set aside. Johan comes to my office on the first day of the next month. Well, the fellow calls himself Johan. I give him the money. There are no receipts"

"Can you describe Johan?"

"A pleasant, well-spoken, middle-aged man with very red hair."

"What language does he speak?"

"Latin. He has an accent, Swiss or Austrian, I think."

"How much do you pay him?"

"Thirty-five thousand denarii four times a year."

"Let's talk about the Bible code. How long have you used it?"

"Since the outside gold started five years ago. Stephen came to Rostock to teach me when George was home on leave. I was still encouraging him to leave the Political Department. We learned the code together."

When Mikail heard that George could read and write the code, he pointed out, "The Sodermann correspondence goes to George Hoffman, who can read Bible code. The strings of numbers and letters in it look like the partners' code."

Pannonius shrugged, "All codes look alike to me. I'll give you a note to the professor." When Mikail explained what he wanted, the professor pulled out a random page of the Sodermann transmittal and another of the partner code. He held them up next to each other and said, "Your friend Pannonius really should know better. All codes do *not* look alike, any more than all music sounds alike. "Then he grinned and said happily, "But these two do." In minutes, he had deciphered a few words and said, "Not a big file. "You'll have it tomorrow."

Duval had lent Mikail a small office that hadn't been used for years. It smelled musty and needed cleaning. The furniture was all odds and ends, a rickety desk in which every drawer locked with a different key, an ancient, unsteady table, a stack of chairs, a file cabinet and a safe. The only change Mikail was considering was putting in a cot. With the office Duval had lent him an assistant. Unlike the office, Hildegard was young, good-looking and wonderfully efficient. Pannonius quietly told Mikail that she was Louie's mistress sent to spy on them.

The professor brought the transcripts the next morning with a note that the Mayor needed to talk to him about very important matters in two hours. Mikail groaned. Victor would have to finish the rest of his work. He had known Victor four days and felt it had been forever.

The Sodermann messages were from an unidentified sender in Aachen to George Hoffman. Mikail called the sender "Sharpie" because he so obviously enjoyed his own cleverness. One message almost jumped off the page. On February 28th, Sharpie advised "Friend tells me M[agister] M[ilitium] finally agreed send five thousand Castle S[aint] G[eorge], one half horse, rest foot. Tell friends immediately." The message then described the route the Romans would take and the dates for departure, rest stops, and expected time of arrival in such a way that the recipient could work out where the Romans would be at any time.

In return, Sharpie wanted to know, "when your friends will have big day so we can help." Once, Sharpie specifically told George, "Discover what Andrew knows without putting yourself at risk." Another enjoined, "Do this in a way Andrew does not find out." On four occasions George was told, "Deposit made with your cousins," which presumably meant Parides. The last entry asked, "Was meeting at castle successful?" There were no return messages from Imponza. Apparently such messages used another route.

Sharpie had asked for information on the Paladin's expected movements. This upset Dorcas. It could mean that an assassin was stalking her father.

The Empress also received a copy of the transmissions. She told Dorcas to have a semaphore sent to Saint George to order a search of the entire castle.

"Why do you want to do that?" Dorcas asked. "We already warned my father about assassins. Anyhow, he's in Cluchia, not at Saint George."

"Just an idea," the Empress said.

Chapter XII

News From Vienna

Alejandro de Ausundas, Mayor of the Palace, was another of the Emperor's old friends. He was short, round, cheerful and fond of proverbs. There all semblance to Sancho Panza ended. By birth the bluest of blue-blooded aristocratic Spaniards, he was said to be extremely ambitious, a womanizer, a man with few morals besides loyalty and the possessor of a truly vicious mean streak.

Mikail had met him only two days ago, but Ausundas greeted him cheerfully by his first name as if he were an old friend. "Sit down, Mikail. Martin read the Sodermann transmissions and thought you young people could use help from someone experienced. This is a heavy load for two Imperial aides."

"I'm no Imperial aide," Mikail said. "I'm just a junior political officer picked up by a whirlwind and deposited in the Imperial palace."

"Then congratulations are in order," the Mayor said smoothly. "I thought you knew. You're doing the work of an Imperial aide, and you'll have the title and money next week. Pannonius arranged it. He also thinks that tax examiner Bibenda should work for you full time. Is that all right?"

Mikail swallowed hard and nodded. His salary had just been tripled.

The Mayor went on, "Titles are not really that important. Sodermann will have to wait. We need to talk about Vienna. Julian Parides has vanished. Stephen's final message told him to run and run he did. Perhaps his clerks know where he is, but they're all Greeks and won't talk. McMahon's sure they're spies. We asked him to send us Vienna's partner correspondence. It came in yesterday and once we finished reading the translations Pannonius and I went straight to the Emperor. Here's my copy. Read it. Meeting's here in an hour. The clerks arrive later today."

"Vienna's not like Rostock then," Mikail said.

"It damned well is not," the Mayor growled. "It's more like Aachen. Aachen paid out 310,000 denarii in cloud money four times a year. In Vienna, it's approximately 200,000, which means we have to assume at least another five to seven recipients. Between the two, we have fifteen to twenty important, well-paid traitors. Maybe more. Fifteen or twenty Witans, Counts or members of the Emperor's consistory on a foreign payroll! It's monstrous blossoming treason. And we never suspected it!"

At the meeting the Mayor assigned Pannonius and Mikail to help Duval interview the clerks. Following the chief clerk's lead, the other six had refused to answer questions and continued to insist that as Byzantine subjects they were entitled to see their ambassador. When Duval came back a day later to ask his subordinates how they were doing, they had nothing to report. "Watch and learn, my children," Duval said. "I'll get them to talk."

At three o'clock the next day, the clerks were brought into a windowless interrogation room. Duval had spent the morning working and setting his stage. He had paced out distances and fussed over placement of chairs. Finally, he placed seven of them for the clerks with his own hand so that they formed a close semicircle near his armchair, and he could talk face to face with them. Hector Phillipadros, the chief clerk, was in the middle of the semicircle, but his chair was recessed so that a junior clerk who turned around to look at him for directions would make himself conspicuous. Two tall soldiers stood behind Louie's armchair, with another at each end of the semicircle. Behind Louie's armchair was a row of chairs for his assistants. A black-robed examining magistrate sat in the middle of the row, with empty seats to his left and right to emphasize his presence.

Duval did not enter until the clerks were seated. He sat down, careful to keep all at eye level, and spoke in an earnest, conversational tone: "My name is Louis Duval. We brought you here to find out whether you are going to answer all our questions fully and truthfully. That will decide whether you live or die. There is no advantage in holding you once we know you will not cooperate. You will then be executed for treason. I will not torture you nor threaten you with torture. I could because you are not Roman citizens, but men do not tell the truth under torture. Nor will I put on an unnecessary show. I am going to give you an immediate choice between life and death here and now. If you want to live, you will tell me what I want to know. I would much rather not kill anyone, but if I have to kill some of you to make the rest talk, I will do it."

He let this sink in before going on, "Nobody gets away with stalling. You are spies who have been caught. You will be given no access to the Byzantine ambassador or to anyone else. Your only choice is to cooperate now or be indicted for treason *today* at the end of this meeting. An examining magistrate is here to issue indictments against anyone who does not obey. Trial follows automatically in three days. Execution immediately follows conviction. Not being Roman citizens, you are not entitled to an appeal. We even brought the magistrate here to indict you. Please stand up, judge."

The magistrate had been rehearsed. He stood up, glared at the seven men for a long minute, and sat down.

Duval went on. "You owe no loyalty to Julian or to the company. Certainly they have shown none to you. Julian abandoned you. Your masters warned *him—him,* but not you—that trouble was coming. He didn't tell you, because your flight would have called attention to his own. He left you behind to die for him to get a few hours lead. He wants you dead, where you can't talk. I want you alive where you can. I am your only friend and best hope, but you must make your deal with me today or die."

The room went motionless. Duval paused before he warned, "You have never been so near death as you are this minute. You take a terrible chance by not confessing quickly, because once I have found out what I need to know, I have no reason to be merciful to a traitor who has spurned a fair chance to purge his crime. On the other hand, if you do cooperate, not only will I spare your life, but I swear that you will be given a chance to start a new life with a good chance to prosper. You should have no trouble making that choice. Don't think you can't lie to me. I can read the code in which your partners communicated, and if I catch you lying it counts as not cooperating. Your life is in your own hands. Who wants to talk first?"

119

He stopped. For two minutes no one moved or spoke. Duval sat quietly, waiting.

Then one of the youngest clerks raised his hand. "I'm not going to throw my life away," he said. "All I did was work with amber, but I think I know where Julian Parides is."

"Take this young man outside, Mikail, and get his testimony."

✳

"My name is Leonidas Angelos and I'm not going to die for the Parides family. I'm not a spy or a member of the family like Hector. Julian Parides is probably living on the second floor of Anna Kaufman's house just outside Brigittenau. I helped him move boxes there from the office a couple of months ago. He needed someone to drive the cart and move the heavy boxes. We made three trips."

"How do you know it's a hideaway?"

"I heard Mrs. Kaufman tell Julian his room was ready, and Julian said to her, 'One of these days soon I'm going to be staying for a long time.' She said, 'Don't worry. We have plenty of food and our own well.'"

"Do you know what was in the boxes?"

"No, but they were very heavy."

"Why did Julian pick you?"

"I was raised on a farm and can drive a horse and cart and I'm strong and can lift heavy weights."

Mikail talked to him for another hour without getting much more.

✳

When Mikail returned to see how Duval and Pannonius were faring, he found them alone, talking with Hector.

"You're not a fool, you know I mean it. So why are you being so stubborn.?" Duval asked.

Mikail interrupted. "Leonidas told me he's a member of the Parides family."

Hector sighed, "Yes, and I have a wife and children in Smyrna. If I betray them, my own family will kill my wife and children."

"Why didn't you say so in the first place?" Duval said in a reasonable voice. "We can work something out."

"How could you possibly do that?"

Duval laughed. "You have to die first. Everyone sees your body. Then they go away, and you arise to talk to me and live a long life as someone else. I've done it before. You may not see your family again, but you definitely won't see them if you're dead, will you?"

Hector sat thinking, but not for long, before saying, "You win."

Duval made him shake hands. Then he turned to tell an open-mouthed Mikail, "Meurice and Gerard are outside. Tell them we are going to need the pig's blood and the trick sword. They must put the screens exactly where I showed them."

Turning back to Hector, he told him, "Don't worry. It worked before and will work now, but you have to do exactly what I say. I want everyone to see your gory body, but not for too long or up too close. We will rehearse three times without the screaming. Take a little time to collect your thoughts and work up a nasty temper. You have to mean every word you scream at me. Make sure you hate me."

Once his actors knew their parts and the last rehearsal satisfied him, Duval had Meurice bring the clerks. As they were walking to the interrogation room, they heard Hector screaming at Duval. Then Hector burst out of the room and ran past them down the corridor and around a corner with Duval and two guards following in hot pursuit. Pannonius, Mikail, and the clerks' armed escorts rushed the clerks into the interrogation room and locked the door. In a few minutes Duval came back, enraged. His angry red face frightened the clerks as he told them, "He didn't get away. He didn't even get far. I want you to come and see him. Then maybe you will understand how serious I am." He led the clerks around the corner to a dark place in the corridor where blood was seeping under a screen.

Duval removed the screen and pointed to a body lying in shadow next to the wall, saying angrily, "Take a good long look." Hector's body lay with a sword in his heart. Blood was spilled all over the body, the floor, and the walls. "Does anyone want a closer look?" Duval asked. "No? Then put the screen back, Gerard, and these gentlemen and I will go back to finish our business now, one way or the other. Meurice, clean up the mess this fool made of himself."

Duval appeared to control himself and sat the clerks down again. He conspicuously removed Hector's chair and told them, "Your friend Hector didn't want to cooperate. You've seen how that ended. Your young friend Leonidas is alive and well. He's cooperating. Which do you prefer? Tell me in your own words right now." He called on each of the clerks by name one at a time. If the clerk refused, Duval kept talking and continued to raise the pressure until he agreed to cooperate. In the end, all but one of the clerks agreed. Duval sent the last holdout back to his cell with an hour to change his mind. and departed. He left Mikail and Pannonius to finish the clerks' preliminary examinations. By the time interrogations were over, the Byzantines had been fully connected to the conspiracy against the Emperor. The clerks did not know the names of the men who had been bribed. Julian had kept that last, most important secret to himself.

❋

Hector was waiting for Pannonius in the prison of another building. A pair of comfortable chairs had been left in his cell. Duval had a bottle of brandy and two glasses waiting. "You won't forget this day in a hurry," he said as he poured. "It may make you feel better to know nobody made a fool of you. I meant everything I said. Now that we're going to be working together, let's start with a drink. I respect the way you tried to save your family."

Hector finished his brandy in a gulp and held his glass out for a refill. Then he said, "Well, if I've changed sides, I'm not going to stop halfway. I gather you found a lot of money at the office?" Duval nodded. "There's a couple of hundred thousand more in the attic of Mrs. Kaufman's house. She's the widow of my predecessor. Julian had something going on with her. He kept secret files there too. They're in the attic. You should find them very useful. Not only do we run our own operation, but Aachen's outside gold goes through Vienna. The Byzantine consulate in Vienna receives the gold and sends a van to bring it over. We store it until the van comes to take it to Aachen."

"Who drives the van?"

"A man named Emmerich Bader. He works for Stephen or the Byzantine embassy.

"Where does Bader live?"

"In Aachen."

"Does he help distribute the cloud money for any other Parides branch?"

"I don't know. It's possible."

"Does he have any kind of accent?"

"Yes. South German."

"Does he go under any other name?

"I've heard him call himself Johan."

"What color is his hair?"

"Red. Too red. Maybe it's dyed or a wig."

"What do you know about distribution of cloud money from Aachen?"

"Not much. I once heard Stephen complain to Julian that his main government connection in Aachen was too greedy."

"Who's the connection? Do you know his name?"

"No, but from the way Stephen talked about him, he must be an important bureaucrat. Not a soldier."

"Do you know anything more about who gets pensions from the Aachen branch?"

"No. Look in the attic Julian's files should have something."

"What do you know about distribution from Vienna? Who receives the bribes?"

"As I told you, I don't know their names. And we never said bribes. We always said 'pensions.' I think Julian made distributions in Tyrol or Upper Austria, because he brought back wine from there after his trips. And I'm sure he went to Saxony. He made jokes about hunting in Saxony where you always kill two birds with one shot. I think he meant that there were two or more pensioners in Saxony."

"How many pensioners received Vienna cloud money?"

"Eight. Julian called them 'my eight rich men.' One must be a Count. Julian once joked that for what he was paying he should get the whole province, not just its Count."

"What was the province?"

"It has to be Dalmatia. Julian liked to talk mysteriously about 'my official friend in Dalmatia.'"

"Were any of the pensioners Witans?"

"Probably. Julian used to meet people in late June and early July at the railroad station. They could have been on the way to Aachen for the Witanagemot."

"Did you remember any names?"

"No. Stephen once mentioned the names of two of them. It was a long time ago, but I might remember if I heard them again."

❋

Developments kept coming. That night the Mayor asked for an immediate audience with the Emperor. He took only Duval and Pannonius. "We have an informant in the Byzantine embassy," he said. "They have a boarder they're keeping out of sight. Our informant got a sight of him. His description fits Stephen Hoffman."

The Emperor asked, "How do we flush him out?"

"Two ways at least," was the Mayor's reply after a bit of thought, "The direct way would be to tell the Byzantines we know they are hiding him and demand his delivery as a concealed criminal under threat of closing the Embassy. He's a Roman citizen, not a Byzantine subject, so we are under cover of the law. The other is to start a rumor that we intend to take drastic action against the Embassy and see if he runs. I assume you're not willing to close the embassy over this."

"There's an advantage to leaving him there," the Emperor observed, "If he runs we know the embassy is going to close. That would indicate that they know the Byzantines are about to invade."

"If it's a tradeoff," the Mayor said, "I'd rather have him telling us who those Witans are."

"The bribed Witans are a problem," Duval admitted, "but consider this: now the Byzantines have problems with them too. How are they going to pay their bribes now that Parides is gone? The trouble is that the next round of bribes is not due until July. By then it's Witanagemot season."

"Not at all," the Emperor said, "we just make sure that everyone knows we have closed the money spigot. If we get the news out now the Aachen gossip mill will do our work for us."

The Mayor changed the subject. 'Yes, yes, the bribed Witans are a problem, and there will be honest men who agree with them too. But we don't know who the leaders of this conspiracy are."

"Of course, we do," the Emperor snapped. "You're being too subtle, Alejandro. Their leaders are my cousin Frederick in cahoots with the Byzantine ambassador. I don't say there aren't others; probably there are. But Frederick and Simonides are leaders and probably the principal ones. Haven't you noticed that this damnable operation seems to have started when Simonides came here as ambassador? I am going to call in my dear cousin too and threaten him for leading a party against me. He may think we know more about him than we really do and say something foolish. My wife has been pushing me to do something like that. And I must turn Giuseppe around. He has always been my chief helper with the Witanagemot. They follow him. He's a Grandee by birth and a natural leader. If worst comes to worst, I can call in the soldiers, but we have spent over a hundred years getting them out of politics, and I don't want to go down in history as the Emperor who brought them back."

"Then the offensive it is," said the mayor. "When do we start?"

"When I tell you," the Emperor said. "I don't want to give them a chance to run once we strike. We still have about six weeks to Witanagemot. It has to be soon, but we will only get one chance, so let's be sure we plan meticulously."

Chapter XIII

High Winds Before the Storm

THE EMPEROR'S MORNING SCHEDULE was as predictable as his inevitable breakfast of toasted waffles with fruit and honey. The clockwork in the best timepiece ever made in the Empire—which he owned—was no more regular than the beginning of the Imperial day. He rose at six-thirty, breakfasted with his wife, and rode for an hour unless it rained, in which case he fenced. After changing he walked into his office at precisely eight thirty. Morning routine comforted him. He liked to say that his day needed an unvarying foundation of certainty, because once it began every moment brought surprises.

His office staff started work at seven, and by eight thirty, they had separated the paperwork into neat piles: unfinished work, incoming messages, correspondence, reports, petitions, and documents awaiting signature. Secretaries were poised for his dictation, and uniformed messengers braced awaiting his orders. The Empire's premier bureaucrat, after glancing at his schedule of appointments and agenda for the day, sat down at his desk and dutifully worked through each of the piles.

Meanwhile, Albrecht and Duval, his two senior aides, did their own paperwork. At exactly nine thirty on this Wednesday four weeks before Witanagemot, they entered the room unannounced in accordance with custom, only to find the Emperor and Empress alone with Giuseppe Sforza, the Imperial Chancellor slumped on a couch and weeping uncontrollably. Chancellor Sforza, who always looked twenty years younger than his seventy-one, had become a shattered old man. The Empress was kneeling near the couch with her arms around him, trying

126

to comfort him, as the Emperor murmured to his old friend in a voice so low they could not make out what he was saying.

Confused and uncertain whether they should be there at all, the aides stood in the middle of the room until the Emperor noticed them. He snapped, "Look on my desk," and went back to comforting his friend. On the desk was a semaphore message:

Pass immediately Empress and Emperor. Body of Andrew Kloffheim found covered in castle cellar. Medical officer thinks dead at least month. Fuller search discloses blood spots first floor. Cause of death stab in back. No weapon found, presumably removed. George Hoffman signed in and out main gate March 27th consistent with probable death date. Reasonable assumption private meeting in empty room first floor. Kloffheim killed there. Body dragged into cellar and covered. Please give Gloria, children, deepest condolences. No one here ever believed Andrew traitor. Gomez

Becoming aware of the newcomers in the room, the Chancellor composed himself. "Andrew was my son. He must have discovered something and given George a chance to explain himself. Instead, the bastard stabbed his old friend in the back. How did you figure it out, Jenny?"

"Louie's people kept finding out one terrible thing after another about Hoffman, but never anything negative about Andrew. No one had seen him leave the castle. Put together, the likeliest possibility was that Andrew was still in the castle and, therefore, presumably dead."

The Chancellor continued to weep. Finally, the Empress said, "Giuseppe, you've had pain enough. The children know me. Let me go with you and be the one to tell them and Gloria about Andrew."

"Let's do it before I lose courage." He walked over to a carafe on the desk, poured a glass of water, took a sip, and said, "Martin, you're too kind to ask me at a time like this, but I know your need. Now that my loyalty is clear you'll want my help with the Witanagemot. Of course, I'll do everything I can. I would have done it anyhow. Things are not going well this year. I doubt the Mayor has warned you about the extent of our problem."

The Imperial couple exchanged glances. *(They know,* the Chancellor thought.) "Do you think the Mayor is disloyal?" the Emperor asked.

"That's the wrong way to say it," the Chancellor replied. "He doesn't like to give you bad news. Or perhaps, he can't believe it. He's not disloyal, although if he ever thinks we're a sinking ship, he won't go down with us. Until then, he's absolutely loyal."

The Empress interposed, "We are keeping Gloria and the children waiting," and left with the Chancellor. The Emperor mused, "The Church forbids divorce. What would have happened if Giuseppe died before recognizing his son? You know the law, Albrecht."

Albrecht answered at once, "Of course. No illegitimate child may receive more than any legitimate one under a will. Without a will, the acknowledged illegitimate son takes one-third of a legitimate son's share. Unacknowledged children take nothing. Thus, I myself cannot leave more to the child born to the woman I have lived with for the last ten years than to the child whose mother left me two years before his birth."

"There must be some way we can change the law," the Emperor said.

Albrecht groaned, "For God's sake, Martin, not now. Witanagemot's less than a month away. Don't we have trouble enough without inflaming the Church and letting Frederick's friends call you a libertine? Do that, and the Witans will leave their mistresses' warm beds at dawn and vote to censure you. What do you intend to do before convocation?"

The Emperor laughed before turning serious, "I need to take the initiative. People start to assemble two weeks before Witanagemot convenes on the fifteenth. Early in the first week of July, I will call in Cousin Frederick and try to frighten him enough to keep him busy protecting himself, instead of plotting against me. Next, I call in Simonides. If he's hiding a fugitive from Roman justice, we have a hold on him. But, Albrecht, suppose the Mayor's wrong again? This Parides bribery thing's the size of a mountain. Did my cousin promise to make him prime minister? Is he setting me up? Or am I just being a suspicious old man? No, he's my old friend." He frowned, "Enough. It's nothing but nerves. I have to concentrate on preventing a vote of censure and avoid being assassinated. That's not hard to understand. We need one hundred Witans. Giuseppe's always taken care of this, but he needs help this year. Work with him, Albrecht. He will want revenge for his son.

Louie, can your young men get me the name of just one specific Witan whom Simonides has bribed? Just one to throw in his face?"

Duval answered, "We have a name if you need one, but he's not a Witan. Aurelius de Nossier, your Count in Dalmatia, took Byzantine money. It's an unpleasant surprise."

The Emperor grimaced "A Greek army over the border and suddenly in Dalmatia would soon be behind Aetius. Italy and Austria would be left unprotected. That's why they kept all that money in Vienna. Recall Nossier."

"It's been done," Albrecht murmured.

Duval continued, "Justin Parides is hiding out near Vienna. MacMahon will arrest him today. We already know that eight men took bribes here in Aachen. Now the Viennese chief clerk adds eight more. That makes sixteen. We can be sure that the bribe money is coming from the Byzantines. You can safely say so to Simonides. We also have the name of the Byzantine representative who transported the gold. As delivery boy he would know who received the bribes. We're trying to find him. Parides' chief clerk in Vienna says there is at least one province with more than one man on the pension list. He thinks it's Saxony. So you could safely throw 'Saxon Witans' at Frederick and Simonides without specific names, but I expect we will have several names soon."

"Good," the Emperor said, "keep at it. The more I have when I talk to Frederick and Simonides the better. Are we ready to make the Witans aware that we have turned off their Byzantine gold?"

"Why wait?" Duval said. "Put the story into circulation now. Organize a leak and let the rumor mill do our work. And the Chancellor might pass the story along to his friends among the Grandees. He can pass it off as a friendly service. The right people will hear it. If we start now Frederick and Simonides will be nervous when they meet with you."

The Emperor wondered, "Should I tell the First Speaker? It shows the Witanagemot respect, and he will be sure to get the news out to the very people we want to hear it."

Albrecht politely disagreed, "Certainly tell him, but do it *after* the story starts to get out. Otherwise, he might tell Frederick, and together they might try to hush it up. But once the story is out, the Speaker will need your help to protect the Witanagemot's reputation. Help him then, and he'll be grateful."

Later that day, MacMahon found Justin Parides in Brigittenau and briefly took him into custody before Justin killed himself with poison concealed in his ring. There were more than 200,000 denarii in Mrs. Kaufman's cellar and an attic full of confidential files and documents. A hasty search found treasonable correspondence with three Saxon Witans. Hector's veracity was confirmed and the Emperor had the names he wanted.

The Aachen Watch knew Emmerich Bader from a tavern brawl some years ago. He had since then twice changed his address and, not surprisingly, had recently vanished from his usual haunts. A general search was ordered, and a large reward offered.

Hector had been stashed in the attic of the small palace hospital in a comfortable suite built long ago for an important prisoner. He and Pannonius had finished their day's work. Hector had been very forthcoming in explaining how the two Parides companies were connected through intermarriage and joint ventures. Pannonius was ready to return to his office.

Two sets of corridors connected the palace buildings, broad, well-lit public corridors that most people used, and a system of parallel back passages originally built for servants. Narrow and poorly lit, the back passages were usually nearly empty, except for equipment and supplies left for the cleaning staff, storage cabinets, and an occasional passing servant or courtier. Pannonius had taken to using the backstage corridors to keep his movements secret. Just as he entered the tunnel underneath the Garden Wing a masked man in dark garb, crossbow in hand, leaped out of the shadow of an outsized wall cabinet ten yards in front of him. Seeing a pile of boxes at the side of the corridor, Hugh dove for his life. He had not quite reached safety when he felt a line of burning fire pass across his scalp and felt blood begin to flow down his brow. As he started to scramble back to his feet, he saw the assailant running at him with a raised knife in his right hand. Pannonius tried to sidestep the knife as he rose, and luckily, the man was either inexperienced or overanxious. His thrust missed his victim's heart, but the knife entered Pannonius' torso near his left shoulder and as he twisted to avoid it, he heard the knife scrape against his shoulder bone. There the knife snagged stopping further penetration. Without thinking, Pannonius reached out to grip his attacker's throat. His right hand did not have strength enough to choke him, but its force pushed the would-be murderer backward and off balance, causing him to stumble, fall, and drop his weapon. Pannonius, rising, looked around and spotted the nearest exit. He ran for it.

While he was stumbling away, his pursuer picked up the crossbow from the floor and wasted valuable seconds seeming to debate with himself whether to wind it or to use his knife. Deciding against the crossbow, he slung it over his shoulder, and picked up his knife. Knife in hand, he ran after his victim. The brief respite had given Pannonius a head start, but the villain nearly caught him when he tripped over a bucket and mop left out for the cleaners. Inspired, he picked up the bucket and, ignoring the pain, threw it with all his strength at his pursuer's ankle. The man staggered, quickly recovered his balance, and came on again, head down, holding the knife in his raised right hand.

This time Pannonius did not run. Armed with the mop, he grasped the stick just below the mop top and pushed its ball of string into the knife. Fear and rage overcame his pain and gave him strength to force the attacker's knife hand up and to the side, where he could not use it. Falling back a few feet, the man came on again more slowly, trying to seize the mop with his left hand while keeping the knife in the right. Pannonius reversed his hold on the mop and stepped back to swing the pole like a quarterstaff. His wounded shoulder screaming in pain, Pannonius now used both arms and swung hard. Adrenaline and anger gave him force enough to land a vicious blow on his opponent's right wrist. The pole splintered on impact and Hugh broke off the split wood to thrust its jagged edge at his enemy's eyes as if it had been the point of a sword. His foe gave ground and Pannonius decided the exit was near enough for him to chance the threat of an unwound crossbow. Shouting loudly in hope that someone might hear him, he ran for the exit, his attacker at his heels.

Pannonius reached the door and exited the back corridor by running up a few steps that branched off to the exit. He found himself in an empty grand reception room only a few steps ahead of his pursuer.

Pannonius knew the large door on the far side of the room must open onto a public corridor. Once there, he should be safe. Tired and bleeding, he started to run for it. Behind him, his assailant picked up one of the small gilt chairs standing in rows and threw it at his legs. The unexpected impact knocked Pannonius off his feet. When he got up, he saw the man standing near the door, sneering under his half mask and starting to wind his crossbow. Pannonius seized a poker from the set of tools at the nearby fireplace and yelling at the top of his lungs charged his tormentor. Seeing a howling, bloody-faced madman coming at him with metal in his hand and murder in his eyes, the assassin turned and ran for his life.

His enemy gone, the bleeding Pannonius opened the door to the public corridor and looked around. Now the pain was almost unbearable, and he was half-blinded by the blood flowing from his scalp. He had come out near Mikail's new office, and feeling agony with every step, he stumbled into it, leaning against the wall for support.

Hildegard was working alone. She screamed when she saw Pannonius, but set to work at once. She found Mikail's spare shirt and cut it up to make a bandage for the shoulder wound and a compress for the bleeding scalp. People had heard her scream and started to gather. Hildegard sent one of them for a doctor and begged a bottle of brandy from someone else to wash out the wounds. Pannonius was gritting his teeth against the pain from the alcohol she was applying to his scalp when he surprised Hildegard by starting to laugh. It had just occurred to him that Elizabeth had been a true prophet after all. Janos' instruction in sword and quarterstaff had saved his life—even if both sword and staff had been a common mop. As a matter of honor, he was going to have to tell the old man, and Janos would never let him forget it.

Somehow, Dorcas got to Pannonius even before the doctor. She found him in Mikail's chair. Hildegard was pressing the compress onto his scalp wound and the room reeked of brandy. Dorcas snatched the pad out of Hildegard's hand, drenched it with an enormous sopping of brandy, and pushed Hildegard aside to take her place. Her first words were, "Who did this to you, darling?" Hildegard looked at her and sweetly said, "Call me when you need me. I'll be waiting for the doctor outside," and left, quietly closing the door behind her.

The doctor's opinion was, "Close call, but I would have expected worse. Your scalp wound is nasty. I'll have to sew it up. Plenty of blood and plenty of mess, and you'll have a scar, but no deep penetration. That shoulder wound will take much longer to heal, but, again, nothing vital. Whoever tried to kill you, didn't do a very good job of it. You have lost a lot of blood, young man. So eat meat for the next month." He washed out the wounds with distilled water and vinegar, salved them, sewed up the flesh wound, and bandaged his patient professionally.

As news of the attack spread, people kept arriving. The doctor tried to shoo everyone out of the room and managed to expel everyone, except Dorcas and General Biakarione, who was examining the wounds with an experienced eye. "You're lucky, Hugh," the general said. "An amateur did this. A professional would have killed you. Any idea who it could be?" Pannonius tried to shrug, but it hurt too much. "In the last few weeks," he said, "I've gotten too close to too many people's secrets."

When the doctor ordered everyone out of the room, a badly shaken Dorcas would not move. The patient was left alone with a very different young woman from the quick, self-possessed one to whom he was accustomed. "It was worth being stabbed to hear you call me darling," he said gently. "You know how I feel. At least I've tried to tell you so. I love you, I always will. I would rather have your love than everything in the world, and, suddenly, it seems I have it. Isn't it strange? Someone tries to kill me, and it turns out to be the happiest day of my life. The best times in my three years in Dacia were the two times you came to visit your father. I was so very happy just being with you."

"Time for me to confess," she said, studying the floor. "I kept every one of your letters to read and re-read. You must have written me every day. How did you ever get anything done? Every one of those letters sounded as if you were talking to me. They made me realize how much I missed you and needed to see and talk to you. It's been wonderful being second memory to the Empress, but I missed you. The Emperor's niece is every male courtier's idea of a prize or a challenge. There was always some man who wanted me or said he did, but your letters proved you wanted me for myself. No one knows me the way you do. I couldn't be sure of anyone else, but I knew one thing. You loved me. Bless those letters. They kept me from being interested in anyone else."

"If I'm lucky enough to have you feel that way, dear heart, why did you keep your feelings hidden when you were in Dacia?"

"Because my father, my uncle, my aunt, and my brother all wanted me to be with you and let me know it by pretending not to notice. You were so obviously the right person for me that there had to be something wrong. It all had to be a terrible mistake. I had known you forever but love had to come from someone I never met before, didn't it? So there was no way it could be a good idea. Besides, I had always been the Proconsul's little daughter living at the end of the world. And suddenly, I was somebody important and in the middle of everything. God, it was fun, but I was so glad to see you when you came back, and when I saw you wounded, I felt I had been wounded. Denying my feelings made no sense at all. But weren't there any girls for you in Dacia, Hugh?"

"None at all. They export the good ones to Aachen."

"When did you first know you loved me, Hugh?"

"I think I always have. I realized it years ago, when I noticed that I was happier when you were around, and the feeling lasted long after you left. The light was brighter and the colors clearer wherever you were around. I was always plotting to find ways to see you. I cared about what you thought of me. But you were exploring the palace and the world. I knew I would have to wait. It wasn't unbearable. What I dreaded was that you would find someone else. Without you, I'd have ended up a middle-aged functionary, good at his work but with nothing else in his life. You see so many of them here."

"What do we do now, Hugh? Our lives here are so dominated by palace intrigue there isn't much room for anything else. All the important people will think our being together is so cute, just like an amusing piece of theatre. It's no way to start a life together."

"Once this is over, we go away from Aachen for a few years and don't come back until we have made the two of us into a single life."

"The Empress won't like it."

"Maybe. But she's not mean, and she loves you. She even likes me. The problem will be Louie. He hates training new people and has no shame about managing other people's lives. He will use every dirty trick he can invent to stop me from getting out of his clutches."

"You'll have to marry me, Hugh, if you want to get us both away."

Aching, he knelt. With a broad smile, he declared, "Dorcas, whom I love; Dorcas whom I have always loved and will love forever, Dorcas whom I cannot live without, will you marry me?"

"Yes," she said. "Yes, of course, Yes, always." The news had taken time to reach Mikail, who was at the other end of the palace compound. He came on the run to find his friend sitting in the best chair, heavily bandaged but gloriously exultant, with a glowing Dorcas on another chair next to him, but somehow managing to snuggle against him. All the other visitors had gone, tactfully leaving them alone. Mikail lacked their tact. Besides, it was his room.

"What happened?" he asked. Pannonius told him, adding he was only alive because his assailant wasn't a professional killer.

Light broke on. "Oh my God," Mikail exclaimed. "Sharpie tried to kill you himself."

"Who's Sharpie?" Dorcas asked.

CHAPTER XIV

Playacting at Peace

IN MID-JUNE KAIDU UNEXPECTEDLY asked for a meeting. The Paladin agreed at once and designated a large farmhouse he owned about fifty miles from Saint George for the meeting place. The Romans were first to arrive on the day set for the meeting. As they waited for the Mongols to ride in, the Paladin and General Lauzac were chatting on the porch with a civilian, an older man with a clever face wearing an elaborate sky-blue and green silk jacket over dark striped breeches and a deep blue sash with many decorations pinned on it, the formal court uniform of a Roman Senior Ambassador. The Paladin wore both his gold belt of office and the red cloak of command while Lauzac was in full dress uniform. No Roman wore arms or displayed a weapon. In front of the house a white flag flapped in the light breeze.

A few feet away from their seniors the junior officers had gathered, talking among themselves. The nameless captain who had debriefed Mikail at Saint George was doing what intelligence officers have always done best; he was worrying. "They're late. Suppose they don't come."

The Paladin must have overheard him, because he smiled and turned to say, "Don't worry, Toby. He called this meeting. He's just showing his independence by being a little late."

Twenty minutes later, a procession of fifteen mounted Mongols led by a rider with a white flag was seen arriving. The Paladin led his delegation down the steps to meet them in front of the house. He stationed the Ambassador to his right and Toby, who was to act as

136

interpreter, to his left. The other Romans formed a line about five feet to their rear.

All the Mongols were in military uniform, except Kaidu himself. A short, broad-shouldered older man with a strong face and a hooked nose, he wore a robe tucked into loose riding pants. When he dismounted he pulled a magnificent silk robe embroidered with dragons and clouds out of the belt of his riding pants and patted it into shape. Then he put on an odd hat with eagle feathers and walked over to the Romans, stopping about ten feet from the Paladin to face him directly. A young Mongol officer positioned himself to Kaidu's left. The others formed a line behind them.

The young officer stepped forward, bowed, and began, "Proconsul, officers and gentlemen, I am Bat, protocol officer and interpreter. As such, I take upon myself the duty to introduce His Excellency Kaidu, Vice Minister of the Right, Commander-in-Chief of the Western Provinces, and brother-in-law to the Great Khan. His Excellency has directed me to advise you that he holds plenipotentiary powers." He then introduced each man in the delegation in turn. When his name was called, the Mongol stepped forward and bobbed his head. No one except the interpreter bowed to his enemies.

When Bat had finished the Paladin took a step forward to make his own introductions. "I need not introduce myself to his Excellency," he said, "since we have long known each other. Next to me is Senior Ambassador Giovanni Mazzeo. As you know, a board of three senior ambassadors, of whom he is one, heads our Diplomatic Service. Neither the Senior Ambassador nor I have plenipotentiary powers. In requesting this meeting, Vice Minister, you did not indicate whether you wanted a formal meeting or a meeting of principals. We are prepared to meet either alternative." Then he introduced each of the Romans by name, except Toby, whom he introduced as "our interpreter." Although the Paladin spoke Latin throughout, Toby helped him by translating an occasional idiom into Mongolian. He bowed when the Paladin introduced him. No other Roman bowed.

When the Paladin finished, Kaidu said, "I do have a specific proposal to make and would prefer a regular meeting to present it. Of course I cannot expect an immediate answer since you do not have plenipotentiary powers. I would also appreciate a subsequent private meeting."

Both delegations trooped up the stairs to a table in the house's largest room, which had been prepared for a diplomatic meeting. Kaidu immediately got down to business, "The Great Khan has authorized me to propose a cease-fire in place for six months during which a meeting can be scheduled to discuss our grievances that led to the present situation." Then he wasted fifteen minutes on a rambling speech.

The Paladin let him wind down before answering tersely, "I cannot see how a cease-fire in place while enemy forces still occupy Roman soil could possibly be acceptable to my Emperor. And I know of no significant grievances the Great Khan had before he invaded Roman soil without any prior complaint. Had your Khan notified us, we would have explored his grievances and tried to satisfy him. I suggest your withdrawal to your own territory and a subsequent meeting to discuss the amount of payment to the Emperor and those of our citizens injured by the actions committed by your forces."

As soon as he could do so politely, the Paladin cut further discussion short, saying, "I think we have said everything profitable to say at this time. I am duty-bound to transmit your proposal to my Emperor. Why don't we sit down under the tree over there and talk?" Under his breath, Ambassador Mazzeo muttered, "His proposal is absurd, and he knows it. This is all about what he's going to ask for now." The Paladin mouthed, "I know."

Two chairs had been placed in the shade of a huge chestnut tree, and as host, the Paladin had arranged for glasses, a bowl of fruit, a pitcher of water, and a carafe of wine to be prepared. Once they were seated, the Paladin opened the conversation with "Kaidu, what is really on your mind?"

Kaidu bit into an apple and answered, "Let's start with the death of young Subatai. As you surely know by now, he was the son of Odsetag, my older sister. Worse, her only son. Odsetag has managed to inflame our younger sister, Nahunta, the Khan's second wife, who is using her influence to turn this raid into a war. What can you do to help me?"

The Paladin was not sympathetic. "Not much. Your nephew was a military officer carrying messages to an enemy army on Roman soil. He died on Roman soil as an invader. The man who killed him acted in self-defense. Any attempt to take personal revenge will make things a great deal worse. Besides, aren't you the head of the Hutus? Won't your younger sister listen to you?"

Kaidu sighed theatrically "No, she doesn't always listen to me, but she has always done whatever her older sister told her. She remembers you, Aetius, from when we were all young and she isn't personally hostile. A gesture would help. Could you return the boy's gold tally? Subatai was the youngest ever to receive it. His mother is very proud of it."

"It's already in Aachen," the Paladin responded. "I could write her, promising to support its return as part of the final settlement. Any mother would want to know how her son died, and I can tell her that. But, in exchange, I want your express promise here and now that there will be no personal revenge. Soldiers die, and their mothers mourn. That's the way it is."

"Thank you," Kaidu said, "I will explain that a future return of the tally will be conditional on her taking no revenge. She won't like it, but I think she'll accept it."

"Have you anything else?" the Paladin asked.

"Yes. You think I planned this raid and I won't deny it, but it was planned on orders. I don't take bribes from the Greeks. I want to talk about how we all get out of this situation. The longer it goes on the more likely a real war becomes."

The Paladin's face was not sympathetic. "Then just get out. Announce it unilaterally."

"They will not do that," Kaidu said flatly.

"There's an old diplomatic saying that people who box themselves in have to live in a box," the Paladin responded. "Your choices are to get out or to fight a major war for someone else's benefit. It may be to our advantage to help you get out, but my Emperor won't reward unprovoked invasion. On questions of appearance, of course, he's always reasonable."

Kaidu repeated himself, "What you say sounds perfectly reasonable, but they won't do it."

"Then switch sides," the Paladin suggested, "cut a deal with us at the expense of the Greeks. That certainly won't show weakness."

Kaidu's face showed how unwelcome he found the proposal. "Again, what you say sounds perfectly reasonable, but the Byzantines have spent a lot of money to ensure that particular suggestion is in nobody's interest. How could we move the route of the Silk Road even if we wanted to?"

"My Emperor won't get into a bidding contest with the Byzantines, least of all one over bribes," the Paladin replied. "Your best course is to pull out. As for the Silk Road, the only reason it doesn't already have two outlets is that the Great Khan himself has forbidden it."

"Again, they just won't do it," Kaidu repeated." You've always been clever, Aetius, find a way."

The Paladin sighed, "How can I do that while you say no to all the things such a way entails? You have the initiative. Make a proper proposal."

The meeting ended after some further, desultory conversation, with Kaidu and the Paladin formally bowing to each other. Both men took care to bow at exactly at the same angle. The Paladin was so unusually tall (particularly when compared to Kaidu) and Kaidu so unusually broad (at least as compared to the Paladin) that the sight was comic. No one dared laugh.

As soon as the Mongols left the Paladin convened his delegation. Ambassador Mazzeo was the first to speak, "What he really said is that he would like to get out of this situation, but can't make any proposal we can accept.

"Then why did he call the meeting?" the Paladin asked. "Why not take him at face value?"

"Because," Lauzac explained, "he's trying to show motion where there isn't any. He was careful to never make an offer from which you could start negotiating. So he stalls while pretending not to stall. Can we believe him when he says he took no bribes from the Greeks?"

"No. Or if he hasn't, then his clan has," the Ambassador interjected. "Nevertheless, the Paladin's right. Kaidu's really put himself in a box. He planned this raid and probably made promises to his Khan. He hasn't kept his promises and may have to make adjustments with respect to the Silk Road. That would leave his Khan worse off than before. He may well lose his position and maybe even his head. So he asks us to get him out as the price of his working in our favor."

"His head's safe while his sister is second wife, and he is the head of the Hotun tribe," the Paladin said," but suppose she's out of favor or seriously ill? That would explain this overture at this time. I like the idea that this opening is a flight forward to get himself out of trouble. Can't we find out what the Khan's likely to do?"

Mazzeo chuckled. "There's no reliable way to find out what the Khan really thinks or will do until he acts. He makes that kind of major decision in the harem with only a few close advisors present. And those advisors are mostly his relatives. It's unenlightened and leads to some strange decisions, but it certainly maintains secrecy. What are you going to do now, Aetius?"

"Nothing. Doing something for the sake of doing something always leads to mistakes. We wait and see."

BOOK IV

Witanagemot Season

July to September 1812

CHAPTER XV

Witanagemot Season

JULY AND AUGUST IS Witanagemot Season, a season just as real in Aachen as spring or summer. The Season begins on the first of July, when the rich and important people of the entire Empire and their families begin to gather in Aachen. They will stay in the capital until the first of September (called Exodus Day) or even a bit longer if the money lasts. Adults wait for the Season counting days and hours in the same way their children wait for birthdays. There is something young and a little naughty in the city's air. It is the city's Lupercal, a time to strut, love, misbehave, and transform your life. "I met you in Witanagemot Season" is the first line of a thousand sentimental ballads, whereas "Oh, I met him (or her) during Witanagemot Season" is the punch line of a thousand off-color jokes. Later in the year, people will excuse their frivolities with a shrug and, "That was during the Season."

The city becomes noisy and crowded. Whether Witans or not, wise men make early reservations at their favorite inns. If you have a house, your friends and family descend on you, often without an invitation. You find room for them anyhow. Some householders leave the city for the Season and double their yearly income by renting out their homes. Important aristocrats own palaces in the better neighborhoods just for the Season. Prince Frederick turns his palace into a hotel for Grandee Witans.

The streets are filled with cheerful young crowds, who don't want to go home and don't have to. They can dance the night away because the main squares are illuminated and the city pays for street musicians.

As the night passes there will be more and more couples embracing in the shadows just out of the light.

The Imperial family lead the revels. They make it a policy to keep in the public eye and attend all important social events. Family members who do not live in Aachen are recalled to help with the festivities. A busy Emperor makes time for a private audience with every single one of his hundred ninety-five Witans, while his Empress entertains their wives and finds a thousand ways to admire their children. Families and old friends hold reunions and talk all night. All kinds of folk find all kinds of reasons to be in Aachen. Alcuin University goes on vacation, making its halls and dormitories available to visitors. Elderly professors, rectors, and chancellors find themselves back in the rooms of their youth. All too often they behave accordingly and end by contributing their pebble to the Season's mountain of scandal.

Aachen's theaters, opera houses, concert halls, and places of public entertainment open early and close late. The lovers of music congratulate themselves on living in an age of gods and heroes. Although Hayden has been dead two years, his presence is still felt, while Mozart is very much alive. His twenty-third opera, *Achilles Among the Women,* will debut this season. No one has heard it, yet everyone already knows that it is about Achilles' erotic misadventures when he hid among the women to escape the Trojan War. The Aachen gossip mill says that after three hilarious hours of comedy, high and low, a brokenhearted Achilles accepts glory and death as his inevitable fate. The opera concludes with *Like Gold Shining on Black Velvet*, a very long trio sung by Achilles, his mother the goddess Thetis and the centaur Chiron, his teacher, about the wonder and beauty of love and the certainty of death. Those who have heard it say that it is Mozart's best work: profound, heartbreaking, and piercingly beautiful. Imperial attendance would be assured even if Mozart's sister Nanerl were not the Empress' friend and piano teacher.

Beethoven, the age's other great musical luminary, will likewise be introducing an important new work. Despite poor hearing, he will conduct. Beethoven has carefully timed his premiere so as not to conflict with Mozart's and the week of talk that will follow it. The two great men profess enormous respect for each other, but their relationship is fragile. It's hard, perhaps impossible, to be friends with them both. Certainly the Empress has tried and failed [Beethoven knows whose friend she *really* is] but, persistent and tactful as always, she will go up onto the stage herself when the music ends to present the great man with a bouquet of roses and the praise of the citizens of Aachen. Beethoven, who would have been mortally offended if she had not, will profess astonishment. Then, overwhelmed by this completely unexpected honor, he will ask her leave to dedicate a new piece that, somehow, he has had the foresight to rehearse, as a musical present to our beloved, music-loving sovereigns. Empress and audience will settle down to enjoy it. When it is over, the Empress will go back on stage to lead the standing ovation.

For those whose taste is less elevated, the circus is in town. In fact, three circuses will be performing this year. Taverns stay open later, and there is cabaret and a kind of vaudeville in some of the theatres. When the comedians make a good political joke, it races all over town within hours. Their favorite targets are the Chancellor and the Mayor. Neither of them can take a joke. Their inevitable overreaction always adds to the merriment. The comedians even make mild jokes about their Sovereign, something inconceivable out of Season. For those whose amusements are not elevated at all, there are, as always, all kinds of houses of ill repute. Too discreet to name names, the madams of Aachen will proudly tell you they entertain "a much better class of customers during the Season, dear," and every year a juicy scandal or two proves them right.

There is music everywhere. Every tavern, beer hall, wine garden, and beer garden has a band and often singing waiters as well. The city pays strolling musicians to wander the streets day and night, playing the fiddle, mouth organ or flute. Most are amateurs or semiprofessionals, who can't make a living any other time, or out of town musicians enjoying a free trip to the capital. Acrobats are popular this year.

Aachen has little of what we would consider political journalism. It is a city of no newspapers but few secrets. There is no official censorship because so little political news is printed. Instead people gossip. The Aachen gossip mill is an institution. Being unintellectual (Paris is the Empire's intellectual capital) Aachen's gossip traffics in personalities and scandal. Scandal can have drastic consequences if it involves a Witan. The First Speaker is a most upright—some of his Witans would prefer to say up-tight, at least privately—man, fiercely protective of "my" Witanagemot's reputation. He promptly sends the disgraced Witan home.

When the rich and mighty assemble, they spend money. The capital's dressmakers, couturiers, tailors, milliners, shoemakers and boot makers have devoted their entire off-season to inventing new styles. Their customers will set the style throughout the Empire when they take their purchases home. Shops stay open late during the Season. There are no reduced prices until the last two weeks of the Season. Then everything goes on sale. The same concentration of money attracts the cream of the Empire's confidence men, fraudsters, fortune hunters, and courtesans. Mothers worry about their daughters—and their husbands.

The rich do more than shop. Deals are done. Money changes hands. Backs are scratched and often knifed. Financial and mercantile dynasties arrange sales, exchanges, joint ventures and combinations for themselves, and marriages of convenience for their children. Great and imaginative schemes are hatched in palaces and taverns.

This cocktail shaker of youth in a river of alcohol into which all manners of people and schemes have also been poured produces a frothy mixture of brawls, drunken excesses, and every possible variety of private scrape and public disorder. Somehow the Watch keeps order, but no watchman goes on leave during the Season. For all that, the city is a happy place. It's a wonderful time to be young. Dignified, elderly gentlemen and well-upholstered matrons sentimentally remember their youthful escapades. Young miscreants are surprised at their elders' understanding and tolerance, at least until Exodus Day.

In this hyper concentration of excitement and youth, love affairs proliferate, some as transient as shipboard romances and others that will endure for life, regardless of whether they end in matrimony. Many do end that way. Others don't, and then there are tears and accusations of seduction on Exodus Day, but the midwives of Aachen smile. They know they will be busy in April and May.

Witanagemot Season's high society centers around three great balls. The night before the Witanagemot opens, the Imperial couple give the First Ball for Witans and other distinguished visitors and their spouses. On the tenth night, the First Speaker sponsors the Speaker's Ball at the Imperial palace, ostensibly to introduce new Witans to the Emperor and Empress. On the day that the Witanagemot adjourns, the Hall is immediately cleared to permit the First Speaker to preside over the Final Ball, given "to express the gratitude of our loyal and faithful Witans to our rulers." Failure to receive an expected invitation to one of the great balls is a social disaster.

There are private parties, balls, and receptions every night. Two are of particular importance. Prince Frederick keeps open house at his palace four nights in each week. The entire political world is welcome. On the third Tuesday of the Season the Emperor comes to dance with Agatha, Frederick's wife, while the Empress dances with Frederick. They used to stay all night, but of late their appearances have become brief.

The Byzantine ambassador, Simonides Kephas, gives the other famous private party. His invitations are as sought after as those to the grand balls. A famous poet and a witty and charismatic man, Simonides cuts a great figure in Aachen's social life. He is beloved by society hostesses. The Emperor and Simonides used to be good friends, but the mill says the Imperial couple may not attend this year.

Nevertheless, the Season's main event is the month-long meeting of the one hundred ninety five Witans in Witanagemot Hall. The Emperor himself comes to open their session and address them. Before and after it opens, he talks with the Witans individually and in groups. The Witans talk with each other and, both individually and in committees, they meet with the men who rule the Empire. Sometimes the Witanagemot disagrees with the Imperial government or even with the Emperor himself. Usually disagreements remain informal but the Witanagemot sometimes formally requests a change in policy. In extraordinary cases, it passes a motion of censure. Censure of the Emperor is very rare but extremely serious, because it comes close to calling him a tyrant and therefore an oath-breaker who should be deposed. After thirty days, the Witans adjourn.

The Witanagemot enacts no statutes, passes no laws, and elects no consuls. Its approval is required only for a few very specific actions. At first look, it appears to have few ways to enforce its will upon the Emperor or anyone else. But it's not that simple.

As the Emperor would be quick to explain, the Witanagemot is *not* the Roman Senate. Nevertheless, the Witans are powerful and ambitious men who remember the powers of the Roman Senate and, regardless of what they may publicly say, hope some day to hold those powers. Meanwhile, they constantly seek to imitate the Senate. Every Emperor abominates the very idea. The smallest movement in that direction draws his attention. He knows what it means. For example, Roman Senators wore a purple stripe at the bottom of their togas. During the last reign, the then Speaker tried to add a purple stripe to the Witans' ceremonial robes and the Old Emperor thunderously put a stop to it.

The Emperor would explain to you, as he often does to the Witans, that the Witanagemot is only an assembly of his counselors, and nothing more. Rather than being descended from the Senate, its roots are Frankish, deriving from the king's right to call on any man for his advice. As a matter of law the Emperor is absolutely right. Nevertheless, the reality is that any Emperor who disregards the Witans or treats their opinion without respect does so at his own risk. The Witanagemot contains all the most powerful aristocrats of an aristocratic Empire *en bloc*. It speaks for the aristocratic class, the only people with real power, other than the Emperor and his officials. As such, the Witans expect him to discuss with them any important change he expects to make in the direction and governance of his Empire. Every Emperor knows that a hostile Witanagemot can wound or destroy his authority, because its opposition legitimizes opposition elsewhere. Censure is an effort to illegitimatize the Emperor himself. No matter what he says, every Emperor knows a quiet Witanagemot is a dozing tiger and fears it. In particular all Emperors fear the creation of an organized opposition, just because it is can lead to a censure. On the other hand, if the Witans can be persuaded to give advance approval to a change of direction, opposition to the new policy elsewhere is hard to justify. Karl VII and Clara, his wife and successor, had the Witanagemot approve the first panRoman policies. The Grandees still regret it.

In his coronation oath, every Emperor also swears, "I will summon a Witanagemot yearly and respect the rights and privileges of Witanagemot Hall." And rights and privileges there are in abundance in that ancient and stately edifice. The chamber's ceiling is so high that speakers must raise their voices to be heard. [In Rome the Senate house was small and unpretentious by comparison. But Roman senators did not need to shout to be heard.] Within the Hall, the First Speaker is lord and master. Even the Emperor and Chancellor bow to him there, although the Emperor always says "out of courtesy" as he does so. No Witan may be called to account for anything he says or does there, except for an actual crime or treason.

The penalty for carrying a weapon into a Witanagemot in session is instant death. An ax lies on a cushion in front of the First Speaker to symbolize his power. At times, it has been more than a symbol. A First Speaker once used it to decapitate a Witan on the spot when he drew a knife on another member.

In his oath, each Witan swears, "I will be the Emperor's loyal and faithful Witan and give my advice for the good of my soul and his soul and for the good of the Empire." No Emperor who ever reigned has not had occasion to repeat that oath in a sarcastic or outraged tone. In his own estimation, the Emperor puts up with a great deal from his Witans. He does so by necessity, not choice. The Emperor of New Rome knows he must take care not to be perceived as a tyrant. His subjects call themselves "citizens of Rome" and consider themselves free men. They call him "Sir," and when they kneel to him, they carefully, and with difficulty, avoid bowing the neck as they do. It is in great contrast with the Byzantines, who prostrate themselves, call their Emperor "the holy one," and kiss the hem of his robe. Worse still, the Byzantines call their Emperor "Master," as if they were his slaves. The Romans think them beneath contempt. "To tell the Emperor the truth is no treason" is a Roman proverb.

In his coronation oath, the Emperor swears "to rule with justice, to be no tyrant, and to rule the Roman people with love." No institution has the power hold him to account when he breaks that oath, but the Witanagemot comes closest. Unpopular and oppressive Emperors have been deposed or assassinated and after the deed, the Witanagemot has created legitimacy for the usurper. Every Emperor dreads a runaway Witanagemot and knows how easily that process can start when the mighty of his empire gather together,

Charles Martel IV is liked personally, but his policies create friction. His panRoman policy—more accurately panRoman policies, since they are a bundle with a common purpose—is a touchy subject. Long ago, the Emperors took back many of the rights they had sold or been forced to grant the higher nobility, such as exemptions from general laws and the rights to coin money, to erect private fortifications, and to impose private tariffs on roads and rivers. The process was long and slow, and its memory still complicates the relationship between the Emperor and the Grandees. They sit in the Witanagemot or send their sons there and have never really accepted the policies or their subordination. They have a very Whiggish predisposition to feel they represent the cause of liberty, and that any Emperor would be a tyrant if he could. So it behooves the Emperor to step warily when he deals with them.

But however tricky his relationship with the Witans may be, the Emperor will open the Witanagemot this year on July fifteenth in magnificence. For the people of Aachen, his procession and the ceremonies in Witanagemot Hall are the soul of the Season.

At exactly ten A.M. the main gate to the palace will open and a golden carriage carrying the Imperial couple will enter Palace Square to the sound of cannons that declare Imperial power and glory. The sound also lets the First Speaker know that the Emperor is on his way and it is time to finish his own opening ceremonies. Long before the cannons roar, the crowd along the mile-long route from the palace to Witanagemot Square is a human hedge ten deep on both sides of the route. Aacheners are never quiet folk. Today they will be very noisy. The crowd will tell you what it is thinking. They will applaud the Emperor (a good sign: silent crowds presage rebellion), but the Empress is their darling. The Emperor sits stolidly and waves in a formal way. The Empress waves to the crowd without reserve. She even throws kisses. The crowd loves it when she does. They throw kisses back.

On a white stallion with purple tack, blanket and saddle, the Grand Marshal leads the procession followed by two squadrons of Imperial Guards, one on white horses and the other on brown. The riders wear full dress purple and white uniforms. Similarly garbed, the mounted trumpeters of the Imperial Guard ride behind them. Their trumpets will sound three times: once as they leave the palace, again when the carriage passes into Witanagemot Square, and finally, with a triumphant fanfare as he enters the Hall. The horsemen ride slowly. Most of the procession that follows them will be walking and many of them are not young.

After a space come the high officials of state on foot. One might expect the Chancellor to lead them, but he is already in the Hall as a member *ex-officio* of the Witanagemot. First come the Emperor's Consistory walking four abreast. There are about sixty-five active Consistorians at any time, but eighty or more will march because retired and former members have the right to parade. It is not unusual to see a retired Consistorian wearing his state robe being pushed in a wheelchair. The crowd always cheers him. Consistorians wear dark blue robes of state and thin gold belts of office. After the Consistory come the senior members of the Imperial Household led by Albrecht Desle and Louis Duval. The Household's light blue robes are belted with purple sashes. Military aides wear full dress uniforms. As a just promoted aide, Mikail will be in the very last row. He almost did not march; the Household wardrobe only managed to patch up a robe for him at the last minute. Near drunk with pride and desperately wishing that Karita and his mother and sisters could see him, he focuses on not appearing to strut and on mentally composing the letter he will write home tonight.

Now come the high officers of state. The broader his gold belt, the more purple his robe, and the nearer the Emperor he marches, the more exalted the officer. A flesh-and-blood table of organization of the New Roman Empire is on display, dressed in silken robes of office, purple sashes—never mind how hot the day may be—and golden belts. Once the civilians have passed, the military follow in the place of honor nearest the Emperor. The most important generals and the members of the Military Council march, walking six abreast. Behind his generals comes their commander, the Magister Militum in shining silver. He alone wears no silken robe, golden belt or medallion. His emblems of office are silver armor and his shining sword held point up in the salute position. His is the only weapon ever allowed in Witanagemot Hall.

The crowd hushes. It is almost time for the Emperor and Empress. Before their carriage walk two files of twelve lictors in blood-red tunics, a rare bow to the Roman republic. To be a lictor is the highest honor an enlisted soldier can hope for. Each lictor carries a fasces held out stiffly in front. The fasces is a bundle of sticks with which to beat anyone who insults the officer of state the lictor is guarding, and is tied together around an ax used to behead a miscreant. From ancient times the fasces has been the Roman symbol of lawful force and legitimate authority. [Its modern meaning is very much another thing.] Next comes the First Lictor, the senior noncommissioned officer of the Roman Army. He is always deep in middle age, serves for five years, and invariably ends as a confidant of the Magister Militum in office.

In Witanagemot Square the procession stops in front of the Hall. His lictors lead the Emperor to the steps of the Hall. There they must stop. Their ceremonial axes are weapons and it is death to carry a weapon into the Hall while the Witanagemot sits. A sign announcing the prohibition was placed next to every one of the Hall's seven doors the day before the session opened.

Finally, the open golden carriage drawn by twelve great white horses arrives bearing the Emperor and Empress, smiling at the crowd. The Emperor wears Charlemagne's thousand-year-old crown. It is very simple and very old. [You can see it today in the Hofburg treasure chamber in Vienna.] The Imperial couple wave and bow. The crowd cheers. The Empress herself is small, lively, and dark, with lovely eyes and beautifully coiffed. She always dresses in an elegant gown, but she's an impatient woman, and there is always something just a bit out of place. When another squadron of mounted Imperial guards in purple on black horses follows, the procession is over till next year.

Later, when they return to the palace through empty streets, the procession will consist of no more than the Imperial couple in their carriage, the cavalry and the lictors. They move quickly through almost empty streets. Even the lictors are now mounted The crowd dispersed hours ago to have fun for the rest of the day and the coming night. It's Witanagemot Season.

CHAPTER XVI

Four Audiences

As commanded, Frederick presented himself in the Emperor's private office on Thursday of the first week in July. The family resemblance between the two men was striking. The visitor was younger by some fifteen years which was evidenced by the way Frederick carried himself, his high color, his hunter's physique, and in the rude health he projected. Where his uncle's hair was black (probably dyed), the nephew's hair and moustache—he wore no beard—were glowing reddish brown. Yet even seated the Emperor seemed taller with features that were firmer. His assurance was regal, while the prince's demeanor showed discomfort. Frederick fidgeted.

"Good morning, cousin Martin." Frederick said. "May I ask why you have summoned me?"

The seated Emperor did not rise or motion his nephew to a chair before answering, "I have quite a lot on my mind, Fred. Some very disagreeable things have come to my attention. I wondered whether you might be able to enlighten me about them." He waited three beats and went on, "We have discovered an extensive bribery scheme by the Byzantines. It seems to have been going on for several years and extends to a considerable number of Witans and other persons of influence. A number of your friends in the Witanagemot have been receiving what the Byzantines like to call 'pensions.' This *bribery* (the sharpened tone of voice emphasized the word) seems to be restricted to those who share your political opinions. If my mind ran that way, I could even describe it as a plan to buy supporters for your point of view or even a conspiracy. Would you be in a position to offer me any help?"

He seemed to notice for the first time that his visitor was still standing. "Please sit down. We will be here a while."

Frederick sat. "Cousin Martin, I have not been a party to any conspiracy against you. I have never concealed my differences from you. I'll be glad to disabuse you of any belief that I am plotting against you, if you will only tell me what I have done."

"No, I am not going to tell you what I know," the Emperor said in a quiet voice. "It is more than enough for me to bring you here to ask you directly. I prefer to prevent public scandal."

The prince flushed. "I am not going to have a voluntary heart attack for your convenience."

"I thought you'd bring that up," the older man sighed. "Sometimes, being Emperor is cruel work. You might remember as much before you aspire to the throne. Regardless of whatever your mother has told you, here is what happened: Your father planned my death. He didn't succeed, and when we caught him, he had to die for it. I killed him because I had to kill him. Plato said, 'When you shoot at the king you must kill him.' And let me add that that if you do so and fail, the king must kill you. Your father tried to kill me, and I gave him the choice of dying by taking poison or dying as a criminal. If he chose poison, we promised to say it was a heart attack. If he voluntarily chose the heart attack—no need for sarcasm—there would be no retaliation against his wife or his children. The choice, such as it was, was his. He elected to protect your mother, your sister, and you, Frederick. He trusted me enough to believe I would keep my promise and I have. I saw to it that your sister was married to a good man and that you had a prince's education. I arranged for you to have a good career with all the privileges of a prince. You are a member of my Consistory and the Witanagemot. A member of the Imperial family cannot marry without my consent, but I made no objection when you married one of the richest women in the Empire, although it gives you the means to cause me great mischief. I have done nothing to stop you from opposing my policies. Nor will I as long as your disagreement results from an honest difference of opinion. What I won't tolerate in my own family is conflict intended to organize opposition, or a family member leading a party against me. I think you're are doing just that, and I won't have it."

"You've never trusted me," the prince remonstrated.

"Fair enough," the Emperor replied, "but I knew what your mother was telling you. Most of all you resent that I didn't make you Crown Prince instead of my son. I think that's what this is all about."

"I am more qualified than he is. You passed me over for someone who was not even of age and unqualified. And before that, I wanted a proper Roman military career and you wouldn't let me have it." The prince was a powerful man in vibrant middle age, but for a minute his sulky face resembled that of a disappointed child.

"I was afraid you would connive against me and build a party if you were Crown Prince. And, I must say, your present behavior shows I was not far from wrong. As for giving you a military career, all Roman history warned me against it." The Emperor paused and his voice softened, "Put yourself in my place. I have worked hard to treat you decently. We are flesh and blood. You know I love you and Agatha."

"I think the panRoman policies are wrong."

"I don't care and won't hold it against you. What I mind is your organizing those Witans who feel the same way into a faction against me and, above all, trying to use honest disagreement to depose me. Freedom of conscience is one thing. I freely grant it to others and won't deny it to you. Organizing opposition to me is another step. That goes beyond the limits. Trying to depose me is treason, but conniving with the Greeks against not only me, but the Empire, is past all limits. Now Fred, answer me yes or no. Did you know about what the Greeks were up to with these bribes? If you did know, or if you heard about it, or even suspected it, you had a duty to warn me. Tell me the truth now. If you do then so far as I am concerned, no offense existed. But if you say you didn't know and I find out that you did, or worse, were complicit, then you are outside my protection and forgiveness regardless of family harmony."

"You think I knew about it".

The older man nodded. "I am afraid so."

Frederick's voice rose in anger. "You have an investigation running and this is a trap."

"We're alone in my private office. If this were a trap, I would have witnesses present. Do you want to look under the tables and in the closets? I won't be offended. It's the prudent thing to do. But you have my word that we are alone. We have had one unbearable tragedy in this family. I cannot imagine enduring another. Even if you don't care about your own life, think of your wife and children."

"You should not have killed my father!" his visitor shouted.

"Your father left me no choice. He tried to kill me," the Emperor retorted, "and if you want to avoid feeling anything like the bitter regret I feel about your father's death, then you should not be a party to an attempt to depose me. When I tell you that you won't like the wrenching regret that follows, I speak from knowledge. I loved your father, I really care for you and Agatha and Conrad. Can't you understand that even if you succeed—which you won't—you are starting a civil war? My son and brother will still have armies. Do you want to become Emperor of Rome over the bodies of the Romans?"

Frederick stood up and said stiffly, "Sir, I did not know, and for that matter I still do not know, that the Greeks were involved in my opposition to you. I certainly have not taken money from them. How can I help you by answering questions about something I know nothing about? May I go, Emperor?"

The Emperor sat silently. Finally, he spoke, "If that still is your answer to my question. Please remember that it is your duty to report to me anything of this kind that comes hereafter to your attention, or if you remember something that you did not tell me. This I say to you as your Emperor. As your closest kinsman and one of the principal victims of the hateful situation in which we find ourselves, I tell you: Go home and think over your answer."

The Emperor's voice became less formal as he went on. "I'm offering you forgiveness to avoid civil war in my family and in the Empire. So I will make a final offer. Sooner or later, I will have to talk to the Grandees to compromise on the panRoman policies. I will use you as the go-between and give you public credit for being the one who arranged the grand compromise. I'm going to have to make concessions, and I will credit you with having persuaded me. That will assure you an honorable place in Roman History. Go home and talk to Agatha tonight and give me your decision tomorrow." It was a generous offer, one Frederick had not expected.

"That is more than generous, Sir," he said. "I thank you for it and I will think it over as you command, although I do not think that I will change my answer. With your permission, I will leave now." He bowed and left the room.

The Emperor sighed and then went to the door to tell the duty aide to find the Chancellor.

In a few minutes the Chancellor walked into the room, asking, "How did it go?"

"Badly, though I think I came close, really close at the end, when I played the last card the way you suggested. I have to thank you for the idea, but in the end, he rejected the credit for mediation."

"Everyone knows that hate makes us do wicked things," the Chancellor said, "but the way it makes us do stupid ones is just as bad. You know how this is going to end, Martin. You will not like what you will have to do, but there's no other way. Think about Jenny and your son. Above all, don't hesitate. It's too dangerous."

"You've gone over the evidence with Louie and his boys. Don't I have enough to exile Frederick now?" the Emperor pleaded. "Killing him would be killing Clovis again. I cannot bear causing another death of my own family. Do you know that Aetius still sees Clovis's face in his dreams? He says he can't look into his eyes."

"You have nowhere near enough evidence for exile," the Chancellor replied, "and even if you had the best of reasons, were you to exile their leader just before Witanagemot, the resentment among the Grandees would make them impossible to handle. You will have to find your own way out. I don't think there is any."

The Chancellor changed the subject, "How are Duval's boys doing?"

"We're on with Simonides for this afternoon. Louie will be there. Talk to him before the meeting," the Emperor said.

Pannonius was busy with the work he had to get done by the end of his day: to try once more to persuade Demetrius to help the investigation; to re-interview the Parides clerks to see if they remembered anything new; to initiate a further review of the Saxony Witans; to keep an appointment with the prefect of the Aachen Watch to see how the search for Emmerich Bader was going; to settle a dispute with the Political Department about access to files; and to talk to Hector about a new line of approach to finding the names of suspect Witans. Then too, Louie was asking for written reports to show the Emperor and there was paperwork in connection with Dacia.

Most of all and much more than anything else, he wanted to see Dorcas, to listen to her voice and to tell her how much he loved her. "You wanted to be at the center of things, didn't you?" Pannonius told himself, "You're a fool, Hugh, and always have been. Horace is the only sensible one in the family." (Horace, the priest, was his brilliant older brother.) Well, Horace might be the clever one, but if Horace had chosen celibacy, he certainly wasn't right about everything. Pannonius started scheming about ways see Dorcas.

The Emperor's afternoon audience with the Byzantine ambassador would be much more formal. Giovanni Mazzeo would stand next to the throne. The Chancellor, the Mayor, both of his senior aides and the usual note takers, junior aides, and the host of diplomatic professionals present at every important ambassadorial audience would all attend. The Byzantine Ambassador would bring his own smaller train. The Emperor calculated that people would talk and the rumor mill would spread the news all over town by nightfall.

Albrecht had arranged the room so that the Byzantine Ambassador would face the Emperor alone, standing on a small square of carpet. The carpet was stage dressing, a first hint of Imperial displeasure. The Emperor kept Simonides waiting while he and his advisors spent an hour rehearsing exactly what they would say. Then Albrecht dispatched a flunky to summon the ambassador.

Simonides Kephas, Duke of Epiros, was a personage of importance. Someone once said of him that he lived his life knowing that he would always be the richest, cleverest, best-dressed and handsomest man in the room. He was immensely rich in his own right and a boyhood friend of Leo Nikephoros, the Eastern Roman Emperor. A great wit and true poet, he had written a famous sequence of love poems in his youth and had, himself, translated them into elegant Latin verse after he was posted to Aachen. A hostess whose house he frequented enjoyed an unassailable social position. Senior Ambassador Mazzeo had once told the Emperor that Simonides was the best diplomat he had ever met saying, "reads everything, knows everybody, states the issues in own favor with every appearance of fairness, lies smoothly and is impossible to embarrass or intimidate."

"He's a snake and a piece of work." the Emperor had responded brusquely.

"He is, isn't he?" Mazzeo had replied fondly. "I admire him so much."

The ambassador swept into the room, instantly noticed where the carpet had been placed, commented on it by an ironic flip of an eyebrow and placed himself in its exact middle before making his elaborate and exceedingly graceful bow. Chairs had been provided for his entourage but none for the ambassador.

The Emperor began, "Tell me Simonides, do you know the Parides family or the Parides company?"

"Certainly," the ambassador replied. "As I am sure you know, there are two Parides families, one in Constantinople and Smyrna the other here in Aachen. They are distantly related and intermarried. Both companies deal in amber and precious metals and transmit money and finance merchants."

"So much for the businesses. Do you know the families?"

"I do, Sir. In which of them are you particularly interested?"

"The one in my Empire. The one headed by Stephen Hoffman."

"I know the other family better. I have had business dealings with the people in Aachen and know Stephen though not well. I've heard the family is not in your favor at present."

"They are not. When last did you see Stephen Hoffman?"

"I don't know. Not recently."

"Have you had any dealings with Stephen Hoffman in the last year?"

"Possibly, but not in the last six months."

"Has anyone else in your Embassy or who represented your government had any dealings with him?"

"I would have to look into that."

"Do you know a man named Emmerich Bader? Is he employed by your legation?"

"That name is not familiar to me, Sir."

"What services have the Parides people or company performed for you or the Embassy or your government in the last five years?"

"Ordinary money transmittal. I believe your government has used them for the same purposes."

The Emperor's tone sharpened as he spoke, "Ambassador, though I am sure that you know everything I am going to tell you, let me give you the reason for this summons. We have discovered that both Parides companies and their families have been engaged in a massive bribery campaign within my Empire for the last five years. They have bribed people at very high levels. Astronomical amounts have been disbursed to fund a party against me, personally, and to create agents of influence within my Empire.

"That alone would be enough to justify almost any action but there is worse because it involves you personally. You are concealing a Roman citizen sought for crimes against the Roman state in connection with funding your treason against me. Stephen Hoffman is being hidden in your Embassy even though he is a Roman citizen and a fugitive from Roman justice. You knew we were searching for him yet gave him sanctuary. Then there's a man who helped distribute the money, one Emmerich Bader. We think he is an employee of your Embassy. He too is a Roman citizen, one with a criminal record. We can only hope we don't find him inside your embassy as well.

"This is far past anything I can possibly tolerate. I will declare you *persona non grata* and send you home. The question is what more should I do? I could close the embassy or allow no one to enter and only Byzantine subjects to leave. I could send in a search party or I could detain you for acts that go beyond any imaginable cover of diplomatic privilege. If it were my father with whom you had to deal our Empires would probably go to war. I certainly will do something drastic, but before I take any action, I will accord you the courtesy of a reply."

The Byzantine Ambassador showed neither surprise nor discomfit. "Isn't he wonderful! Wonderful!" Ambassador Mazzeo whispered to the Emperor. "Or perhaps he's been warned."

"Let me go through these accusations one at a time, Sir. First, I deny that we have either Stephen Hoffman or Emmerich Bader in our Embassy or under our control. Neither is, or was, our agent. I wish I could permit a search party to enter our premises to put these slanders to rest, but, as I am sure you must know, I cannot. My Emperor would never permit it. It would be a violation of all diplomatic right, custom and law. He would consider it an act of war.

"I know nothing about the flow of funds through either of the Parides companies. I had no involvement; my Embassy had no involvement; and my government certainly had no involvement. As for the not-very-veiled threat of military action, I have nothing to say. It has been a long time since the Eastern and Western Roman Empires actually resorted to arms against each other. These false accusations should not provide the basis for so extreme an act."

The Emperor remained motionless, wrapped in thought. Minutes later, he spoke. "I am sorry, Ambassador, that it comes to this," he said in a voice that contained no regret, "but the truth is you've been caught in unforgivable acts. Worse, this torrent of bribery started when you came here. You leave me no choice. I hereby declare you *persona non grata*. I will not strip away your personal diplomatic immunity, but you will have to return to Constantinople immediately. I must stop this intolerable interference in my Empire's internal affairs. I'm going to put guards at the entrances to your embassy and verify everything and everyone going in or out. And when your diplomats leave the embassy, they will have an escort. I have more than enough justification to close your embassy, but a time of stress is a bad time to cancel communication. You may go back to your embassy now to determine who will represent your Emperor hereafter. Senior Ambassador Mazzeo will be there in three hours to work out with you the details of your departure and the extent to which we will allow the ongoing functioning of the embassy. I expect you to deliver Stephen Hoffman to Roman justice. Otherwise, I will take him. If you wish a final personal interview with me, I am willing to grant it." He rose and left the room.

Ambassador Mazzeo walked over to a troubled-looking Simonides, whose face had fallen when the Emperor left the room, to ask, "Do you want an exit interview with the Emperor, Simon?"

"Of course," Simonides said. "He as much as told me to ask for it. Something like this has been in the air for a few days. I also have a personal problem. Will he listen if I mention it?"

"I'll raise the issue. Professional courtesy. I know who she is," Mazzeo said. "On the diplomatic side, you will have to pick someone to act in your absence, because we don't want to lose our ability to communicate with Leo. Why not take your successor to the exit interview? That way you can retain some continuity and sidestep publicly presenting him to an angry Emperor. If I come over in three hours, will you be ready to talk to me?"

"Oh, yes," Simonides said, "I won't pretend that I expected this today, but the Parides situation has been boiling and, well, you know the Aachen gossip mill. We have talked among ourselves about what to do if things went really wrong. Will you be at the exit interview, Giovanni? You have enormous experience and your assistance would be a great help. I need to know exactly what I am to advise my Emperor. That's more important than the things he said to me today in public. How angry with me is he really? I mean personally. We used to be friends."

"Very angry," Mazzeo answered, "but he won't take it out on your personal matter."

"Well, it's been a nice career," Simonides said dryly. "He's furious with me, and what my lord and master Leo Nikephoros will say when I get home will be worse. Someone always pays for a fiasco. This time it's going to be me. It'll be back to writing poetry for the rest of my life. Anne would be a great consolation."

Action and adrenaline always improved the Emperor's mood. He was downright jolly when he called a meeting of his counselors after Simonides left. "The news will be all over Aachen and the Witans will know that we have found them out. The First Speaker will demand an immediate audience for tomorrow morning. When he does, Albrecht, tell him noon tomorrow. That's after Simonides. He will think we know which Witans been bribed. Do we know yet?"

"Only what we've told you. The Count of Dalmatia and three Witans in Saxony is all we know for sure. There's more to come."

Ambassador Mazzeo asked, "When I see Simonides, what time should I give him for his exit interview? He also has a personal problem."

"Nine o'clock tomorrow morning. I don't want to lose tempo. His personal problem is Anne Savigny, the jurisconsult's wife. Jenny says that Anne has left her husband and was going to run away with him. I can't permit Anne to leave with him; that would be siding against my own jurisconsult. But I won't stop her from leaving Aachen alone, if she sneaks away and doesn't make a public fuss that forces me to do something. You can hint as much."

"Why say anything at all?" the Ambassador asked.

"Because then Simonides will owe us a favor when he reports to Leo, and my jurisconsult will have to stop brooding and start doing my work again. Besides, Jenny likes Anne. All the women seem to feel that if a woman can have Simonides, she shouldn't be forced to settle for anyone less."

The exit interview with Simonides was a brief, serious affair. He brought his successor, Nicholas Evangelos, a career diplomat. The Empress joined the Emperor and Ambassador Mazzeo.

As soon as he had finished introducing his replacement, Simonides went straight to the point. "What do you want me to tell Leo?"

The Emperor spoke in a slow, careful voice, speaking for the record, "You may tell him that although we have no designs on his territory nor any desire to interfere in his internal affairs, I am most concerned that the reverse is not true. Please tell him that the New Roman Empire will not withdraw from Dacia, Dalmatia, Sicily, or any other territory under any circumstances. I think Byzantium has connived with the Mongols. The results so far have been unfortunate for the Mongols and will be unfortunate for Leo, if he goes on. We are content to let the Eastern Empire stand in its present boundaries for the sake of our common history and as a buffer between the Caliphate and ourselves but if Leo takes military action, I will change my mind. The Eastern Empire, its ambassador and its embassy, have been caught interfering in my empire's domestic affairs for over five years in a conspiracy that they funded with an enormous amount of Byzantine money. Denial is pointless. All this is obvious.

What do I want? I want to make sure this conspiracy comes to an immediate end and is never repeated. I want Byzantium to keep its hands off my internal matters. Any attempt to steal Dacia with the connivance of the Mongols, or otherwise, will lead to my annexing a province or two from his Empire. I have ample military force to do so. If his crime ends and is not repeated, there will no reason to employ it.

"My present inclination is to shut down your embassy, permitting your diplomats to take only personal items with them and providing them with temporary quarters until we complete our search for criminals. I did not say this at your public audience, but, believe me, I will do it. Or you can deliver Stephen Hoffman, alive and willing to talk, with no reservations."

Simonides took a deep breath and collected his thoughts before speaking, "I don't deny that you are entitled to expel me, and I recognize that you have great cause for anger. Let's assume that you would find Stephen Hoffman in the embassy. He might not be alive, of course, but let's not consider that ugly alternative. Stephen will not cooperate. The Parides family is extremely well connected, and everything they have worked for over the last hundred years has just been destroyed due to their patriotism. My Emperor has an enormous obligation to them, and there are well-placed people in Constantinople who will remind him of it. Please believe me when I say the course of action you propose will have all the wrong consequences. It will only fuel the hawks at home who foolishly want war for Dacia.

"But of course you must do something. As an alternative, suppose I delivered a piece of paper with the names of twelve Witans and made sure that we also identified and broke off communication with any agents of influence. Which would you rather have? Stephen Hoffman, who will not talk easily or quickly if he is still alive, or the very information you hope to get from him now, before the Witanagemot begins? Give the First Speaker the names. Then he will see they do not attend, and no Witan will be in a rush to sell his vote. I can't guarantee you will have your way on the panRoman policies, because your Witans really hate them, but we won't aggravate your difficulties. And, by the way, Frederick never took a copper from me, although he must have known that some of his people had their hands out. When you finally release them, we will take Stephen and Demetrius back to Constantinople. Nobody's died over this so far, except one man who foolishly killed himself. Let's keep it that way. On a personal level, I apologize to you. I did what I was sent to do. I have often regretted that assignment. As it happens, I found joy here, but that's not a political issue."

"What about agents of influence?" the Emperor asked.

"You know about Dalmatia. I know of five others in your government. One of them is another Count. Their names will be on the list. I can't tell you the names of anyone Constantinople is running directly, because the whole idea there was not to tell me or my Embassy. This I do know: there is a major agent of influence in your government, who is also a spy and I am certain he is on the civil side. We called him Odysseus, and he worked directly for people in Constantinople, who kept my embassy out of the loop. The same is true of Emmerich, who is not in the Embassy. I don't know where or who Odysseus is. They were careful not to let me know."

The Emperor looked at the faces of his wife and ambassador before replying, "I'm inclined to consider your offer. We will find you a place to repent for the next hour or two while we talk over your offer. Please cancel this year's Witanagemot reception."

In the end, the Emperor's advisors were in favor of acceptance. Simonides sat down and wrote out the names, shook Ambassador Mazzeo's hand, and departed.

The Emperor proved a good prophet. Within two hours, the First Speaker requested an emergency audience. The Emperor received him alone at noon. Andivius Hedulio, First Speaker of the Witanagemot, was a dignified man in middle age with prematurely white hair. There was never anything uncertain about his speech or his precise movements. He stood ramrod-straight, never raised his voice, was invariably courteous, and spoke in a rich baritone. The Emperor once told his wife at breakfast that in all the years he had known him he had never caught the Speaker out of character. She replied that his wife probably said, "Speaker, please pass the salt." The Emperor understood his wife's way of communication and passed the salt.

Impeccable manners were part of the First Speaker's persona. He began by thanking the Emperor for the courtesy of the early audience and portentously asking, "for your assistance in averting the consequences of terrible misbehavior by men whose conduct I cannot condone." Then he pleaded, "Don't make a bad situation worse. The gossip is already all over Aachen. I heard it from four good sources before I asked you for an audience. It will injure the reputation of the great institution I have the honor to represent. Of course, there's always another scandal for the mill, but any public arrest or disgrace of Witans or too brutal a disclosure from the throne at the opening of the Witanagemot will take us years to live down."

The Emperor played to the Speaker's vanity by gracefully telling him that he always paid careful attention to his requests, reflecting both his personal esteem for the Speaker and his respect for the great and ancient institution he represented. He confessed in a hushed, conspiratorial tone that he had been given the names of certain Witans by the Byzantine Ambassador himself. He would give the Speaker the list in the very strictest confidence so that he might make sure none of them attended the Witanagemot. In fact, it would be for the best if they were not seen in Aachen for a very long time. Perhaps the Speaker might tell them so. When he did, he might add that they would certainly have to pay the treasury double the amount they had received from the Byzantines. If those Witans vanished from Aachen, the Emperor suggested, there would be as little public scandal as possible. He dropped a second heavy hint that he did all this out of his personal respect for the Speaker. Relief showed on the Speaker's face as he hurriedly agreed. After a few general remarks, he left with profuse expressions of gratitude rippling behind him like a spill of oil over rough water.

Hardly had the door closed than the Emperor mused to his wife, "It isn't often I get someone to do my dirty work for me who thanks me for the privilege. It happened twice today."

Chapter XVII

Brother and Sister

DAVID AND DORCAS DA Costa had been close all their lives. As children, they were so inseparable their parents called them "the almost-twins." David was fourteen months older, but Dorcas was precocious. Though he was clever, she was a prodigy. They remained close until David went to boarding school at thirteen. For a long time, their paths diverged. After David finished school, he went on to the University of Pavia but he came home every year for the long summer vacation to see his sister.

Donna disliked all girls' boarding schools, having had an unhappy time at her own. She and Aetius missed their son and kept Dorcas at home as long as they could. Dorcas missed her brother and complained of being lonely. The Paladin finally told his wife, "She's so much smarter than everyone around her that she's lonely. What's worse, everyone defers to the Proconsul's daughter. It's making her difficult and conceited." Donna agreed, albeit unhappily. They sent their daughter to the palace school as a boarder. Once there, Dorcas' intelligence and personality made her a star. She spent her adolescence by growing up in the Imperial palace with summer vacations in Dacia. Universities did not take women. Instead, at age eighteen, she became a junior lady-in-waiting to her aunt, the Empress. Her quick wit and endless energy recommended her to the Empress. She, in turn, came easily and naturally to love her aunt. Her career at court was an enormous success. By the time her brother arrived three years later, Dorcas was a person of importance; everyone in the palace knew her or if they did not, they still used her first name when they spoke about her.

David took another path to Aachen. His boarding school was Vittarino's School in Mantua, an ancient foundation where generations of the aristocracy had sent their sons for four hundred years. The masters were not at all in awe of their highborn students and provided them with an education that was superb, if a trifle reactionary. Meanwhile, the young aristocrats polished one another. Attendance assured any young man who graduated a lifetime supply of good connections, as well as a natural aristocratic style. The headmaster put Prince Frederick's son, Conrad, and David in the same suite, and the cousins grew close. David graduated speaking and writing a good clear Latin, with a solid knowledge of modern and ancient Roman history and literature, an ability to handle numbers and abstractions, and no discomfort whatsoever in the presence of the great and mighty. He also acquired a high opinion of his own worth. After graduation, he and Conrad roomed together at the University of Pavia.

For his graduation present, Conrad prevailed upon his father to offer David a place on his staff in Aachen. His son's friendship with Conrad had always made the Paladin uncomfortable. Although he did not want to make Prince Frederick's relationship with the rest of his family even more uncomfortable, he disapproved and said so. Unfortunately, what he saw as his father's arbitrary objection helped persuade David to accept the position. The extent of Frederick's opposition had not yet become evident, and Conrad's mother had outflanked the Paladin by first obtaining the Empress' approval. The Emperor shrugged, made the best of the situation, and gave David his blessing. When the Paladin tried to persuade him to change his mind, he told his brother, "You're making too much of your subjective feelings." But the Emperor developed a vague feeling of disapproval towards his brother's son.

When David first arrived in Aachen, the Emperor invited him to the Wednesday family dinner. He could hardly refuse him an invitation when his sister was not only at his table, but usually was the life of the party. The Empress' sister and her family, and the Paladin had standing invitations whenever they were in Aachen. On the other hand, Frederick and Agatha had never been invited, nor had Conrad or his sister. In time, the Emperor came to regret the invitation, but when he did, it seemed that it was too late to do anything about it.

Once on Frederick's staff, David adopted all the opinions of his party and argued with his uncle every Wednesday. The Emperor did not appreciate the loss of tranquility at his own dinner table and started to wonder how discreet David would be about repeating what he heard. His appeal to Aetius for help was met by his brother's reply, made with a certain satisfaction, that David no longer took direction from his father. Eventually, Wednesday dinner became stressful, and the invitation was withdrawn. David was mortally offended and now, alienated, sided with Frederick in every way. The Prince realized the treasure he had been handed. How could he be accused of plotting against the Imperial family when one of its members was on his own staff? He kept David away from anything too closely connected with the dangerous opposition.

None of this made the slightest difference in Dorcas and David's devotion to each other. They publicly dined together once a week and avoided forbidden subjects. One evening, Dorcas told her brother, "I will be bringing Hugh Pannonius this week. Please don't make any difficulties. I am going to marry him." Then she told Pannonius, who simply said, "Louie won't allow it. He'll suspect us of plotting against him." Dorcas listened. When he was finished, she said quietly, "Please find a way, dear."

Pannonius took preventive medicine and went to see Duval, who, predictably, had been unhappy. "Not that I mind your marrying into the family of my superior," he said (making Pannonius realize how much he did mind), "but please consider how that particular meeting will appear. Must you do it?" Improvising quickly, Pannonius replied, "Yes, I must, but it will be private—nobody there but family. I am sure David doesn't want to take political advantage of it." Duval had made a grimace of disbelief, and Pannonius thought of Aunt Luisa.

Dinner at Aunt Luisa's house it was. David arrived to find his sister chatting with the hostess, while her fiancé was amiably accepting being lorded over by an ancient butler, who was crouched in a fencing stance and illustrating his advice with the poker. The suddenness of his sister's engagement would have unsettled David at any time, and the rumors swirling around Aachen made him alert to innuendoes, whether intended or not. But, he knew that if his sister had decided to marry Hugh Pannonius, marry him she would. Having met Aunt Luisa before, he greeted her with a kiss, then, with some trepidation, walked over to congratulate his sister and Hugh on their engagement. Dorcas knew her brother too well to miss what he was feeling. She told him, "All I want is the men in my life to like each other."

"That's fine with me," David said. "Hugh and I know each other. Let's keep the politics out of it tonight."

Pannonius agreed at once. They talked for most of the evening. David had a great many questions about his father and Dacia. To his surprise, Pannonius discovered that David was not angry with Aetius. Like his father, he regretted the rift, but saw no way to heal it. When Pannonius told David how his father felt, the atmosphere warmed. Nevertheless, the political situation hung over everything all evening. Just before he walked Dorcas back to the palace, Pannonius turned to David and tiptoed onto forbidden ground, "Please listen to me for a minute, David. I really must say something about politics for your sister's sake. If you get hurt, she is going to be hurt. We are headed for a dangerous confrontation. Whatever you do, please, David, be careful. Don't let anyone use you."

David scowled, "You're threatening me."

"No, just asking you to be realistic," Pannonius insisted. Don't let anyone hide behind you, or pull you into anything you don't want to be part of."

Pannonius walked Dorcas home down empty streets in the bright light of a full moon. It was a perfect romantic moment, but he sighed and plunged in. "I thought I had to say it," he told her. "Did I go too far? Frederick is using him as a facade."

"What you did was right," Dorcas replied. "He paid no attention when I warned him. If he's caught in disloyalty to the Emperor, it would be a perfect revenge for Frederick against my father."

"What has revenge to do with it?"

Now it was Dorcas' turn to worry about going too far. "There's a secret you have to know, if you're going to marry into my family. It happened long ago, but it explains a lot about Frederick and Conrad," she said, and told him about the death of Clovis.

"Darling, that's not a safe secret to know," Pannonius said quietly. "Does David know?"

"Of course, he knows. So does Conrad. David told me that he and Conrad took an oath not to let it touch their friendship. He thinks it's like the brotherhood oath father swore with the Emperor, but Frederick's not a party to it, and Conrad is his father's son before he's David's friend. Should I be afraid for my brother?"

Pannonius was silent. When he spoke, it was with increased intensity and seriousness. "So far as I have seen, Frederick has only used him on public projects. But when everyone has to pick sides, with whom will he stand? If he's too close to Frederick, he can do something or say something in a moment of excitement that will ruin him. If we stay too close to him, it can rub off on us too. But, darling, whatever happens, I am always on your side."

"Is there any chance it won't reach David?"

"Yes, but David should be putting some distance between himself and Frederick and he's not doing it. Frederick's game is to get the Witans to jump from being against the Emperor's policies to being against the Emperor himself. A motion to ask the Emperor to discontinue the policies would have lots of support, but Frederick wants to get the Emperor censured as a tyrant. That makes it personal, and when it happens, he's is going to take a deep interest in everyone around his cousin."

Two miles away, Frederick was holding a meeting of the officers of his party in his home, the Hiegenstier Palace. The Hiegenstier was named after the Seventeenth century prime minister who built it. Hiegenstier had died widowed and childless leaving his newly built palace and his great wealth to his only relative, Clovis's grandmother. Ugly, uncomfortable, oversized, and expensive to maintain, the Hiegenstier was the pride and misery of Frederick's life. Although it was well built from materials of the very best quality, the palace astonished viewers with its ugliness. Passing architects made cheap epigrams at its expense ("When is the best time to view the Hiegenstier?" "Midnight on a foggy day."), but nobody ever managed a truly amusing joke. The building's ugliness was too honest. Perhaps some day it would be considered fascinating, but even after more than a hundred years, that time had still not come. Owners of the Hiegenstier had usually grown up in it and always thought of it as somehow connected with their status as great aristocrats. Who else would own anything so enormous? Who else would choose to live in it, but someone whose ancestors had lived in it? For that matter, who else could afford it? So, eventually, its owner always came to think of the Hiegenstier as a embodying all the old-fashioned virtues, unique, honest, direct and dignified. This point of view was not widely shared. The owner's wife invariably hated the Hiegenstier. Agatha, Frederick's wife, was no exception.

The Hiegenstier had been constructed a hundred and ten years ago in a style then popular for public buildings. The dark reddish brown granite, with inserts of an even darker red stone for emphasis, used in the body of the building contrasted with the stained white marble frames of its many windows and doors. A facade of giant, Corinthian, purple marble columns faced the street. Numerous white marble allegorical statues had been built into the facade or installed as newels at the top of the palace to hold in place a balustrade of miniature Ionic columns carved from yet another reddish-brown stone. The three kinds of red stone had weathered differently, and if they had ever harmonized with each other, they did so no longer. Time been no kinder to its deeply carved columns, statutes, and artistic details (such as the dripstones on the roof shaped into spitting gargoyles). They accumulated grime from generation to generation no matter how hard the palace's owner tried to clean them—and Frederick and Agatha had mounted several serious, very expensive campaigns. Accursed and unrepentant, the building continued to remind passers-by of a man with a three-day beard.

Hiegenstier had been obsessive about his privacy. The public suites faced dark interior courts. He had paid Grilling Gibbons a fortune to come from England and design and carve the paneling. The results would have been magnificent had he not insisted on too dark a wood. After Gibbons departed, well paid but sullen, Hiegenstier made things worse by hanging escutcheons with his coat of arms over the beautiful paneling. Gibbons had also carved magnificent doors that would have been notable had they not been overpowered by oversized lintels in exotic marble whose colors clashed and into which the Hiegenstier arms had been carved. The marble floors were inset with mosaics of colored marble, but the stone was so hard that both family and servants insisted on covering the mosaics with thick flannel runners to ease the pain of walking. The wife of an earlier owner had tried to meet the marble problem. She had purchased magnificent Oriental rugs and placed them over the finest mosaics. The dark public suites were filled with oversized Seventeenth century silver furniture, wrought at a time when fashion sought grandeur and disdained comfort. Nothing else looked right in the rooms, so there they remained, the last unmelted members of their tribe.

Frederick's grandmother and her husband had tried hard to humanize the brute. They had built additional suites of public rooms in what was then a modern and luxurious style. Time had cruelly converted those rooms, too, into uninviting sprawls as dingy and graceless as the rest of the palace.

The top two floors were living space where consecutive generations of wives had enjoyed a freer hand and more influence. Money was no object; the men of the family were always rich and always married well. Consequently, for the most part, the rooms on those floors were almost comfortable and sometimes even elegant, although they were cold in winter and stuffy in summer. David lived on the third floor in a two-room suite, with Conrad down the hall.

Frederick maintained a fine table and a famous cellar by way of compensation. Over many years, Agatha spent a fortune vainly trying to make the Hiegenstier livable. At last, admitting defeat, she had an extension built, a new wing where the rooms were airy and comfortable, and moved her husband and herself into it.

In a small dining room of the extension, Frederick was meeting with five senior members of his party. The men had dined, and the servants had been excused. Wine had been left on the table with a pitcher of water to dilute it for those who preferred to drink it that old-fashioned way. Platters of dry figs and dates, preserved ginger and bite-sized pieces of dried, salted fish had been left on the table

The atmosphere was clubby. The six men, all of them Witans, had known each other for many years. Frederick presided, but he had diplomatically arranged for a round table. Augustus Wittelsbach, Francisco de Medici, Louis de Bourbon, Mariano Visconti, and Otto Hapsburg were all were heads of great aristocratic clans. They stood at the very apex of aristocratic society, so rich, powerful and influential that they expected other aristocrats to follow them. They were reaching the important business of the night.

Frederick finished a detailed description of this meeting with the Emperor and summed up, "Martin indicated that he is willing to negotiate terms for the panRoman policies with the Witanagemot. Personally, I think the best we might get from him is a weakening of his demands or a lengthening of the time for them to become effective. I doubt he'll roll back the policies back enough to satisfy us. But we might secure peace for a time, and with it a chance to strengthen ourselves further. He will not offer us what we really want, a reversal of the policies sufficient to cause the balance of authority to shift away from the Emperor to the greater aristocracy, in other words, to ourselves. So what do we do now? Do we want to weaken or delay the policies, or do we want to depose the Emperor, which is the only way we can get the full extent of what we really want? Or, if we cannot achieve that, would we agree to a change of Crown Prince, preferably to one of us?"

"Martin is only sixty-two," said Medici. "We will be strong in this Witanagemot despite the loss of what the Byzantine gold could buy. We should decide what to do now."

"He made you an offer, Fred," Visconti added. "It's still open. Do you want to accept and try to steer the negotiations in our favor?"

"My wife likes that idea," Frederick replied, "but he will still have the last word on what he agrees to, and wins more than we do in any settlement. On the other hand, we are not entirely safe personally. I don't think any of us took Byzantine money, but we all knew about it. We could ask him to put the whole matter to rest as part of any settlement. That's something to consider, if we do a deal."

Visconti asked, "Is anyone in favor of settlement? Because I think we must settle or fight now." He looked around the table. Nobody spoke. He went on, "I say we should fight, but where we are going is very close to treason. I myself am willing to do it, but I'd like each of you to agree before we go further." Visconti went around the table. One by one, the magnates agreed, some by a nod and others with an explicit declaration. Then he ruthlessly demanded, "If you don't agree, you should leave the room now. If you stay, you are with us to the end." Wittelsbach gasped, but no one left the room.

Frederick picked up the lead, "If we don't want to accept any offer, then we want him inflexible to make censure a black and white choice for the Witans. He's clever. Therefore, he will offer to negotiate at some point to avoid such choices. How should we respond when he offers?"

"By making demands that will be popular with the Witans, but he can't accept," de Medici said.

"And by filing a motion of censure as soon as the imperial speech is finished and he has left the Hall," Visconti said. "He will expect us to try for a vote against any expansion of the policies, and then use that vote as a fulcrum for a censure. He wants to forestall the second motion by talking compromise, but only if he loses the first vote. So, let's move for censure first and not give him a chance to get a compromise moving."

"I like it, but Witans will say that we're being inflexible and hasty, and that any conflict is our fault," said their host. "How do we meet their complaint?"

"By telling them that a motion for censure can always be negotiated or withdrawn, and that all we are doing is trying to bargain from strength," Medici answered. "Then we wait for him to do something that we can claim to be a provocation. As soon as he does, we push the censure motion and give the Witans no time to consider leaving us."

"That would call for great skill and delicacy," Frederick said. "We have to be very careful. One wrong step, and we may be finished."

"One consolation is that exile is the worst that can happen to us." Hapsburg said.

"Don't be too sure," warned the prince. "He can be bloody when he thinks he's in danger. I've told you my father's story."

Soon after, the meeting ended, and Frederick went upstairs. "We closed the door behind us tonight," he told his wife.

"Be careful what you do, dear. I love you," Agatha said. "Martin made you an offer. You thought it was a fair one, considering the source. Why didn't you take it?"

"Because if I do, I'll never be Emperor."

❋

David returned from his dinner with Dorcas and Pannonius dispirited and confused. He had always feared being caught between his father and Frederick. It did not help that Caroline Wittelsbach had gently told him she had was thinking of marrying an older man she did not love because of family pressure. He damned Aachen and cursed the day he first came there. He walked home, wondering whether he shouldn't throw up his career and find a quiet place far away from Aachen. But he had no idea of what life as a country gentleman would be like. And Caroline might change her mind if he were on the winning side. Wittelsbach women had a way of marrying winners. He told himself that the Witanagemot would start in ten days, and then he would have a better idea of where things stood. It didn't help much.

Chapter XVIII

~~~~~~

Diplomacy Starts To Work

ON THE FIRST OF July, the Mongols unexpectedly asked the Paladin for a second meeting. The Paladin accepted immediately and scheduled the meeting to start as soon as Ambassador Mazzeo could be recalled and bring with him Isaac de Bergeros, another of the three Roman senior ambassadors

The parties met at the same farmhouse as before. In designating it as the place of meeting, the Paladin had acted out of sentimental reasons. He had inherited the house from Donna, who had grown up there, and it was full of pleasant memories. When he arrived, however, he was dismayed to see how everything was in a state of total neglect. The farm workers had fled from the invading Mongols, taking the horses and stock with them. They had left behind partially plowed, unseeded fields in which the untended furrows were thick with weeds, while the plow-broken earth made the air unpleasantly dusty.

The day of the meeting was very hot. Much the same group of Romans was waiting on the porch, trying to restrain their hopes. Again, a troop of Mongols was seen riding in, led by a rider bearing a white flag, but this time, two unfamiliar Mongols in court robes accompanied Kaidu. At the ritual of introduction, they were presented as Ochir and Bekter. The ambassadors smiled when they heard their names.

When the introductions were finished (the Paladin let Toby make the Roman presentation), the Paladin began, "We are honored by the presence of such important representatives of the Great Khan. Have you any suggestions on how we should proceed?"

179

Although obviously much younger than Kaidu, Ochir responded directly to the Paladin as head of delegation to head of delegation, "I have plenipotentiary powers and substantive proposals to make. I suggest that three senior members of each side meet with their three equivalents. The meeting should be closed, with only one interpreter and one note taker for either side." Roman faces brightened; this sounded as if Ochir meant business. The men trooped up the stairs to the large room, and Ochir sat down between Kaidu and Bekter on either side. Across the table, the Paladin sat between the Senior Ambassadors. He left General Lauzac below to signal this was a meeting of diplomats to settle terms of peace. In the same spirit, all three Mongol negotiators wore robes. The interpreters and note takers sorted themselves out at the ends of the table.

As host, the Paladin opened the discussion: "The purpose of this meeting is to find a mutually satisfactory way to resolve present hostilities. When last we talked, I suggested a number of ways by which we might extricate ourselves. The Vice Minister did not think them inherently unreasonable, but he did not believe them practicable at that time. Since you have proposed this meeting, I would hope you have either changed your position or have other proposals for a mutually agreeable solution."

Ochir asked, "Have you full authority to negotiate with us, Proconsul?"

Senior Ambassador Mazzeo responded, "Our Emperor knows about this meeting and has approved our presence. We have an excellent idea of the kind of proposal he is likely to approve, and three senior Roman decision makers—the Proconsul and two of our three senior ambassadors—are present at his direction."

Ochir nodded. "Our situation is not really that different. I have the advantage of having just spoken to the Great Khan. You rejected an unqualified ceasefire in place. I assume you have not changed your mind (the Paladin nodded his head), so let me ask the next question. Would you change your mind if we agreed to send an ambassador to New Rome immediately to negotiate the issues between us and establish an acceptable expiration date for the ceasefire?"

The Paladin's voice was cautious. "Certainly, that would be a step in the right direction. In itself it is not enough. For one thing, we have to agree on the issues to be negotiated. We may or may not be able to do that today. And then, the question becomes how long a ceasefire? A brief ceasefire for negotiation is one thing, but we cannot consent to protracted negotiations while foreign soldiers remain on Roman soil."

Ochir briskly pushed straight ahead. "Then I can improve the atmosphere immediately. My Khan has authorized me to state that he has no desire to leave any military presence on your side of his border a minute longer than he must. Suppose we simply left and restored the Zone to its former status. What then?"

"Without a peace treaty?"

"For argument's sake, yes."

The Paladin's voice remained cautious. "Again a step, this time a long step, in the right direction but still not quite enough. We need to resolve all disputes to prevent any recurrence. If you have any grievances, they should be disposed of. We ourselves have grievances to be resolved as a result of this invasion. For that, we need a treaty, and if I may suggest so, for the same reasons, so do you."

"But there has been no declaration of war."

"That's the merest of technicalities with armies in the field and soldiers dead in battle," Aetius replied. "Wars end by treaty because otherwise they are not ended. We both want this one ended. If you are worried about the technicalities, don't call it a 'Peace Treaty'. Call it something else."

Now it was Ochir's turn to be cautious. Suspicion showed on his face. "Again for argument's sake, yes. That means, as you have said, an understanding on the items that need to be negotiated. Yet, what is there to be negotiated here except withdrawal and restoration of the Zone? Neither of us has any problem with either item. Is a treaty under those circumstances anything more than a formality? If you are asking the Great Khan of Mongolia to pay some kind of tribute in order to forestall an attack on his lands, he will not do it."

"I understand your sensibilities," the Paladin said (there may have been the faintest wisp of sarcasm in his tone), "but we have farmers who have lost their year's crop and livestock, not to mention their homes. Look around you. This particular farmer can afford the loss. Most can't. Someone is going to have to make them whole. If you don't, my Emperor must, but what was not his fault ought not to be his expense.

Providing humanitarian help directly to poor farmers as a matter of grace won't hurt the Great Khan's prestige. Quite the contrary. Then, we both need a much clearer set of rules for the Zone. And finally, it is outrageous that we have to trade with the Great Khan's subjects through Constantinople. It causes the smuggling that destroys the Zone and increases the likelihood of another conflict between us. Incidentally, it also impoverishes the Great Khan's subjects and injures his revenue."

"Let us see if we can work out a list of issues to be discussed," said Ochir.

And that was all there was to it. After more than thirty years of refusing to even talk about the Silk Road, the Mongols agreed in a casual, almost off-the-cuff fashion to open the Road, if the terms satisfied them. For two hours the diplomats worked toward establishing a comprehensive list of issues to be considered. Then they recessed and the Paladin took advantage of the recess to talk to his two senior ambassadors. Isaac De Bergeros was an expert on Rome's Eastern relationships and fluent in Mongolian. A short, stocky person with a reputation for being plain spoken, he was older than he appeared, but his motions and words were still brisk.

"So far so good. I am astonished that they are willing to talk about commercial relations so quickly," the Paladin said. "They refused to even consider the subject last time. How do you feel about it, Isaac?"

"They are giving us a real opportunity. They may even have taken your suggestion to change sides. I wouldn't be greatly surprised if they proposed an alliance against Constantinople."

Ambassador Mazzeo interposed, "Aetius, could you manage a chat with Kaidu?"

Taking his advice, the Paladin sought out Kaidu. "I'm delighted by these developments but a little surprised," he said. "Can you tell an old friend how it happened?"

Kaidu looked coy. "Someone told the Khan a few home truths about the late Prince Subatai that his wife forgot to mention," he smiled. "Someone else brought to the Khan's attention the fact that Byzantine bribes were not being shared with the royal treasury. The Khan had been told otherwise and got very angry. My sister cooled down when you offered to return her token. I take it that offer still stands."

At the Paladin's nod Kaidu continued, "Good. The Khan asked Ochir to look into the situation. Ochir concluded there was nothing for us in this half-war. So the Khan told him to get it settled on terms that did not humiliate us, and if he couldn't, to tell him what a real war involved. That's a warning old friend; you can only push so far. By the way, Ochir's probably going to be our next Prime Minister."

Meanwhile, Bekter, a very senior Mongolian diplomat, sought out Senior Ambassador de Bergeros. Bekter had a very different tale to tell. "Always good to see an old friend," De Bergeros. began. "It's been about three years hasn't it? I was still in Kiev when you were promoted and sent home. Are you representing your Ministry today?"

"Yes. Ochir is the Great Khan's man. I'm the diplomat the Ministry gave him."

"Who's Kaidu representing"

Belter laughed, "Nobody, Isaac. Nobody but himself. Ochir brought him along to make sure his name is signed on any deal we make to prevent him from intriguing against it. He's an inveterate troublemaker. The Byzantines bought him long ago. They paid top price too. No matter what he tells you, he was the moving force behind the plan to invade, and he's trying to keep this thing going. He promised the Great Khan a quick success, and the Byzantines promised to help us with our troubles with Kiev. But Kiev is the same problem it's always been, the Byzantines are a disappointment and Kaidu lost a third of his army. The Khan wanted to kill him, but his sister saved his life. Yet, here he is, still scheming away. The man's got the courage of a lion and the flexibility of an snake."

"And Ochir?"

"Very high in the Khan's confidence. He's been told to clean up this mess up without paying too much. You can get a commercial treaty, but he wants one favorable to us. The Khan can turn around if he thinks it's not going to work out."

"Oho," said De Bergeros, "And did Ochir send you to warn me to protect his back against our asking too much?"

Belter smiled, "If that were true, I couldn't tell you, could I?"

De Berger's responded with, "God bless our honorable profession." Both diplomats laughed.

For the rest of the afternoon, they all worked hard to prepare a list of items to be discussed in connection with any final negotiation. Finally, the Paladin brought the talk to a conclusion, "I think we both know now in general terms what we want to talk about in connection with a treaty. I suggest we inform our respective military that an immediate truce is in effect and put in place the process for a final negotiation."

"I agree," Ochir said. "My instructions were that if we get to a point where final negotiation seems to be in view—and I think that we will be there after spending a few more minutes polishing the draft—to accept an offer of a truce, begin withdrawing our army, and advise you that the Great Khan will send an ambassador to New Rome to negotiate a final treaty. I will advise you when his ambassador will arrive in New Rome as soon I myself know. It will be convenient to hold the commercial issues for separate negotiation. We will both need to consult with our experts on that subject. This has been a good day's work. And now I, for one, wouldn't mind a drink."

In two hours, the Mongols were gone, and the Paladin was left with his two ambassadors. He told them, "Isaac, you should stay to handle any complications. You know these people, and your spoken Mongolian is superb. Giuseppe and I should go home and start working on the commercial terms, leaving you here to accompany the ambassador. Whom do you think they will designate as ambassador? Ochir himself?"

"Yes," both senior ambassadors chorused.

"I think he's right about separating the commercial issues. Resolving them will take time and an immediate truce reduces the chance of an accidental provocation. We have to talk among ourselves about what exactly to ask for. Wouldn't it be glorious if we could turn this Byzantine treachery into a direct connection to the Silk Road? I think they're starting to change sides"

"They already have," said De Bergeros. "Let's have that drink."

Chapter XIX

Last Minute Preparations

AMONG THE OTHER THINGS happening in Aachen during the first two weeks in July were these:

It was a perfect day for early July, hot but comfortable. Late morning rain had washed the air and settled the dust in the little square. The noisy children Sharpie detested had gone home for dinner. The trees were in full leaf, especially his favorite, a seventy-foot umbrella-shaped elm. The square was always empty at this time of day and there were almost two good hours till sunset. A man could sit on a bench near the fountain, look at the elm and be alone with his thoughts. This was Sharpie's favorite place to think something through.

He had a lot on his mind. He was certain he was still safe. He ran through his checklist: no one was following him, no one at work showed suspicion, his house had not been searched, and he had done everything to cover his tracks by tricks that George and Emmerich had taught him. Nevertheless, he felt conspicuous. He was afraid, though he managed not to show it. He told himself that he had always been underestimated and was smarter than they were, but that scoundrel Hugh Pannonius was too clever by half. George had been terrified of him and that younger brother he had acquired, the Fleming with the odd first name, was learning too quickly. His good luck might not last. He had tried to deal with Pannonius himself, but the bastard had gotten away. He was lucky but so was his enemy. That wasn't fair. Before he went into hiding, Emmerich had told him that he was going where Sharpie could not find him and warned him that the Byzantine Embassy was now off limits. It shouldn't have mattered. He had always operated outside the embassy. His handlers in Constantinople had given him four different ways to communicate with them, only one of which was connected with the embassy, but now none were working. George was gone; Parides was out of business; he couldn't use the semaphore system to send messages; and Emmerich, his personal lifeline, had vanished. Even if Constantinople wanted to help him, he had no way to ask them. He did know one Witan as deep in the Byzantine service as he was himself, but he was not the sort of man to risk his own life for Sharpie.

So it came down to the same choices he had been revolving in his mind for weeks: to run for it, to try to make a deal with the Emperor, or to continue relying on his cover. Two of the three were not even worth considering. The Emperor would never grant him mercy. They had his correspondence with George, in which he hinted at Andrew's killing. The idea of killing Andrew had been Sharpie's, and Sforza wouldn't sleep until he saw the body of the man who had murdered his son. For that matter, killing Andrew wasn't the half of what he had done.

Running would have been best. But where? He'd never get to Constantinople. How could he outrun the semaphores? England might be reachable, but the English would turn him over without a qualm. The Northmen might be more independent, but the only way to reach them was by ship. Once he was missed, the semaphores would close the ports to him.

He would have to continue to rely on his camouflage. Unlike Emmerich he had not prepared a hiding place. But what good had his hidey-hole been to Julian Parides? So it came down to the fact that they might find Emmerich, and if they did, Sharpie was done for. He had better see that Witan and be careful; the fellow might think he was being blackmailed.

Louie Duval could not say that he had gotten out of bed on the wrong side, because his troubles had started while he was still abed. When he woke up, Hildegard had been fully awake and thinking for half an hour. She needed to get a few things off her lovely chest. Louis ruefully acknowledged to himself that although he could outsmart anyone else, it was surprising how often he outsmarted himself. He had done it once again when he had sent his mistress to spy on Pannonius and Mikail. In her twenty-seven years, Hildegard had pretty much gotten any man she really wanted. She liked both Mikail and Pannonius and would have taken either of them as a way out of her present unsettled position. Unfortunately, both were models of constancy. Mikail talked about Karita all the time, and the sight of Dorcas and Pannonius together elicited powerful feelings of sadness and envy. Why, she now demanded of Louie, couldn't *her* man be like that? Feeble attempts at *not before breakfast* and *not now* were dismissed with an immediacy he had rarely heard from her. "You make an absolute commitment to your work," she observed. "Why can't you, why won't you, do the same for me? There isn't anyone else for me, and I don't think there is for you either. I'm good for you, and you know it. What holds you back?"

Louie recognized that he was about to be told to make a decision or she would leave him. He couldn't honestly say he shouldn't have expected it, but the fact was that he hadn't. Because it wasn't as simple as she thought. He showed her his real feelings when they were alone, especially in bed. She knew how much he cared for her, which made her feel entitled to ask him to make a life with her. What she did not know was that twenty-five years ago he had been married and had lost both wife and child within a single year. He remembered his sense of desolation perfectly. He never talked about it, but he had made himself an absolute promise never to give hostages to fortune again. But Hildegard melted whenever she saw a child, and Louie knew with perfect clarity that she would insist on having children once they were married, no matter what she promised. He was nearly fifty, too late for him to be a father, even if he had wanted to be. Well, if he were going to lose her, he wouldn't be a coward. "It's not that I don't like you enough," he said. "I do. It's that I'm too old. I can't be a father at my age"

The pain showed on her face. "You don't have to worry about *that*," she assured him, "I can't have children. If you hadn't been so wrapped up in yourself you would have figured it out in the last two years. Don't lie to me, Louie. Men always want children, no matter what they say, but I told myself that that if I couldn't have children, at least I might have a man who really cared about me. How foolish of me to look for love at court. I'll leave after the Season is over and go home, you need me till then. There is one thing I won't do; I won't break in my successor."

By now they were walking around the room. His chest felt tight and for a minute, he couldn't talk. "Oh, sit down," he said in exasperation. "Nobody is telling you to go. I don't want you to go. Stay past the Season. Stay for good if you want. What you don't know is that I lost a wife in childbirth when I was young. My little boy survived, and just when I was starting to heal, he died. It destroyed me. I won't ever forget it, and I will never take that chance again. If you're fool enough to want to stay with me, I'll give you anything you want, even marriage."

He paused, She looked at him with wide-open eyes and an O-shaped mouth as he added, "And the hell of it all is that I must be with the Emperor at nine-thirty. I can't even take you back to bed."

Now she did sit down. "The job," she said with a laugh. "The Goddamned everlasting job. This isn't going to be a marriage, Louie. It's legal bigamy with me as junior wife. I don't get you till you're seventy."

He was pulling on his clothes in a hurry. "If you're lucky, maybe then, but never blame me for what you just brought on yourself. What did you just say about courts?" But he had sense enough to kiss her long and hard before he left.

Dinner arrangements at the Hiegenstier changed every year on July first. Before then, the family usually dined at home alone or with a few close friends and David dined with the family. Once the Witanagemot Season began, things were different. For the rest of the Season, the Hiegenstier was transformed into Grandee party headquarters. Frederick still ate in the main dining room, but now his dinner guests were limited to the members of the Grandee caucus. His family and their friends dined separately, David among them. These arrangements unpleasantly reminded David of his expulsion from the Emperor's family table. He kept his feelings to himself, but it made him sulky and sorry for himself. He worried whether he should have tied himself so closely to Frederick. The dinner at Aunt Luisa's had increased his unease.

On the other hand, lunch was pleasurable. It was served buffet style in the small ballroom. All tables were open seating, and an attempt was made to integrate people, which made it a good place to pick up news and meet fellow diners. On this day late in the first week of July, however, the only empty seat was at a table where Augustus von

Walsenburg was holding forth. David sat down with low expectations. The man was a Witan and Grandee party functionary, whose job was to pass the word on the prince's positions.

David had met him casually, but, to his annoyance, Walsenburg did not even recognize him. The fellow was one of Frederick's favorite hunting partners and much too noisily proud of his connection with the family for David's comfort. David thought him a loud, vulgar lout. He also felt that Walsenburg's use of an unjustified "von" and the way he carefully referred to the senior Grandees were snobbery in a country yokel without that much to be a snob about. All he ever talked about was hunting. But not today. He thought he was among friends, and if what he was saying was not treasonous, it was not very far from it either. Every other sentence began with "If only our good Frederick were Emperor . . ." David tried to pay as little attention as possible, but then Walsenburg said something in his loud voice that David could not miss, "Number One and that bastard half-brother of his who killed the man that ought to have been our Emperor."

David fled quickly to his room to think. Now he knew that he had been lied to. Not only had his uncle told the lout the holiest of family secrets, but he was using it against the Emperor. Frederick was carrying a personal grudge against the Emperor and his father, although both he and Conrad had told David their differences were merely differences of opinion over policies. David could not longer deny the facts. The man was organizing opposition to the Emperor and might be contemplating worse.

He had been a fool. Now what was he to do? If David walked out, everyone in the political world would wonder why the Paladin's son was quitting Frederick's party and house. He could he explain his action without the reasons underlying it becoming public knowledge? That was the last thing the Emperor and his father would want. Should he talk to Frederick? No, he had told Walsenburg the secret in the first place. If David asked him about his intentions and actions, it might bring on the very scandal David wanted to avoid. He would tell Dorcas the facts as soon as he saw her. That was his duty, but he did not want to spy on Frederick and Conrad. Though they had lied to him, they had been kind. Once the shock wore off, it occurred to him how excellent was the advice Pannonius had given him: do nothing until after the

Witanagemot. In the meanwhile, make sure nobody uses you or your name and don't be dragged into anything you don't understand. *And I thought he was being impertinent,* David thought sorrowfully.

❋

The Chancellor was having dinner with five old friends, all Witans. Since the Season began, he had been spending almost all his time meeting with Witans.

"The panRoman policies will be the most controversial subject," the Chancellor said. "We are trying to find out how the members of the Witanagemot feel about them. What issues do you have with them?"

"I worry about the Emperor having too much power," one of his friends replied. "Martin's no despot and doesn't want to be one, but the next Emperor might be. We should stop where we are."

This wasn't what the Chancellor was looking for. He wanted to hear about specific issues, to find whether there was any ground for compromise. He politely said as much.

Another Witan, a man named D'Alianza from lower Portugal, joined in, "What upsets me is that part of his program that deals with things on my own property. Proposals to limit what he likes to call feudal tenures strike directly at my interests. Right now anyone who rents land from me has to provide me with a set amount of labor on the estate for maintenance of roads and improvements as in addition to money rent. If you take corvée away from me, I can't raise the tenant's money rent to cover it. He hasn't got the cash."

"We all know that corvée is always inefficient and often goes to improve the owner's land, not to make public improvements," the Chancellor replied. "That's illegal. But suppose the labor went exclusively to work on the roads and other public parts of your domain. The work's got to be done anyhow."

"That's worse," D'Alianza objected. "You take the right to use the labor away from me and give it to the Emperor. I get nothing at all."

The Chancellor thought for a minute and tried again, "All right. Suppose we converted all corvée into a money charge, and split it between you and the Emperor."

"Then something that used to be mine is now partly Martin's," D'Alianza said. "That amounts to an increase in my taxes."

"All right, we end all corvée, tax land with a fixed fee, and you get it all in exchange for a promise to maintain specific road and public improvements. Does that meet your objections?"

"No," D'Alianza answered. "It still comes down to putting an obligation on me that wasn't there before."

"But corvée is unjust and inefficient. It should go."

"I can see that. Yet without it, the Emperor has a right to control and inspect roads and improvements on my land, and I have to make them when my Count—who, by the way, doesn't like me—thinks it necessary, and do them to his satisfaction. Sooner or later, that will cost me a lot of money. It also puts my peasants in direct relationship with Aachen, going over my head. Long run, that can't be good for me. The fact of the matter is that no matter what you propose, Giuseppe, something that used to be mine will belong to Martin."

The discussion went on for two hours, with the Chancellor probing to find what kind of ideas were likely to be acceptable to the Witans, and what would anger them.

Nearby, the Mayor and Albrecht were having a similar conversation with a different group of Witans, while in his study, the Emperor was talking with a Grandee who had always been opposed to the panRoman policies, looking for a way to get him to change sides. He was having unexpected success.

The prince and the senior members of his group were having their own conversations with Witans, trying to encourage opposition in men with a lifetime of going along with the Emperor. Most Witans made sure to talk with both sides. Frederick himself avoided participating in the interviews, fearing to be seen as leader of an opposition party, though his pretense was wearing thin.

The day after he spoke with the Chancellor, D'Alianza had his interview with Francisco de Medici. Where the Chancellor had sought opportunities to compromise and to discover the Witan's sensitivities to specific policies, de Medici was trying to incite him to oppose Imperial power. D'Alianza, an experienced politician who had understood the Chancellor perfectly, knew just what de Medici wanted. On the whole, he was inclined to be on the Emperor's side, but Frederick some day, perhaps even some day soon, might be Emperor in his cousin's place. It was unwise to offend him. He let de Medici lead the conversation.

De Medici opened with, "This isn't about the integrity of the Roman Empire. It's all about Martin's desire for more power at the expense of people like us. Don't you think this push toward imperial power has gone far enough, Rodrigo?"

"Certainly, there are things I don't like," the Witan replied, "but he says he's willing to talk to us. What's so wrong with talking?"

"We won't get anything unless we lever it out of him. We should be talking from a position of strength."

"And how do you propose to develop such a position?"

De Medici said, "I understand a motion for censure will be filed,"

"Isn't that overdoing it? A motion for censure says that the Witanagemot thinks the Emperor is a despot. Nobody really thinks Martin is a despot. I don't."

"Maybe not yet," de Medici said, "but he's going in that direction. He'll speak sweetly enough to us. When he gets what he wants, however, it will be too late to stop him."

D'Alianza didn't like what he heard. "Anyone who votes for that motion makes an enemy of Martin for life. Why should I support such an obvious accusation of despotism, when I don't even think he's a despot?"

Speaking slowly, choosing his words carefully, de Medici said, "Probably we will never vote on it. It just gives us a stronger hand to trade with Martin. But if the Witanagemot does vote that way, you're in the majority. Then, if Martin leaves as Emperor, you are in a favored position with his successor."

Now it was d'Alianza's turn to think before speaking. "In other words, Francisco, you would like to replace Martin with Frederick. I know you're not alone. I know what Martin is, and what he will do. I don't know Frederick except that now I do know he's exceedingly ambitious. I'm sure you'll find people who will be willing to go with you. Not me."

"Will you keep your mind open?"

"I always keep my mind open. But if you are asking whether I can see my opinion changing, I cannot. Aren't you taking a terrible risk if you go much further?"

De Medici pondered, "All right then, let's assume no motion is filed. We negotiate with Martin instead. Will you join a group of Witans to bargain with Martin.?"

D'Alianza went right to the point. "I'll talk to your group and probably join it on specific issues which involve money in my pocket. If you are asking whether I will follow the prince into a confrontation with Martin, my answer is no."

"Could you be persuaded to change your mind?" de Medici asked. *He's offering me a bribe*, thought D'Alianza. He was not offended, but responded immediately, "No. There isn't enough money to make me fight an Emperor who holds all the cards."

De Medici had found out where this Witan stood. He was not quite finished. "If that's how you feel, so be it. Let's go to the specifics then, Rodrigo. What bothers you most about the policies?"

D'Alianza relaxed. "Now, that's a question I can answer comfortably. His proposals to change feudal tenures take money out of my pocket." The rest of their conversation was not very different from his conversation with the Chancellor.

Dorcas was very nervous about approaching her aunt with the news of her engagement. She had told the Empress what David had said about von Walsenburg. Her aunt had flushed with anger, but said only, "Please thank your brother. I know it was his duty, but it can't have been easy for him. Frederick is a fool who is going to make us all unhappy." After a short pause, the Empress went on, "It's a man's world Dorcas, but men can be such fools. They should listen to their wives more often. The Emperor listens to me. I expect Pannonius will listen to you." Dorcas had thought the conversation over, when the Empress paused. Her ever-restless hands picked up an old vase to rearrange flowers that had fallen out of place. When the Empress mentioned Pannonius, she dropped the vase, and the sound of the valuable antique smashing on the marble floor made an exclamation point.

Without thinking, Dorcas immediately said, "I'm not paying for it," and the women started to laugh together. "Then consider it a wedding present," the Empress smiled. "Your face has been telling the world the news for the last few days. Of course, you will have our blessing, but I'm afraid we need your fiancé right now."

✳

Sharpie and his Witan friend were alone in a back room of a Great Street tavern after hours, a place no one would ever have expected to find either of them. They were using false names and pretending they were out-of-town merchants negotiating a cargo of wool from England. Their level of mutual trust was very low. For all that, they were getting along swimmingly. They had come to realize they had the same problem: if Emmerich were caught, it would mean their death. They were talking about Emmerich without daring to say his name.

"Our heads are very loose on our necks," Sharpie said. "Better to save them together." Sharpie went through the alternatives he had been considering and suggested cooperating in flight.

The Witan saw things differently. "I have no desire to run. As things stand I am a rich, important man with a great estate. The money I got from the Easterners went into improving and enlarging it. I have no desire to spend the rest of my life as an exiled pauper. Once we run, we can't return so long as this Emperor lives, unless Emmerich were to die before they catch him. I can't see how we could manage that. We don't even know where he is. It would be easier to kill the Emperor himself."

Both men stopped cold, suddenly realizing what the Witan had just said. "Who would do it?" the Witan whispered. "The Greeks were supposed to send professionals to keep us from being involved."

"Put that idea aside for a second," Sharpie said. "Who else is at risk from Emmerich? Frederick always kept himself away from the work."

The Witan's voice dropped to a whisper. "That's what you think! How do you think the Greeks knew which Witans they could pay off? The chief led them to their targets. He never spoke directly to Parides or Simonides. The chief told me, I told Emmerich, and he told Simonides. Who's at risk if they catch Emmerich? Everyone. Emmerich knows everything. If he talks, they find out about everything and everyone. I'm pretty sure that Frederick did more than introduce people. I think he took money and used it to pay people so they wouldn't know it came from the Greeks. I know five more Witans they haven't found out about besides me, plus the Count in Bari. There may be more. Only Emmerich and the chief know. You're right. We must kill him, but how?"

"I've been thinking, and I have some ideas," Sharpie said. "We would have to kill his brother too. We would need the prince's help." He then sketched out what had been running through his mind.

The Witan listened and thought about it, looking for an obvious flaw. "It could work," he conceded. "Don't worry about the chief. The Greeks didn't seek him out, he went to them. Ever since it all started five years ago, the chief been the one who pulled the strings. Don't you know they killed his father? Now he's waiting for the executioner, just as we are. I'm staying in his palace, I'll talk to him tonight."

CHAPTER XX

The Emperor's Speech

THE FIFTEENTH OF JULY, Convocation Day, is a major holiday in Aachen. In a glorious parade the Emperor and Empress ride in state to Witanagemot Hall and open the Witanagemot. The Emperor's speech from the throne is the year's most important political event, and the most comprehensive public statement of Imperial policy of the year.

The ancient ritual for the opening the Witanagemot is formal, stylized, and ceremonious. The First Speaker likes to describe it as stately, but it has been called hidebound and pretentious—although never by a Witan. Certainly, the stage on which the show is presented is impressive. Witanagemot Hall is the size of a small cathedral. Its famous seven doors face the square. The enormous Ω-shaped central portal contains a pair of great bronze doors. Each of them is triple a man's height and double the size of the doors on either side of the portal. The doors open into a vast auditorium. At the far end of that auditorium is an elevated platform on which sit two golden Imperial thrones and a solid gold podium that only the Emperor may use. (The Roman slang for orders from on high is "straight from the gold".) On the auditorium floor to the right of the stairs leading up to the thrones is the First Speaker's outsize desk. In front of it is another podium that only the Speaker and the Witans may use.

Facing the Speaker's desk are twelve rows of beautifully carved seats for the hundred ninety-five Witans, divided by a broad middle aisle. The seats occupy only the middle third of the great hall, leaving broad open spaces on either side. The Witan who has served longest sits on the right side of the first row, and the newest Witan in the leftmost seat of the last row. Seating by seniority was adopted to prevent the formation of cliques but without success. The Witanagemot has always been infested with them. The only *ex officio* member is the Chancellor. He sits in the middle of the first row.

Michelangelo's huge statue of the Archangel Michael, the Empire's patron, rises in the center of the empty space to the Witans' left. In front of it are a small brazier and a box of incense on a table. When a Witan wishes to speak, he walks over to the statue, takes a pinch of incense, throws it into the brazier, and says a prayer aloud. Then he stands below the statute to wait his turn. It is not unusual to see four or five men standing in a queue This procedure was copied from the Roman Senate many years ago.

Behind the Witans are less impressive seats for alternate non-voting members and the Consistorians of the Emperor's Consistory. Behind them a three-foot high, gilded, metalwork screen runs across the room to separate the front section of the room from the public accommodations. There are two balconies for the public. On Convocation Day the Hall is always packed.

Wednesday, July 15, 1812 was Convocation Day. At eleven o'clock sharp, as the sound of cannon announced that the Emperor had left the palace, the bronze double doors in the great central portal opened and, walking two by two, the white-robed Witans followed their First Speaker into the Hall and down the center aisle to their seats. Walking behind them came the Chancellor, the Archbishop of Aachen, and the Chancellor's page, a young man carrying a leather portfolio that contained the Edict of Convocation.

Once the Witans were standing at their seats, the First Speaker clapped his hands, signaling them to sit down. The Chancellor was already at the lower podium. The Hall's porters closed the central doors and prepared to reopen them for the Emperor.

The First Speaker bowed to the Witans and they rose to take the oath. Once it had been administered, the First Speaker asked the Chancellor to read the Edict of Convocation. The Chancellor read the Edict *verbatim* and added, "I am commanded by the Emperor to advise the honorable Witans that inasmuch as he has convoked this Witanagemot for giving and receiving their advice in accordance with good and ancient custom, all Witans shall have free speech for whatever they say in this Hall, except it be crime or treason. There will be no retaliation hereafter for anything lawfully said within these walls." This speech is part of the ritual. No Witan believes it for an instant.

The First Speaker declared, "This, the Witanagemot of the year 1812, is open" and called on the Archbishop for the invocation. After he finished, the Witans recited their oath and were seated. There was a pause to await the Emperor. Soon, trumpets were heard outside in the square, and the Grand Marshal's voice was heard through the central portal, calling loudly, "The Emperor has arrived." All seven doors opened simultaneously. Once the Emperor has entered, they stay open night and day until this year's Witanagemot is closed in order to show the Witans' willingness to listen to any Roman citizen. The Emperor's train of officials and Consistorians entered through the side doors and walked quickly down the side aisles to seat themselves behind the Witans. Only the Emperor's party and the Witans ever use the central aisle.

The Grand Marshall's voice was heard again calling, "The Emperor is about to enter." The Grand Marshal, the Imperial couple, and Magister Militum entered through the center door to a trumpet fanfare and progressed slowly down the aisle to the stairs leading to the throne platform The Marshal led followed by the Imperial couple walking side-by-side. The Emperor wore Charlemagne's crown. Last came the Magister Militium holding his sword upright in the salute. As he passed the Speaker, the Magister bowed to acknowledge his permission to carry a sword into the Hall. The Speaker did not return his bow.

Everyone but the Witans rose for the Emperor and Empress. The Witans were making a point: under ancient Roman custom the host does not rise in his own house to greet a visitor. This is their house. On his way to his throne, the Emperor passed the standing First Speaker. As he did so, he made a shallow bow, saying, "out of courtesy." The First Speaker returned his bow with a much deeper one. The Marshal remained at the foot of the stairs, and the Magister positioned himself on the third step. He held his sword upright at the salute. As the Imperial couple reached their thrones, the Witans rose as one and bowed. Then all sat simultaneously.

The First Speaker pronounced loudly, "Our Emperor Charles Martel has expressed his desire and intention to address this Witanagemot. Silence and attention for the Imperial address!" These words are yet another compromise. "Intention" suggests that the Emperor acts as of right, whereas "desire" implies he asks for permission. This is a perfect example of the deliberate ambiguities running through the choreography. The Witanagemot struggles for more authority than it has, but usually has to settle for appearances.

The Emperor sacrificed his dignity and donned eyeglasses. Accustomed to public performances, he spoke with resonant authority. "Witans and Romans, greetings. I welcome you with all my heart and wish you health and peace. I ask your prayers for myself, the Empress, the Crown Prince, and the Empire. In accord with custom and as my oath requires, I have summoned you to receive your advice and wisdom on behalf of my people. I will listen to whatever it is that you tell me." This is yet another formula. The Emperor then proceeded to substance:

"This has been an eventful year. I turn first to the events in Dacia. As we all know, the Mongols launched an unprovoked invasion of our Dacia Commandery, intending to ambush five thousand Roman soldiers deep in our own country. This wicked plan was brilliantly devised, well executed, and, unhappily, assisted by treason among our own people. Nevertheless, because of the courage and ability displayed by our soldiers and other Romans, the invaders were themselves caught by surprise and their army destroyed, dispersed, or captured.

"Since then the Mongols have requested a cease-fire. We told their representatives that any peace settlement must be based on their complete withdrawal from Roman soil. We also suggested this would be a good time to settle long-standing issues between us. I am pleased to tell you that a cease-fire is now in effect, and the Mongols will withdraw immediately from Roman soil. Furthermore, they will send an ambassador to settle our differences. He will arrive here within a week. For the first time, they have agreed to discuss our long-standing desire for a commercial treaty to eliminate the requirement that all Silk Road goods must pass through Constantinople."

The Emperor had saved announcing the agreement to open the Silk Road for this speech. The long-desired announcement brought even old, arthritic Witans to their feet, chanting, "Eternal Rome! Eternal Rome!"

The demonstration went on for ten minutes and ended with the entire chamber standing and singing the first stanza of Alcuin's *Hymn to Saint Michael*:

Michael Archangel
Of the King of Kings
Give Ear to our voices.
Hear Us, Michael
Greatest Angel,
That the enemy with cunning craft shall not prevail
To do the hurt he craves.

When the hymn ended, the Emperor continued:

"The next matter of which I must speak is not as pleasant. We have uncovered a far-reaching conspiracy involving Romans and foreigners directed against our Empire and myself. The conspirators have been active for five years. Their actions were coordinated with the invasion. At least one political officer turned traitor and helped plan the invasion. He betrayed and murdered his friend and senior officer, the godson of our own friend and colleague the Chancellor. An attempt was recently made in my own palace to murder one of my aides. This widespread treason extended to Dacia, the neutral Zone between ourselves and Mongolia, Vienna, Rostock, Dalmatia, and here, in New Rome. The traitors contemplated my assassination. Millions of denarii have been spent in bribes to further this conspiracy over the last five years. To my shame, I must tell you that Counts and Witans took foreign money. We know most of the Romans who have taken these foreign bribes and are sure to find the others. You may rest certain that this fountain of corruption has been turned off forever. The guilty will be punished.

"Roman history warns us that were I to die, a dispute over succession might turn into civil war. One way often used to ensure the Empire's unity is to appoint not only a crown prince but also a strong junior co-Emperor to protect the succession from disruption. Accordingly, I will appoint the Empress co-Emperor. We have had female co-Emperors before, including some of our greatest rulers. Helena was co-Emperor with Constantine, Theodora with Justinian, and Clara with Karl VII.

"It is also time we talked about the bundle of policies designed to strengthen the Empire's unity that are called the panRoman policies. Over the past several years, our discussions have grown unnecessarily divisive and acerbic. These differences of opinion have become a risk to Roman unity that must be addressed. I am here to listen as well as to talk, but permit me to open the discussion by giving you my point of view.

"Our Empire has grown over generations to include many different peoples. Were it to dissolve into its constituent nations and peoples as it has several times in the past, there would soon be wars, accompanied by mutual hatred among ourselves. So I ask: what holds us together? Certainly, our common habits and language help hold us together. Every educated man and woman, as well as many with little or no education, can speak Latin. We have the law, which lets us trust each other and is, or ought to be, the same everywhere. Even I can only change the law as it will be in the future and cannot over-rule a judge's decision. Commerce is another very strong force holding us together, perhaps the strongest. The Empire's roads, rivers, and other ways of transportation are open to all. No toll or private tariff stops the flow of commerce or goods. This is an enormous benefit to every person in the Empire. Lastly, if I may say so, the very existence of the Emperor holds the empire together. I do not seek to enlarge my power, but an Emperor there must be so that there can be an Empire.

"Yet, sometimes, all this is not enough. Disunion too has friends and helpers. So strong is the ambition of men for sovereignty over others that there will always be ambitious, able men who would rather rule a part of the Empire than be citizens of the whole. Impatience and dissatisfaction with things as they are—and things are always imperfect—create opportunities for their ambition. Unless restrained, such men can destroy the Empire. It is only a short step from disunion to civil war.

"The panRoman policies are designed to assist our unity. Differences of opinion over specific policies or their specific terms are legitimate, but they can never be allowed to justify disunion or violence or to excuse the formation of an organized party of opposition.

"It is time our differences on these policies were reconciled. I will honestly consider every proposal advanced in good faith with respect to them. Nothing reasonable will be out of bounds; I am willing to make reasonable compromises. My representatives and I have spoken to many of you, seeking to discover what in the policies causes disputes. We found five significant points of disagreement:

First: prohibitions against building private toll canals, railroads, and toll roads. Here, I must confess to having been overly rigid, which is not to the Empire's advantage. This can be addressed.

Second: certain landowners still have the right to appoint judges to resolve disputes on their property, even in cases to which they are a party. It thus makes the landholder a judge in his own case. I receive complaints about this almost weekly.

Third: there are questions relating to public work required to be done by the tenant as one of the duties of tenancy under so-called feudal or manorial tenure. The landlord is supposed to maintain public roads and public improvements. Too often public money or the labor corvée, which also belongs to the public, is misused. Furthermore, landlords sometimes keep fees and charges levied in the name of the Emperor for the rental of land or other income. This complicated subject is the thorniest single issue relating to the policies. While I think the entire subject must be reviewed, I understand that a balance must protect the landholders' existing rights.

Fourth: the question of the right—if that be the correct word for it—for the descendant of a citizen whose ancestor was a nobleman, a status that no longer exists, to continue to call himself by his ancestor's title. Many of you feel that these rights are essential to your position in society. I am open to discussion.

Finally, I have also suggested that the number of persons entitled to vote in the selection to the Witanagemot in each district, which varies widely, should be increased. There are counties in which only ten or twenty voters elect four Witans. As a result, some elected seats in the Witanagemot tend to become hereditary and then Witans represent themselves, not their province. This is a limited problem and should not stand in the way of a general settlement. Gradual change seems appropriate.

Our discussions over the last several years have taken an inappropriately adversarial tone. Many of you have been led to feel that that I am trying to hobble or demolish your traditional privileges rather than curbing abuses. Others fear I will force changes on you by issuing edicts or taking action unexpectedly without your previous knowledge and a chance to dissuade me. I tell you here and now that I will not force any changes in a way that my own loyal and faithful Witans would find unfair or obnoxious. That is no way to treat one's friends. On the other hand, there is merit in my suggestions. Perhaps I ask for too much, but how can it be right to refuse to consider any change at all? I suggest that, after a full discussion of these subjects here on the floor of this august Hall, that the First Speaker appoint a committee of Witans to meet with my advisors to work out, by give and take, a compromise acceptable to all Romans of good will. My promises of free speech and no retaliation shall apply to whatever committee members say or do in private, as if they had spoken in the Witanagemot itself."

The Emperor then addressed other subjects. When he concluded, the members of his Consistory and the galleries exploded with cheers and applause, (as usual Duval had packed them), but the Witans themselves applauded politely, like men who have just been given something important and complicated to think over. The First Speaker was on his feet immediately to thank the Emperor for "this important and historic speech" and to ask the Witans to stand as the Imperial couple exited.

As soon as the Speaker recessed the Witanagemot, his friends and supporters surrounded Prince Frederick. He told them the speech had given him much to think about. Then he and the five aristocrats who were the heads of the Grandee party went on to a conference room, where a light lunch and heavy decisions awaited them.

"Isn't he the clever one?" asked Josef Hapsburg. "He offers us compromise and, without ever saying so, leaves a feeling that anyone who opposes him must be in foreign pay."

Augustus Wittelsbach joined in, "Not only has he offered us a compromise but now there will be a co-Emperor to whom censure for past actions would not automatically apply. Friends, this is not the best time to push a public attempt to remove an Emperor."

Frederick felt the meeting sliding out of his control. He said, "When we will ever get a better chance than now? If we retreat, we lose our only lever against him."

Francisco de Medici responded, "Who will vote to remove an Emperor who has just won a war and brought us the Silk Road? And did it on the cheap at that."

The prince persisted, "We do it on the same basis as before. We say censure is to be held in abeyance until we receive a satisfactory result in our attempts to compromise. Then we make sure there's no compromise."

"No one will be interested in censure until we all know how the attempt to compromise has turned out," Wittelsbach said. "We have been outmaneuvered."

Frederick studied the room, and seeing his dream had no support, gave in to the inevitable, "If we don't go for censure we will want to control the committee. Usually, such committees have three members, so we will try to get two of us appointed. The Speaker won't include me, but he'll consider my suggestions. Who's interested?" After looking around the table, he said, "All right, our choices are you, Augustus, and you, Francisco. I will submit your names to the Speaker."

As the five men got up to leave, an infuriated Frederick said, "That damned man! One speech, and he has us squabbling among ourselves."

That afternoon, the First Speaker proposed three days of discussion, after which he would appoint a committee of five, not three, members to seek a compromise solution, using the Emperor's suggestions as a starting point. He appointed both of Frederick's recommendations, but the three other committee members were all friends of the Chancellor and unfavorable to Frederick's cause. The Prince suspected that the First Speaker and the Chancellor had connived against him, planning it all in advance.

He was absolutely correct.

CHAPTER XXI

The Shape of Completed Fate

A FEW DAYS LATER, the Watchmen of a village near Aachen brought in Emmerich Bader and a woman posing as his wife. They had been living there under false names. When he arrived, Emmerich had explained that he'd been sick and was recuperating. The villagers had wondered occasionally about a sick man who never saw a doctor and spent all day gardening, but never suspected he was a fugitive. They thought him unneighborly but not unfriendly.

In the end, Emmerich's beloved garden occasioned his arrest. A traveler passing through the village had tied up his horse and gone into the general store to make a purchase. He came out to find the local bully going through his baggage, and when he protested, the bully knocked him down and ran away. The traveler raised a hue and cry, and the villagers gave chase. Emmerich was working in his garden when the thief cut through it, his heavy boots crushing plants that had cost Enmmrich so much labor. Outraged, he went for the bully. Although twenty years older and twenty pounds lighter, Emmerich was giving a very good account of himself until his opponent drew a knife and cut his face. His screams alerted the pursuers who caught the attacker and dragged him to the Watch station.

A Watch station was the last place in the world Emmerich wanted to be, but the Watchmen insisted he come with him to sign the formal complaint. His signature and affidavit were duly taken, and Emmerich received medical treatment. Greatly relieved to be going home, he was stopped when the head of the village Watch walked into the room carrying a poster with a sketch of Emmerich's face, offering fifty thousand denarii for his arrest.

When Emmerich saw the poster, he panicked and tried to run away. Identification and arrest soon followed. The town's five Watchmen and their wives spent all night drinking and talking, gloriously happy over their unimaginable good fortune.

By the end of the day rumors were racing all over Aachen. Sharpie and the Witan quaked when they heard them. They met and agreed that if they did not act immediately, they would soon be dead.

"I have already spoken to the prince," Walsenburg said, for he was the Witan, "We are to go over to the Hiegenstier at once. He thinks our best chance is tomorrow night's reception for the Mongolian ambassador. If we are to kill our target before he kills us, we will have to act tomorrow and pray that Emmerich doesn't talk tonight."

"Can we really trust Frederick?" Sharpie asked. "If they can't prove he took money from the Greeks, why shouldn't he save his own neck by betraying us?"

"Because he told the Greeks who would take their money and took Greek money to redistribute to Witans, who would only take it from a fellow Grandee. He thinks the Emperor is looking for an excuse to kill him. He's just as frightened as we are."

State receptions were held in the throne room. They might not rank socially with the three great balls of Witanagemot Season, but every reception began and ended with a wonderful party, and any invitation to the palace gave a woman the right to order a new gown and wear her best jewelry.

After an hour or so of the party the honored guest and the Imperial family appeared on the throne platform at the north end of the room and descended a flight of marble stairs to the Domain, a large floor space just below the platform covered with gold matting and separated from the rest of the room by plush ropes. There, guests who had received special invitations were presented to the honored guest. After the presentations, the Imperial party ascended the stairs, and the honored guest and the Emperor usually said a few words from the throne platform. After the Imperial party departed, there was music and dancing far into the night.

❀

Six were in on the secret: Frederick, his two his brothers-in-law, the de Meynard brothers, Conrad, Walsenburg and Thomas Marsalia, but only five sat in the Hiegenstier discussing how to manage the assassinations. Conrad would not take part. Agatha had begged her husband to abandon the effort. "It's worse than madness," she told him. "We all love you. You have all the good things of this world. Go to Martin. He said he would forgive you."

Her husband was obdurate. "I will not beg my father's murderer for my own life," he shouted. "I have spent every day of my life having to be grateful to the man who killed my father just for not having killed me too And why? Because I exist and am related to him. Some day he is going to kill me too. I know he wants to do it because he has always wanted to do it. His existence poisons my life. So long as he lives I cannot breathe. I cannot stand this pain and fear any more. I will kill him or he will kill me."

"Then don't take my son," Agatha told him in a voice he did not recognize, "I won't let you kill Conrad for your madness. Promise me he will not go to the palace. If you do not, I will go to Jenny myself tonight and reveal the plot." Unwillingly, Frederick gave his word.

Frederick and Thomas Marsalia worked out the details. The prince pointed out their best opportunity, "Martin, Jenny, and Aetius will be standing next to each other in the receiving line. Those are our targets. We couldn't ask for a better chance."

Marsalia agreed, "Simple is best. It leaves fewer things to go wrong."

So the plan agreed upon was the simplest possible—to hide pistols in their official robes and charge their targets. Loose and voluminous, a Witan's summer robe could easily conceal a weapon. It was illegal to carry weapons into the palace, but Witans were never searched, and Sharpie said he had his own methods of concealment.

Members of the Imperial family and relatives of those standing beside them on the receiving line had first entry. Frederick would enter first and, after passing through the reception line, would loiter in the

Domain near the targets, as if waiting for a friend. Witans and the highest members of the court had second entry, and other important officials such as Marsalia, third entry. When the heralds announced second entry, the three Witans would go on line together. When Walsenburg called out, "Now!" they would whip out their pistols, and each would rush his designated target. Standing further back among the third entry guests, Marsalia would act as watchman until the Witans charged, then run forward to cover their rear. He would also kill any victim who escaped the first assault. The prince would not charge, but he would also carry a pistol and act as back-up. There would be five assassins against three targets: the Emperor, the Empress, and the Paladin. If any target escaped, the conspirators were doomed. Once the three were dead, Frederick would deliver a rousing speech, claiming to have freed the Empire from a tyrant. If the Witans in the room followed him, he would have accomplished the first and most difficult part of his task.

When he left the Hiegenstier after an emotional meeting with his wife, Frederick knew his resources were barely adequate. The chance of killing all three targets was not good. But he was willing to fail if he could kill the Emperor.

Everyone but Mikail had gone to the reception. Duval had warned him that Subatai's slayer should not attend. A glowing Hildegard, beautiful in lilac silk, had stopped by on her way to the party to show off Louie's premarital present, a magnificent amber and gold bracelet. Wishing it had been for Karita, Mikail truthfully told her that it was the most beautiful piece of jewelry he had ever seen. He did not add that he himself had bought it in Rostock with the Emperor's money. His silence was not entirely kindness. He thought of Duval and remembered Lucas languishing in Pomerania. When Hildegard left Mikail's thoughts turned back to Sharpie. He was getting up for a drink of water when the key finally turned in his mind, and at last he understood what Karita had tried to tell him in his dream.

As clearly as if he had been there himself, Mikail saw Andrew deciding to update a document he had sent to the mailroom. The day's mail had not yet gone out and Andrew sent a clerk to the mailroom to retrieve his letter. Uncertain which letter he was supposed to bring back, Andrew's clerk brought them all. Andrew found an envelope addressed to Thomas Marsalia marked "personal." Andrew knew he had sent no such letter, and when he opened the envelope, out fell a cipher in George's handwriting. Thomas Marsalia was Sharpie!

But Andrew suspected office politics, not treason. He assumed that Marsalia had found out that the Chancellor wanted to replace him and was plotting with George (Andrew's own friend and protégé!) to discredit him. Andrew sent George an angry message, demanding an immediate explanation. In his reply, George promised to tell Andrew secrets and proposed that, for mutual protection, they meet where no one could observe or hear them. Then, once Andrew's back was turned, George stabbed him and dragged the corpse down to the basement.

Mikail admired his own cleverness for a minute before he recalled that Sharpie had contemplated the assassination of the Emperor. And where was Sharpie now? In the throne room for a reception where the Emperor would be present! He considered the quickest way to get there. Going the long way round to reenter the palace from the public entrance would take him too long, but there was a side entrance to the throne room inside the palace. Long ago, a musicians' gallery had been built inside the room with a staircase running down from the gallery to the floor of the throne room. The gallery itself had long since been removed but the stairs remained, and they would bring him into the throne room near the Domain. Mikail shot out of his chair and ran.

When they thought of that August night in later years, the guests at the reception first remembered the splendor. They recollected how the glorious news of victory and peace with Mongolia had circulated, how elegantly the women were dressed that year, and the weirdly beautiful Mongolian music. But their minds always came back to the way that night ended in dead bodies on the Domain floor and pools of blood soaking into the golden mats. Above all, they remembered the weeping Emperor.

Guests invited to the reception did not pass through the palace to enter the throne room. They entered a lobby whose doors opened to an outside courtyard. Inside the lobby, white-clad chamberlains inspected invitations and checked names against the list of invited guests before admitting them directly into the south end of the huge room. These arrangements were designed to restrict the number of people admitted to the palace itself. Accordingly, most of the guards on duty for the reception had been posted in the lobby, not the throne room.

Guests had started to trickle into the lobby a little before nightfall. By now it was dark and the party was well under way. The room's mirrored walls reflected and magnified the light emitted from thousands of candles. The candles, the August heat, and the natural body warmth of seven hundred people made the room feel tropical, but this night was a celebration and the revelers didn't care. Efforts had been made to keep the room comfortable, and both men and women carried hand fans. A film of moisture made the women's skin glow, while their silk gowns glittered and sparkled in the candlelight. Although protocol demanded long gowns, fashion was kind and encouraged dressmakers to cut their gowns to allow air to circulate. That year's color was purple. Younger women wore violet, lilac, and orchid, the flowery shades, while the older ones preferred plum to set off gleaming gold and polished jewelry. Witans' summer robes were red and gold, while the officers of state wore blue summer-weight robes of state. Other men wore full dress military uniforms or elegant silk evening jackets with ruffed shirts and dark pressed pants. A poet might have described the Emperor's guests as a gaudy, rather disorderly, flower garden.

Although the Imperial chefs drew the line at brewing kumis, the fermented mare's milk that is every Mongol's favorite drink, the waiters' trays carried not only the Imperial kitchens' usual specialties, but Mongolian tidbits as well, such as horse meat barbequed in a horsehide bag, air-dried mutton and beef, and mixed horse and mutton meatballs.

A life-size ice sculpture of a Mongol rider on his pony stood on a wooden stand in the middle of the room. Servants pulled mechanical fans to provide a steady breeze over a large block of ice to keep cool air flowing over the sculpture.

The Master of Ceremonies had provided the guests with a choice of music. In the southeast corner of the room, a twenty year-old prodigy from Modena was playing the pianoforte. In the opposite corner an impromptu group of Mongol amateur musicians played their native music. The group consisted of the ambassador's valet, his secretary, a code clerk, and the embassy doorman all playing Mongolian horse-head fiddles and one of the cooks with a shoulder-held, double-ended Mongol hand drum. The horse-head fiddles' two strings, a "male string" made of twisted hair from a stallion's tail and a "female string" from a mare's tail, produce piercing music with a poignant, pensive sound that suggests great distances and the wind blowing over the endless steppes. The ambassador's daughter and a visiting friend accompanied the instruments by singing. Occasionally they dropped into throat singing in the Mongolian mode in which the singer's voice box produces two simultaneous pitches. (Although the audience did not know it, this was a special treat. Mongolian women rarely throat-sing.) The instrumentalists were amateurs but both singers had lovely, well-trained voices. While the ensemble might not have impressed an audience at home—although the singers were good—its unexpected, unique beauty overwhelmed the Romans, who had never heard anything like it.

Enraged at being upstaged by amateurs, and foreign ones at that, the red-faced prodigy was violently banging at his piano in a way that boded no good for either the instrument's future, or his own.

The Aachen gossip mill was already circulating an accurate account of the Mongol ambassador's three-hour morning audience with the Emperor. The war was over. The Mongols wanted friendship and an ongoing relationship, and so for all practical purposes, the Romans had won. The Khan would exact a high price, but the Silk Road would be open.

Ambassador Mazzeo was chatting with a retired diplomat he had known since they were junior attachés.

"Yes, I was there, Chris," Mazzeo was saying. "After Ochir presented his credentials, he had a long meeting with the Emperor. It was all roses and honey."

"Whatever happened to Kaidu?"

Mazzeo smiled. "Ochir cleaned house. He told our Emperor in the calmest voice you ever heard, 'I dug the whole band of thieves out of their holes and killed fifty of them. They were taking Greek bribes. The Khan did not kill Kaidu."

"The Mongols are a happy and cheerful people," said his friend, "I enjoyed my fifteen years there and made a lot of friends. They play a kind of polo, called buzkashi using the decapitated bloody body of a newly-killed goat for a ball. The idea is to pick up the goat and push the other players out of their saddles and under the hooves of the horses. Same bloody mess for their politics."

Mazzeo nodded his agreement. "As Ochir told it, the Khan announced he did not take Kaidu's life or divorce his Hotun wife out of his great respect and affection for the Hotuns. Neat, isn't it, The Khan announces he is going to honor the Hotuns by *not* chopping off their chief's head and *not* divorcing Odsetag, who, by the way, is recovering from her illness. Of course, he confiscated everything Kaidu owned."

His friend grinned, "The Mongol way to collect taxes."

"Wait, there's more," Mazzeo said, "Before the Emperor could mention the farmers of Dacia, Ochir smoothly raised the subject himself, 'Kaidu betrayed the Great Khan as much as you Romans when he attacked you. Therefore, there is no reason for reparations. However, Kaidu stole a great fortune from the Khan. The Khan will make over half of Kaidu's property to help your Roman farmers as an act of simple human kindness. The other half will compensate the families of our soldiers killed by his adventurism. Now let us talk about more agreeable things.' Therefore, no one is at fault and nobody has to apologize, but our farmers get compensated. The perfect diplomatic result. The man's good!"

"I wonder how much of that fortune will stick to Ochir's hands?"

"Not a question our Emperor will ask if the money's enough. Martin changed the subject. He demanded the return of George Hoffman."

"What did Ochir say?"

"He put on a show. He turned to Sforza and told him, 'Chancellor, *I* have avenged your son. *I* ordered his death myself. George Hoffman is dead. He did not die well.'"

"He's made a friend of Sforza for life."

Mazzeo nodded, "Probably why he did it. George was no threat to him. Uh-oh. Please excuse me, Chris. I see someone I should talk to."

He had noticed Thomas Marsalia. He went over and greeted him, "Thomas, I have sad news. Ochir killed George Hoffman. I know George worked for you and that you were good friends for a long time. Politics apart, my condolences on a friend's death."

Marsalia had been clutching at a fantastic hope that his clever George would somehow escape to Byzantium. Now here at last was the news he had dreaded. He completed his conversation with the old busybody without giving himself away before walking over to position himself for the coming attack. Long experience had taught him how to conceal his feelings. His father was a famous surgeon who passed as a good man in public. But at home he insisted his son show him every form of respect and every overt manifestation of love while regularly beating him, usually for no better reason than his need to hit someone who could not hit him back. Doctor Marsalia dispensed psychological pain with equal skill. While persuading the world that he was a loving father, he never provided affection or encouragement to young Thomas. When his son inevitably showed his feelings, he was beaten a second time and called unnatural to boot

His mother adored her beast of a husband. Anything her son confided was promptly betrayed to the tyrant. That taught him that no one could be trusted, especially not women. Naturally Thomas hated his father, but over time he learned to respect and admire his diabolic ways. A child's careful observation of a parent taught him how to conceal his own nature. Having never received friendship, love, or pity, he saw no reason to dispense them, especially since a good semblance usually got him what he wanted. In only one instance had his father failed. There was one person for whom Thomas did feel true love. Sharpie's diamond-hard carapace almost shattered when the old ambassador told him that George was dead.

When he got away from the old gossip, he was dizzy with rage and pain. His thoughts spun. *Poor George, my poor darling dearest George, George the only one I ever loved, the only one in this dirty world I could ever tell the real truth, who saw me as I am. George saw my heart, understood it, and loved me for it. So lively, so playful, so much fun, so full of mischief and amusing malice. How subtle and unexpected his hands and mouth were for love and how well he understood my needs. What wonderful style he had. My only love and my entire life. That bastard Hugh Pannonius and that disgusting little brother of his killed him. Little brother found out things he shouldn't have found out. Instead of being killed, as he should have been, little brother got away and what he told people at Saint George Castle killed my George. I would die happy if I killed him first. I don't know whether to pray to God or the Devil for it. Not that either of those fakers exist. Belief is for fools. Without George I have nothing in this world. Nothing, nothing, nothing, nothing in this ugly, rotten world. Living without George for the rest of my life will be like being beaten by the old man forever. What difference does it make to me whether these clods kill the Emperor? And how stupid they are. George would have had a better plan. Suppose this one works? It saves my life, but what good does that do me without George?*

Sharpie lusted to murder. He touched his robe to feel the hardness of his pistol.

✳

Mikail was breathless when he reached the entrance to the Gallery stairs. He had not expected to find any one there, but a small, elderly sergeant was on duty with a young recruit next to him. The sergeant was a small self-important minor palace functionary rather than a real guard. Mikail had met him once or twice before. The sergeant stopped him with, "I'm sorry, Mr. de Ruyter, but Mr. Duval specifically told me you were not to be allowed in. And you're not properly dressed, Sir."

Mikail lost his temper. "Sergeant, someone is about to try to kill the Emperor. Do you want to be responsible for his murder?"

The sergeant had spent his entire working life as a palace functionary and Mikail was not the first jumped-up young man from the provinces who had told him a story to crash a palace event. He knew just how to handle him. "Frankly, sir, I don't believe you. I'll send someone to ask Mr. Duval, but you can't pass. My orders are that nobody gets in who's not invited and properly dressed."

The more Mikail argued, the more obstinate the sergeant became. When Mikail stood close to him and raised his voice, the sergeant beckoned his assistant and the two men locked arms to bar his way.

The stairs debouched into the west side of the throne room. From the head of the stairs where he and the sergeant were arguing, Mikail could overlook the entire room. He saw that most of the guests were gathered to his left at the south end of the room where he saw a dense, parti-colored crowd. A few guests looking for quiet conversation had spilled over the rest of the room. At the north end of the room, a short flight of purple marble steps led up to a platform on which stood two Imperial thrones. In front of the steps, plush ropes marked off the floor of the Domain, a large space whose floor was covered with gold colored matting. Inside the Domain, the Master of Ceremonies and the Mayor seemed to be making a final inspection. Such guards as there were, were scattered around the room. Most stood at either side of the entrance to the Domain.

The sergeant droned on. As Mikail watched, the Master of Ceremonies and the Magister climbed up the stairs and left through a door behind the thrones. Noticing their departure, guests began to drift toward the Domain. Mikail spotted Thomas Marsalia standing alone with his back to the thrones in violation of protocol. Something about the movement of his head and his posture suggested that he was a lookout. Now Mikail felt certain that something was afoot. He began to think about running the blockade.

A few minutes later, the Master of Ceremonies returned to announce in stentorian tones, "The Emperor and Empress, the honored guest, and the members of the reception line will enter shortly. Members of the Imperial family and others entitled to first entry should now come forward." Only Frederick and David came forward. David was entitled to first entry because his father was on the reception line, not because he was the Emperor's nephew. The irony of the situation was not lost on him. Dorcas and Pannonius were absent, having taken the evening for themselves.

Trumpets rang out. The Imperial couple entered from the door behind the thrones and appeared on the platform, followed by Ochir, the Paladin, the Mayor, and the Magister. To the shouts of the crowd, the Imperial party descended the steps to the Domain and formed a reception line. His sword drawn, the Magister took his position in front of them. Ochir's two bodyguards had been quietly standing near the foot of the stairs. They moved over to stand behind him, trying to look inconspicuous.

Frederick was the first to be admitted. He passed down the reception line where the Mayor, the Paladin, the Empress and the Emperor exchanged only formalities with him. He had no better success when he sought to engage Ochir in conversation. Seething, Frederick walked away. He found a place within the Domain, thirty feet away from Ochir at the end of the line, and stood there, apparently waiting for a friend.

David received a different reception. The Mayor was in a merry mood. Having known David since birth, he claimed the privileges of an honorary uncle and teased him unmercifully about the beard he was trying to grow before passing him on to his father. The Paladin asked David whether he had seen his sister. David told him that he had dined with Dorcas and Pannonius and thought them happy and well suited. Aetius had anticipated difficulties between his children. Now he was very pleased and told David as much. He introduced his son to Ochir, and they exchanged a few words. The others chatted with him in a friendly way, and then David too was finished.

As he walked away David noticed the Prince still standing in the Domain. He walked over to ask why Conrad was not at the reception. Frederick replied, in a flat voice, "Conrad will not be at this reception." David was already uneasy. The atmosphere at the Hiegenstier that morning had been peculiar and unpleasant. Frederick and Agatha had kept to themselves, lunching alone, which was very much out of the ordinary. Afterwards, Agatha had walked her husband to the door and saying, "Come home tonight," kissed him passionately. David was certain she had been crying. Conrad had gone to the door with his father and afterwards, low-spirited and silent, excused himself.

Disquieted, David turned aside for a minute to think. He wanted to renew the conversation, but he could see from Frederick's face that his presence was unwelcome. Finally, Frederick said in an edgy tone, "David, I'm trying to think about something. Please leave me alone." Now the young man was certain that something was terribly wrong. Stepping away to mull over the situation, he unintentionally put himself between the Prince and the reception line.

❋

The Master of Ceremonies called out, "Witans and others having second entry may advance to the entrance to the Domain." A line of men in red and gold and light blue robes started to form near the entrance. Still standing at the head of the stairs, Mikail decided he had to make a run for it now. Behind the landing, the corridor turned away, and in a few steps he could be out of the sergeant's line of sight. "If you won't let me in, I'm leaving," he said and walked away into the corridor. The sergeant watched him go. When he had passed out of his sight line, he turned to watch the show with his recruit.

"What the Hell was wrong with him?" the sergeant asked no one in particular.

Around the corner, Mikail counted to fifty. Then, suppressing an impulse to shout, he lowered his head and charged down the corridor, raising his legs high to build momentum and increase the impact of his hundred and ninety pounds. He was behind the guards and on them before they could turn around. He pushed the little sergeant into his assistant with all his strength and then pushed them out of his way roaring down the stairs into the room. The sergeant pulled himself up to scream, "You can't do that! You're out of uniform" at Mikail's back. His assistant who had tumbled down the stairs after Mikail's push got to his fee quickly and was up and chasing Mikail. Only a few paces separated them.

Marsalia had turned. Now he was standing behind the Witans and looking at the Domain. Mikail charged through the guests, yelling, "THAT'S HIM! THAT'S SHARPIE! SAVE THE EMPEROR!"

The spread-out crowd was slow to react. A big man, not properly dressed, was running hard towards the Domain, pushing guests aside and bellowing, "SAVE THE EMPEROR!" A uniformed guard was running a few feet behind him, and, some twenty feet behind, a sergeant followed them.

Marsalia was where Frederick had placed him, near the entrance to the Domain, a few feet behind the line of Witans waiting for the Master of Ceremonies to begin the second entry. He heard the noise and turned to see a big man pushing people aside and running hard in his direction. Two guards followed him. Marsalia thought they were accompanying him. At first he could not make out what the man was screaming, but when Mikail pointed directly at him, Marsalia recognized Mikail. "*By God, it's little brother, and he's coming right at me,*" he said to himself. "*Talk about luck.*"

He pulled the pistol out of his robe and started to raise it. An old soldier nearby noticed a man raising a pistol and shouted, "WEAPON!" Mikail, who was only about twenty-five feet away from Marsalia, heard and tried to twist away, but his momentum slowed his change of direction.

The guard running just behind him had seen the pistol too. He made a desperate leap to pull Mikail down, but succeeded only in grabbing the back of his shirt. The shirt ripped; the guard couldn't hold on. Fighting to keep his balance, Mikail skidded and started to slip sideways.

Marsalia was a little slow in bracing to fire. Pistols were not common, and he was unaccustomed to using them. The old soldier shouted again, "LOOK OUT! HE'S GOING TO SHOOT!" He was too far away to slap the pistol out of Marsalia's hand, but his quick-thinking wife threw her steel-framed ballroom reticule at his face.

Her scream, the flying purse, and several other people nearby trying to pull at him broke Marsalia's concentration, but although off-balance and unsteady, he managed to stay on his feet and hold on to his weapon. He aimed for Mikail's chest and pulled the trigger. Although he was starting to fall and distracted by the blow to his face by the reticule, his own nervousness, and the surrounding noise and excitement, Marsalia was too close to miss, but his shot was skewed. The bullet went into Mikail's chest on a rising diagonal to the right of his heart, just missing his lung, and continued upward to exit below his right shoulder, tearing muscles and shattering bones. Mikail fell, striking the marble floor with an audible impact. A wave of screaming guests swamped Marsalia. Several men held him down while someone else seized the pistol. Mikail lay bleeding on the floor. He heard people screaming and a strong voice calling, "DOCTOR! DOCTOR!"

A guard had been posted on the throne platform at the far end where he could overlook the room. When he saw Mikail running towards the thrones, he blew his whistle and pointed. Most of the guards outside the Domain started to run towards the imbroglio.

The Master of Ceremonies was about to announce, "The Second Entry may now proceed." Hearing the whistle, he turned and looked around for orders, but the Magister and the Mayor seemed to give conflicting directives. The Magister called the guards around the Domain's perimeter and ordered them to investigate the incident. Meanwhile, he ran to position himself between the Emperor and the man who had drawn a weapon. Almost simultaneously, the Mayor pointed at the reception line and called out, "Get them out of here at once!" The Master of Ceremonies was momentarily confused. Only Ochir's professional bodyguards were quick to react. They immediately took position in front of their master. Experienced men, they had seen assassinations more than once at the Great Khan's court.

Just outside the Domain, the three Witans looked at each other. Walsenburg hissed, "Here's our distraction. They'll be gone in a moment. NOW!" He ducked under the plush rope and charged at the Emperor. The de Meynards followed him.

The Emperor had been chatting with Ochir and was finishing a thought when Walsenburg charged at him. Ochir's bodyguards did not know whether the armed man running toward them intended to assassinate their master or the Emperor, and they did not wait to find out. They were on Walsenburg like hounds on a fox. One slit Walsenburg's throat in a single movement, and as he fell, the other followed him down and plunged his knife into his heart. Walsenburg's body spurted blood. It sprayed over the Empress. She screamed.

As soon as the Paladin heard the whistle, he realized an assassination attempt must be under way. He was already running for the stairs leading up to the throne platform before Thierry was ten feet into the Domain. Like the good hunter he was, all of Thierry's attention was concentrated on the prey fleeing before him, but had he turned around he would have seen how close the Magister was behind him. When he stopped to raise and aim his pistol, the Magister caught up with him and thrust his sword through his back. Thierry fell forward face down onto the gold matting. The Magister coolly pulled his sword free, and as he kicked the body over, he looked backward to make sure that there was no further attempt on the Emperor. Then he coolly put his foot on Thierry's stomach to steady himself, and plunged his sword into his heart.

Phillippe de Meynard was the last assassin. The Master of Ceremonies had noticed the first two assassins slipping under the rope. Now he was beginning to react. To avoid him, Phillippe had to run a dozen steps to his right before slipping under the rope and coming up opposite a stunned Empress in her bloody dress next to the Mayor. He pulled out his pistol, and when the Mayor saw him cock it and raise his arm to aim at the Empress, he instinctively pushed her down and away from the weapon and charged forward, screaming at the assassin. Enraged, Phillippe fired directly into the Mayor's heart, killing him at once. The Empress screamed and fainted. Led by a furious Emperor, a dozen men fell on the assassin, and one of Ochir's bodyguards slit his throat.

The Emperor walked away from Philippe's body and helped his wife to her feet so he could begin comforting her. The Chancellor, Albrecht, and General Biakarione had been chatting while they waited for their entry. When they saw the mayhem erupt they had run to their monarchs. Soon, the five were together, trying to make sense of the incredible event. The Emperor's back was to the prince.

In front of the Domain, the Master of Ceremonies raised his voice, commanding all guests to leave. The room started to empty. Frozen with shock, Frederick stood massive and blank-faced. He had just watched his friends' brief attack come to nothing. In what seemed no more than an instant, it had started and been over. He never even got involved. Nothing had gone as he had hoped or planned, and men he had known and loved all his life had died in an instant for him to no purpose. David took a step towards the Prince, to whom no one was paying any attention, with the half-formed idea of taking him home, when he saw Frederick pull a pistol from his robe and raise it at the Emperor's back. David did not think. His legs and arms moved automatically. He might have been playing the scrimmage game at Vittorino's School as he tackled Frederick and took him down with a crash. As Frederick struck the floor, his pistol went off harmlessly.

In seconds, General Biakarione and David had pulled him up and were holding a struggling Frederick as Ochir and a dozen others, including the Emperor himself, ran to help. No longer silent, Frederick was shrieking obscenities and telling the Emperor to his face how much he had wanted to kill him. The Emperor turned his back and walked over to the Chancellor. He said nothing, but something must have passed between them, because the Chancellor took the Empress by the arm and gently said, "My turn. Let's get you home, Jenny" and led her out of the room.

The Magister had been kneeling next to the body of his old friend, the Mayor. As the Empress and Chancellor went up the steps, he rose. His anguished face darkened, and he shuddered. He had sheathed his sword, but now he took it out again and, dragging his feet, slowly walked over to the screaming prince. He turned to look into his Emperor's eyes but saw no sign there would be mercy for the traitor. Holding its basket hilt in both hands, he pushed the silver sword into the prince's chest with all his strength. When he pulled the blade out and the body hit the floor the blood started yet another growing red pool on the gold matting. The Magister walked away and sat down on the stairs leading up to the throne platform. His unwiped sword lay on the step next to him. Frederick's blood still glistened on its blade.

Palace guards and chamberlains were moving out the last guests at the far end of the throne room while blood continued to flow and stain the Domain's matting. Always more comfortable in action, General Biakarione took Albrecht by the arm, and the two men went off to arrange for removal of the bodies. A group of guards were standing near the dissolving ice sculpture in the middle of the room. Albrecht beckoned one of them over and told him in an angry voice, "Burn that matting tonight. Tonight! I never want to see it again."

The Emperor remained standing in the middle of his Domain, silent, unmoving, surrounded by a small crowd of officers, aides, and guards. He turned around and, shivering in the heat, stumbled on uncertain legs up the purple marble stairs onto the throne platform. He turned around, looked wide-eyed at those still in the room, and sat down alone, all alone, on his throne No one else was on the platform or the stairs, except for the Magister, still sitting on the first step with his head in his hands and the bloody, unsheathed sword at his side.

Then, to the astonishment of everyone still in the room, Charles Martel IV, true successor to Charlemagne, rightful and duly anointed Emperor of the New Roman Empire, "happy, glorious, triumphant and pious," a man who never showed his feelings in public, stood up and screamed, "Oh, what a bitter life is mine! What have I done, and who has cursed me, that I must I kill those I love to keep the world together?" He began to weep. Those present stood there. They did not know what to say. They did not know what to do. They did not even know what they could do.

His tears fall down and wet his beard.

EPILOGUE

MIKAIL SURVIVED. THE BULLET hit his chest and shattered much of his sternum, but none of the fragments penetrated his heart or lungs. The primary risk in such cases is infection. By our standards, Roman medical care was rudimentary, but doctors did do a great many things right without knowing why they did them. They knew enough to keep hands and instruments clean when treating wounds. No one was quite sure why well scrubbed hands protected wounds from infection, but once the fact was pointed out, the results were self-evident. The chief difference between then and now was the length of Mikail's convalescence.

Frederick's death collapsed organized opposition to the panRoman policies, but not the Witans' dislike for them. Seeing a role for himself, Wittelsbach changed teams to broker a compromise. In the end, the Emperor withdrew his opposition to private railroads and canals in exchange for license fees and a share in their profits, and the Witans surrendered their rights to manorial judges. Questions relating to manorial tenures were compromised by a complicated formula that gave the Grandees rather more than they conceded. All issues relating to the methods of electing Witans were postponed for three years. Wittelsbach received the plaudits the Emperor had offered Frederick. His daughter Caroline took advantage of the moment to point out the advantages of an alliance with the Imperial family. She had good news for David that night.

❋

The Emperor summoned David and received him in a private, narrow audience room sitting in a high-backed chair that looked like a throne. Behind the Emperor's chair was a magnificent nine foot high Malabar Indian screen with ivory inlays showing rajahs hunting, sitting in justice and riding elephants. It had been a gift to the Old Emperor's father from the Mughal Emperor.

The Emperor started talking before David finished his bow. "I suppose you think I brought you here to thank you for saving my life. So, yes, thank you, although I was wearing a mail shirt under those robes despite the heat. I am not a complete fool. I leave that to my nephews. But you would not have been standing next to Frederick if you had not been a part of his cabal and, in effect, acting as a member of the opposition to me. I don't think for a minute you ever suspected that he planned to kill me. I don't even think you realized that he wanted to depose me, let alone that you were helping a plot that was not only treasonable but an attack on your own uncle. But what were you thinking, you stupid boy? By God, I ought to send you to the dampest part of the west of Ireland for the rest of your life to run a horse farm and develop rheumatism. Politics are politics, but I am your uncle, you ungrateful brat! Where would you be without your relationship to me? I have trouble enough with strangers and don't need more from my own family. What do you have to say for yourself?"

This was definitely not what David had expected. He had self-possession and sense enough to say that he had nothing to say for himself. He could only beg his uncle's pardon and would try to learn from his mistakes.

"That's a start," the Emperor conceded. "Now I assume you want a public career and don't want to retire to private life?"

Not quite trusting his own voice, David nodded.

"Then court is not the best place for you at the present. Go make up with your father and go to Mongolia with him. Caroline Wittelsbach will wait. Your aunt will let her family know we approve the engagement. You can announce it. In Mongolia you can learn how real work is done instead of learning how to intrigue. Your father will want to teach you and will need someone for the day-to-day work. When you get back, we'll find a career for you. You did save my life, so you are back in the family. Come to the Wednesday family dinners and bring Caroline. Your father and I will discuss Rhine wine, your aunt will talk about what she is going to wear on her next visitation, and your sister will try to get me to pay for her honeymoon. But there will be serious talk now and then. I expect neither Caroline nor you will pass it on to anyone else. I knew you resented not being asked, but while you were with that devil Frederick, there weren't going to be any confidences."

"I really do thank you," David said, "but what if my father doesn't want to take me?"

"He's more hurt than angry and doesn't want a real breach any more than you do," his uncle replied. "I'll see you Wednesday." David bowed and left the room, confused but relieved.

The door closed behind him, and the Paladin stepped out from behind the screen. "How did you like it, Aetius?" the Emperor asked.

"Perfect. Next week, Moliere. You should have been an actor. He'll be all right, Martin. I promise."

"He's your son and your responsibility," the Emperor said. "I just did what you asked me to do. As for the embassy, I agree with you, it must not leave until all issues are settled. Nothing should be left on the table for them to trade, though they'll try anyhow. And you'll want to stay here for your daughter's wedding, say six weeks? I reserved the Royal chapel, even though the archbishop gave me a hard time. He said it was only for the family. I asked him what the Hell he thought you were."

The Paladin was shocked. "She's my daughter, and she hasn't told me she is engaged yet. How did you find out?"

"Well, for that matter, I don't know that she's told Pannonius yet. But you know your daughter. Dorcas asked Jenny for the Royal chapel as soon as she made up her mind to accept Pannonius. Jenny told me, and I arranged it with the bishop immediately. Look surprised when she tells you. By the way, what does that young man who took the bullet want to do when he gets better?"

A day later Pannonius and Dorcas went to visit Mikail, who was sitting at the window in his hospital room, feeling sorry for himself and missing the excitement of the past several months. Standing very close to one another, Pannonius and Dorcas formally asked him to be their best man, and with equal formality he accepted. Wistfully, he thought of what Karita would look like as a bride. Then he asked where they would be living once married.

Pannonius said they didn't know, but they might not be comfortable at court. They wanted to be alone to knit their lives together and would like to be away from Aachen for a few years. Did Mikail have any notion where *he* was going?

Mikail said he didn't, and he couldn't do anything about it until the doctors got their claws out of him. They had told him he was going to be fine but not to do anything strenuous for another six weeks.

❋

Later that day the Paladin came to visit Mikail, who was still in the downswing phase of his healing cycle and mooning over Karita. Pannonius had been to see the Paladin and formally asked for and received his consent for the marriage. The Paladin was so overflowing with joy that he radiated happiness like an oversized puppy.

The big man pulled over a chair and said he had things to talk about if Mikail felt up to it. His cheeriness was so warming it even reached the patient. Mikail congratulated the Paladin on his daughter's engagement. The Paladin congratulated Mikail on being best man and what did Mikail want to do when he recovered? Mikail said he didn't know. He didn't want to stay at court and definitely didn't want to be a political officer. Could the Paladin use him at the embassy?

"No, an aide's been selected."

Mikail said he would be glad to profit from the Paladin's advice.

Aetius started to think aloud. "Military and legal are out. But you read people well, pick up things fast, have imagination, and don't frighten easily. That makes you a good troubleshooter. Moscow and Kiev are big and important, but nobody here knows much about them. You speak Ukrainian, so you could learn Russian easily. In the meanwhile, take some time off. Why don't you recuperate with my younger daughter, Dacie, and her husband for a few months? They live down the Rhine in the wine country. I spoke to your doctor; he'll approve."

Low as he felt, Mikail had to laugh. "It always comes down to good Rhine wine with you, doesn't it?

"A man should appreciate the good things life gives him," the Paladin said smugly. "By the way, that young woman who started the whole thing has turned up. Karitza isn't it?"

The lights went on behind Mikail's eyes. His chin turned up as if someone had pulled a string. "Ka-ree-ta" he said automatically.

"Yes, Kraitsa," the Paladin said. "She ran away from her father to go looking for you and managed to get through the Mongol lines. A very persistent and imaginative young woman. Reminds me of you. Our people sent her on to Lauzac, who sent her on to me. I interviewed her and liked her very much. Keeping her safe in Dacia eventually turned into a problem, like everything else in the world. So I stashed her down the river with my younger daughter and her family. She and Dacie seem to be getting on rather well. As you said, everything comes back to good Rhine wine."

Mikail's reaction was beyond words.

The Paladin, who was enjoying himself, went on merrily, "I told her you would probably have forgotten her and didn't think you would marry her. She said she didn't think you were going to forget her, and she wanted you in marriage or out of it. Actually used those very words. I thought I was listening to a ghost. A very friendly one. Yes, I liked her very much. After what you have done, your brother is in no position to object to anything you may do, including marriage."

He stood up the better to enjoy the impact his words were having, and left, firing a Parthian shot over his shoulder. "Let me know what you want to do about the job and about going to the country. I'll be around for about six weeks before my embassy leaves."

Mikail was so speechless he could not even say goodbye.

The Emperor sent for Conrad, who was brought in shackled. "I have stopped the investigation," the Emperor said. "If it found what I expect, there would be no way to avoid my committing another crime. I am not going to kill you, but I have two generations of proof that if I don't, your branch of the family is likely to kill me. Ergo, it must be permanent exile. You can accept it or let the investigation run its course. I will not tamper with the judges. Which do you prefer?"

"Exile," Conrad said immediately. "Will you be fair to the women? My mother, my grandmother, and my sister?"

"I don't make war on women. Your grandmother is too good at teaching others to hate. She's going into a comfortable convent. Your mother will be sent to live in her house near Lyons and can't remarry without my permission. That's all. Your sister and her husband don't appear to be involved. I just don't want to see them for a while. I will try to let the feud die with me. Do the same."

"Thank you," Conrad said. "I will. What do you intend for me?"

"Cuba, and your name will be struck from the list of members of the line of true successors."

❋

The Paladin went to see the Emperor and Empress. They were sitting together on the same sofa, enjoying the sloping late afternoon sunlight in the Empress's frilly sitting room. After describing the embassy preparations, Aetius turned to his own situation. "Between this trip to Aachen and the embassy, I'm going to be away from my Proconsulate for six months. Much too long at a time like this; you're going to have to pick someone permanent. You know I want to retire, so when my assignment is over would be a perfect time. Lauzac is doing the military and civil parts of the job under protest, he doesn't want the big job. Whom do you want for Proconsul?"

"Lauzac, of course," the Emperor said. "You always said he would do, and he's performing very well. Where's the problem?"

"The problem once again," his brother replied in a tone too respectful to be respectful, "is that Lauzac has repeatedly refused the job."

"He just thinks he means it," the Emperor said comfortably. "Just tell him that I'm taking him at his word. Since he won't take the job, I'm going to have to give it to D'Atri and he'll have to report to D'Atri. He won't abide that."

"You'll make running the day-to-day operations of the Proconsulate impossible," his brother responded. "If D'Atri takes the job, Lauzac will be furious. If Lauzac changes his mind, D'Atri will be even angrier."

"Oh, I know that," the Emperor assured him. "Then when Lauzac makes a fuss about D'Atri or vice versa, as one of them inevitably will,

I promote the other to the big military job in Tunisia. I've been looking for someone good for months.

"As for your own retirement, what you need is a couple of months off to get to know your grandchildren. In the meanwhile, Aetius, you really ought to learn how to manipulate people. It's part of the job."

Pannonius and Dorcas had a magnificent wedding. They stayed in Aachen only long enough to attend the wedding of Mikail and Karita. The young couple were allowed a year to themselves after which Pannonius would join the Crown Prince in Spain as his principal aide. "The idea," the Emperor said, "is that you will help him learn his trade the way Giuseppe helped me. When the Chancellor retires, Albrecht will succeed him and, eventually, you will succeed Albrecht. My son will have a Chancellor he knows and trusts." Things did not quite work out that way. Pannonius never became Chancellor and retired early, but his great-grandson became Emperor.

Mikail and Karita had a small wedding. The Paladin gave the bride away. Mikail wanted Pannonius for best man, but Lucas made a scene. Karita wrote her father with all the details and a few sketches—she was talented that way—and mentioned that she had been presented to the Emperor and Empress when her husband served as best man in a wedding party in the Imperial chapel. Her stepmother chose to believe Karita had made it all up. Mikail and Karita had three children, all girls, and Mikail doted on them. The Paladin's career advice to Mikail to specialize in the problems of the Eastern frontier was inspired. The peace with the Mongols held, but within two years, the Tsardoms of Moscow and Kiev and the Eastern Roman Empire were unhappy with Rome. For a generation, representing the Empire on its Eastern borders gave Mikail a magnificent career.

To his surprise, Louie Duval found marriage comfortable. When he listened to his clever wife, he didn't outsmart himself quite so often.

Hildegarde's sister even provided him with nephews and nieces. He taught them chess, but they complained that he cheated.

✳

The Emperor abdicated on his sixty-fourth birthday. The Empress succeeded him, but abdicated two years later. They left Aachen to live near Aetius and his daughter in the Rhine wine country. Everyone speaks of them now as the Old Emperor and the Old Empress. The Paladin had long since gone to live with his daughter and make wine, as he had always said he would.

✳

Simonides trudged back to Constantinople, carrying expectations of an ugly interview with Leo Nikephoros. He found Leo not as angry as he had feared. "It was my idea to send you to Aachen when Frederick approached us. It didn't work," Leo explained. "Now what?"

"The less the better," Simonides replied. "We supported and financed an attempt to assassinate the legitimate Western Roman Emperor. It didn't work, but all we've lost so far is money and part of a trade route. Those consequences are bearable. If we continue, we can lose Thrace. We must abandon the idea of acquiring Dacia."

There was a displeased silence. "Maybe," Leo said finally, "in the meanwhile, we have to find you another job."

"No thank you," Simonides said. "I'm going home to Epiros and literature. The great world can take care of itself."

Leo put his arm around Simonides. "Simon, we've been friends since we were boys. You don't really prefer literary life to engagement in great affairs. You'll change your mind."

"Then I must make sure I can't," a smiling Simonides replied. He proved as good as his word. Once back in Epiros, he published *Second Spring*, a cycle of fifty love poems he had written for Anne over the last four years, prefaced by a long "Ode to Aphrodite" praising the transformative powers of love in which Aphrodite herself has Anne's features. The cycle was instantly recognized as the finest love poems in Greek since Sappho, but the scandal it caused was volcanic. Not only were the poems outrageously indiscreet—many being as obscene as the worst of Catullus' poems to Lesbia with which they were immediately compared—but Simonides' reputation for discretion was gone forever along with his career as a diplomat. But every Greek-speaker with any pretension to literary culture read *Second Spring*. Simonides himself translated the poems into Latin. It is said that when Anne's husband read the poems, he walked up and down his library, cursing and reciting Horace on how great poetry outlasts bronze and marble At the time, Savigny was only two years older than Simonides and a man at the height of his powers, but *Second Spring* depicts him as a drooling dotard. Nor is Simonides' description of Aachen kind. Leo Nikephoros never spoke to Simonides again.

Simonides is considered the greatest Greek poet of the Nineteenth century. His themes are love, storms, waves and water, transformation, impermanence and resurrection.

He kept in touch with no one from Aachen except Giovanni Mazzeo who twice visited him in Epiros. At the end of his second visit, painfully aware of how his friend was aging, Simonides wrote "To Giovanni," a short poem about old friendship, and gave it to him as a parting gift. Someone put the words to music, and even today, "To Giovanni" is sung wherever the Greek language is spoken on much the same occasions as when we sing "Auld Lang Syne."

Gaspar soon discovered he had lost his taste for soldiering. He obtained his pension and returned to Imponza, determined to import carpets into the New Roman Empire. While he was preparing for the Silk Road, his wife approached him about returning. "Now we are even," she observed. Gaspar agreed, but pointed out he would be leaving for China in a week. She thought for a minute and concluded, "You'll be lonely. Suppose I go with you?" Over the next ten years, they made four trips to China and created a Roman market for Chinese carpets and tapestries. Gaspar grew rich and was elected mayor of Imponza. He and Mikail remained lifetime friends They liked to say, "We owe everything to each other."

❋

When William Hoffman returned to Rostock he found his wife gone. She had left a letter saying she had returned to Smyrna. She hated Rostock. To her, it represented only death and sorrow. He himself had been kind and understanding, but, in the end, he too had come to represent Rostock to her. She would be better off with her family for the rest of her life, and he without her. As a parting gift, she was setting him free and recommending that he leave the city.

William was not yet sixty, still wealthy, and with connections wherever amber was traded. He knew the Tsar of Moscow loved amber, so he sold everything and resettled in Nizhny Novgorod on the Volga. William's profound knowledge of the amber business and the Tsar's patronage assured his success. He rose to doyen of all foreign merchants in Moskovy, living to a very great age, and left his fortune to found the first boarding school for girls in Moskovy. He talked often and fondly of his wife, for whom the school is named, and of his two dead daughters, but never mentioned a son. As a result, when William died many years later, no one in the city where he lived knew that he had ever had a son named George.

A NOTE ABOUT THE
WITANAGEMOT

THE USE OF THE word "Witanagemot" is artificial. The institution needed a name and none of the obvious choices—legislature, parliament, House of Lords, Senate, Diet, Privy Council and so on—was quite appropriate. All these names carry too much freight. Closest is the House of Lords, but even then there are enormous differences. This Witanagemot does not legislate and its members were elected rather than hereditary. The author finally chose the Anglo-Saxon word "Witanagemot" just because we know so little about the real witanagemot. The Anglo-Saxon Witanagemot was a group of men called to help the king under the general Frankish-Germanic principle that the leader of the tribe has the right to the council of every man in it. Nobody really knows very much about how it functioned

As the text indicates this Witanagemot's membership consists of a set number of witans, usually three or four, elected from each "county" which is the Carolinian term for what we would call a province. There is a public meeting of the county's voters. Voting is oral and public. The ballot is not secret. As only persons of substance may vote, the Witanagemot represents the principal people of substance in the county, i.e. the landholders. Ordinary bourgeois people would not vote or would rarely vote. Hence as a balance a certain number of cities send one representative. There too the voters are people of substance. Rostock's witan was almost always a former Lord Mayor. The central fact is that the Witanagemot represents the aristocratic and monied elements of society.

The origin of the institution was as the Emperor suggests, his advisory council and so the Chancellor is still an *ex officio* member. But the Witanagemot has evolved into something quite different. The Emperor has a true council of course; it is called the Consistory.

The Witanagemot is not a mere show. It is protected by custom, the fact that its members are powerful men who value their status as witans and by the Emperor's coronation oath, the closest thing the Empire, has to a constitution. It is useful to all parties. It can help to get rid of a despot, provides the Emperor with a way to obtain consensus to a major change in government or policy and provides a place for the discharge of the ambitions of the powerful. There is something for everyone in its existence. That is why the Emperor has not sought to weaken or destroy it (or, at least, has never succeeded) despite the obvious ambition of its members to become a real Senate. Moreover the idea that there is something, however remote, that may protect the validity of the Emperor's coronation oath is popular among the Romans. The institution may be considered a success.

The Witans work closely with the Consistory. There are overlaps in membership and the committees of the Witanagemot have a close relationship with their vis-à-vis committees in the Consistory. This allows the aristocrats to have influence and a voice through their institutional access to the Emperor and, what is more important to them in practice, the members of his Consistory. The Emperor finds it useful because it helps him rule with the consent of the people who count and lets him know what they want. A strong Emperor can use the Witanagemot but a weak one is threatened by it because the institution provides a potential launching pad for an attack on the crown by a magnate or a group of magnates. Hence the Emperor's refuses to countenance any organized opposition and takes care to meet personally with every witan.

ACKNOWLEDGEMENTS

MY WIFE HALLIE, MY son Matthew, my daughter Jessica, my son-in-law Jonathan and my friend Joseph Russell read drafts of this book, and gave useful help. That is the least of the many reasons for which I am grateful to them, and to my daughter-in-law, Kimberly.

I had the good luck to be introduced to Paula Trachtman, best of editors, whose help was indispensible.

When an elderly man writes a first novel, the number of people who ought to be thanked is endless. Thanking only some of them would be ungracious, but I hope they all will know who they are and recognize my appreciation.

It is an old and beautiful custom to express thanks to parents and teachers. I would therefore like to thank my father who wanted to be an historian, my mother and my grandmother to whom the past was real and present, and, among many others: Dr. Dorothy Chandler; the members of the Colloquium at Columbia College, especially Moses Hadas, J. Bartlett Brebner and Julius A. Goebel, Jr. for teaching how the past worked and how it goes on working in us. Karl Nickerson Llewellyn did an act of gratuitous and unexpected kindness a long time ago that greatly improved my life.

The idea of writing this novel was inspired by reading *Nostromo* by Joseph Conrad. Compared to that great mountain of imagination this work must necessarily be insignificant, but *Nostromo* it was that showed me what is possible and encouraged me to try.

New York City
May, 2013